JN412391

The Story of Nine Asian Alphabets

The Story of Nine Asian Alphabets

Asia-Pacific Centre of Education
for International Understanding

Hollym

The Story of Nine Asian Alphabets

Planned by UNESCO APCEIU

The original edition in Korean was published by Hollym Corp., Publishers in 2013.

This publication is supported by the Ministry of Education Science and Technology, Republic of Korea.

First published in 2015
by Hollym International Corp., USA
Phone 908 353 1655 **Fax** 908 353 0255
http://www.hollym.com **e-Mail** contact@hollym.com

Published simultaneously in Korea
by Hollym Corp., Publishers, Seoul, Korea
Phone +82 2 734 5087 **Fax** +82 2 730 5149
http://www.hollym.co.kr **e-Mail** info@hollym.co.kr

ISBN: 978-1-56591-408-7
Library of Congress Control Number: 2014930214

Printed in Korea

Foreword

The invention of writing system enabled the humankind to record their thoughts and speech in the form of letters. The written language has played an important role in passing on the meaning of human existence over time. Through writings, we have gained the wisdom of our ancestors, and we transmit what we have learned to the next generations.

Countless languages and writing systems exist, and from them, we are able to learn about cultures and histories. Furthermore, preserving indigenous writing systems is crucial for the humankind because they enable us to gain a deeper insight on the people who use them.

UNESCO has been committed to preserving human writing systems, firmly believing that upholding writing systems will lead to the protection and promotion of diverse human cultures.

Writing systems will also contribute to eradicating illiteracy, enhancing the quality of human life. UNESCO aims to protect marginalized cultures and enhance mutual understanding towards a Culture of Peace.

In accordance with UNESCO's efforts, APCEIU (Asia-Pacific Centre of Education for International Understanding) published this book to enrich the reader's understanding for diverse writing systems and to culture respect for the values presented in them. It seeks to share stories on the writing systems of Asia, explaining how they use diverse letters such as Arabic, Chinese, Cyrillic, Latin, and many others. Among many, nine Asian languages were selected with consideration for geographical balance and/or linguistic affiliation: Hindi, Arabic, Thai, Vietnamese, Indonesian, Mongolian, Chinese, Japanese, and Korean. The writing systems of these nine languages are introduced in terms of their developmental process, unique forms, and calligraphy.

Originally published in Korean as a product of collaboration with the Ministry of Education of the Republic of Korea, this book has been widely recognized by Korean readers since it was first released in 2012. Encouraged by the ever increasing global demand to learn about Asian culture and languages, APCEIU decided to publish an English version of this book. APCEIU hopes that this book will stimulate more interest towards cultural diversity and global citizenship, which can become the basis for mutual respect.

I would like to thank everyone who contributed to making this publication possible, in all steps of its production from researching to writing and editing. Also, I thank those who are working hard to advocate literacy and cultural diversity across the world. In particular, my gratitude goes to Professor Lee Dong-Cheol who advised in the initial planning of this book.

Chung Utak
Director, APCEIU

Contents

Preface

Why Is UNESCO Interested in Preserving Letters?

Writing is important because it can preserve and chronicle the experiences of mankind. People have been able to avoid the mistakes of the past since writing allowed us to keep records of our ancestors' wisdom, and also pass it down to the next generations. Through this preservation made possible by letters, we can also better understand the cultures and histories behind the languages.

In 1999, UNESCO designated February 21 as the International Mother Language Day. As language and cultural diversity are considered universal human values which strengthen social integration, these are essential elements to achieve the objectives of the UN's the Millennium Development Goals (MDGs) and the targets of the UNESCO's Education for All (EFA). The International Mother Language Day has provided people with the opportunities to see the meaning imbued in various mother languages that are endangered across the world. Language allows individuals and societies, to which they belong to, to build their self-identity. Moreover, it is a vital component for peaceful coexistence.

Therefore, preserving various scripts is a source of humanity's strength and opportunities. This embodies cultural diversity, and also plays roles in the exchange of different perspectives, the improvement of ideas, and in the development of imagination. This can not only provide high quality education but can also

International Mother Language Day poster

serve as a way to respond to social change.

To revive endangered languages and expand educational opportunities for everyone, UNESCO has emphasized the value of literacy education. Literacy can be defined as the ability to read, write, and understand simple sentences. Literacy education improves quality of life for those who cannot read and helps create a society that is equal and free of prejudice.

The distribution of illiteracy is nearly the same as that of poverty. Those who have been deprived of educational opportunities have few avenues in society to which they can decide their own destinies. Literacy is a light that illuminates darkness. UNESCO's advocacy for the education of writing systems to promote literacy is not solely for the learning of alphabets, but for mutual understanding, and aims for greater development.

Homo Literariensis (Letter Using Humans)

Around the world, it is estimated that there are around 6,000 languages, but only about 40 can be written using letters. Europe has 208 languages and Asia has 2,304 languages which amount to 29% of the world's total languages. Even though these languages exist, nearly half of them are at risk of endangerment.

Cave drawings could be considered the first form of writing in the history. Drawings of animals and hunting found in caves had shamanistic meanings. In other words, by drawing on cave walls, the artist hoped to be able to hunt these animals and return safely. Pictures were in the early history of a letter and had a very important role. Aside from the shamanistic meanings of these pictures, they became a way to record the amount of surplus products to accumulate wealth. As the scale of the economy grew and society became more complex, cuneiform characters were written on clay tablets and later on reed papyrus.

It is said that the first writing system began in the region of Mesopotamia. Scholars presumed letters were first used in Egypt in 3100 BC, Indus River Valley in 2500 BC, Crete in 1900 BC, China in 1200 BC, and Central America in 600 BC. Through this, we can see that a letter is not just a symbol but a phenomenon that has spread from one culture to another.

About Asia's Nine Writing Systems

The roots of letters can be largely categorized by Egyptian hieroglyphics, cuneiform, and Chinese characters. There are also phonetic writing systems such as the Latin alphabet and symbolic writing systems, which include Chinese characters. There are many different ways to write letters. Phoenician letters, Semitic letters, and Arabic alphabet are written from right to left, while Hindi letters, Greek letters, Cyrillic letters, Hangeul are usually written from left to right. Phags-pa letters and Chinese characters are written from top to bottom.

Letters absorb various cultural aspects of a region and evolve throughout history. It is no coincidence that the three civilizations where letters originated are in Asia. This was possible because Asia was a place where many different religions, cultures, and traditions intermingled for a long time.

Letters are interpreted by both the past and present, and also give hope for the future as well. This book has divided the various Asian writing systems into East Asian writing, Mongolia's Cyrillic alphabet, Southeast Asian writing, the Arabic alphabet, and India's Hindi writing.

1. East Asian Letters

Hangeul : The Korean people had difficulty creating a national identity because they lacked their own indigenous writing system for a long time. It was not until the modern era that Hangeul became Korea's native alphabet. Hangeul's basic consonants

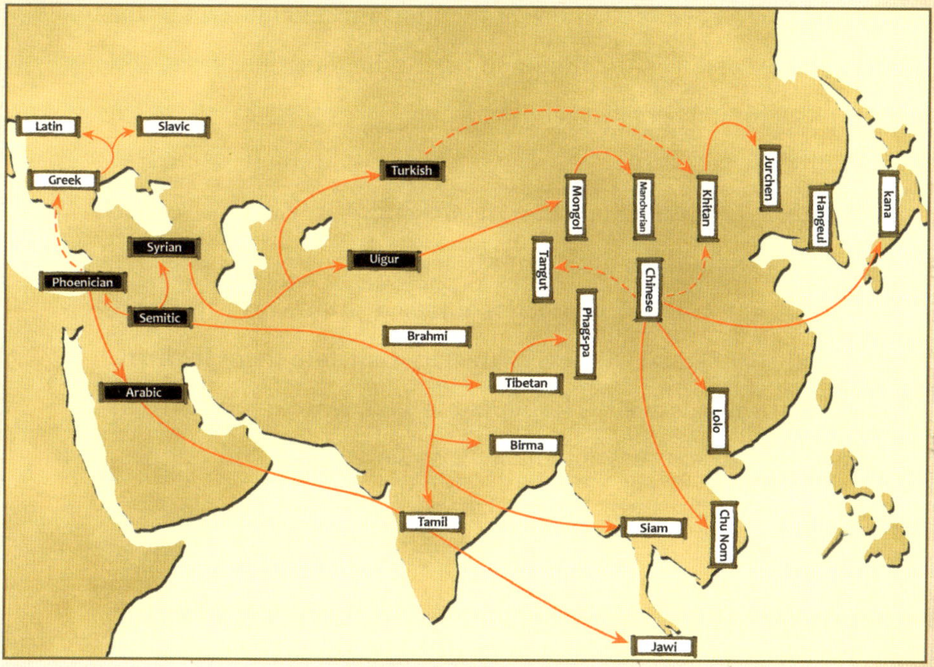

Spread of Asian letters

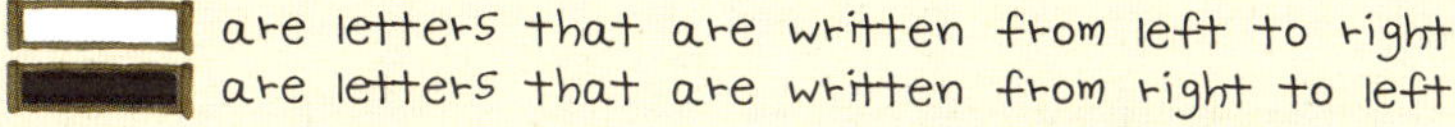

(ㄱ, ㄴ, ㅁ, ㅅ, ㅇ) can be added with strokes to make stronger sounds and as a result, form phonetic letters. Hangeul is so great that it is said that one can even imitate the sound of a ghost using this alphabet. Unlike English, Hangeul has few letters and pronunciations that are exactly alike. Hangeul has been honored as one of UNESCO's Memory of the World recipients. Out of the existing letters, it is the only one where the date, purposes, and people behind its creation are known.

Japanese Letters : In Japanese writing, three scripts called Hiragana, Katakana, and Kanji (Chinese characters) are used. In the year 300, Chinese characters diffused from Korea to Japan. Around 50,000 total Chinese characters exist, and there are many types of fonts as well. The Japanese people adapted Chinese characters to express Japanese. It is said that 2,136 Chinese characters are currently used in Japan.

In Japan, letters are also used like pictures or as part of pictures. The Japanese *mojie* is also often called the original emoticon. In Japan, Chinese character puzzles are also often enjoyed by the Japanese people. Japanese letters are very familiar to Japanese people, as it functions as storage for knowledge and are used for playing games as well.

Chinese Characters : Chinese Characters are used by the largest number of people around the world. Compared to other writing systems, Chinese characters feature numerous characters. It is estimated that ten thousand characters are in use today. According to Chinese legend, Fuxi (伏羲) had a leading role in writing the Eight Diagrams of divination in 3000 BC, and Changhil (Changjie) created Chinese characters based on these Eight Diagrams in 2700 BC.

Chinese characters were based on the images of objects (called pictographs). Later, the images became symbols that held meaning beyond the images themselves. Therefore, calligraphy and painting are linked to one another. When Chinese characters are written artistically, they become calligraphy and when they have profound depth, they become pictures. A Chinese character is like an oriental painting in which the letter's meaning is expressed through pictures.

2. Mongolian Letters

When thinking about the Mongols, images of Genghis Khan taking charge of the nomad tribes usually come to mind. In the nomad tribes' languages, the ancient Turk alphabet was the first letters created by nomadic tribes. Even with the tradition of using indigenous writing systems, the Mongolian language currently uses Cyrillic letters. The Mongols, as a nomadic characteristic, used various letters. During the Yuan Dynasty, the Phags-pa alphabet, developed by the Buddhist monk Phags-pa, was used. Also, the traditional Mongolian letters (Mongol Bichig) is currently used in Inner Mongolia. Since 1994, after gaining political independence from the Soviet Union, the Outer Mongolia used the Mongol Bichig. However, the Cyrillic letters, used since 1941, were much more familiar to the Mongolians. Because Mongol Bichig was written vertically, it proved to be difficult to computerize the letters. As a result, Cyrillic letters, used since the socialist revolution, are still in use in Mongolia.

3. Southeast Asian Letters

In Southeast Asia, Chinese influences are mixed with Indian cultural influences. Vietnamese letters are influenced more so by Chinese characters while Thai letters are heavily influenced by Indian letters. Thai is also connected to Lao and Cambodian languages. On the other hand, Indonesia, located among several islands, uses many different languages, but the Indonesian people speak Bahasa Indonesia and use the Latin alphabet for writing.

Vietnamese : In Vietnam, with the growing stability of the ancient monarchy, the use of Chinese characters spread. In the 10th century, like Korea's Idu, the Vietnamese used a script called Chu Nom, which changed the Chinese characters' sounds and meanings to fit the Vietnamese phonemes. For example, 石 (*dan*, rock) and 多 (*duo*, many) is written together to read *duo*. *Duo* is Vietnamese for "rock." In other words, the sound for 多 and the meaning of 石 are combined to create Vietnam's own writing system. Those who are not able to read the symbols can understand them just by listening. The current Vietnamese national language in use is called Tieng Viet. In the early 17th century, French missionary Alexandre de Rhodes created the letters for it by using the Latin alphabet.

Thai : The letters of the Thai language originated from letters of the Khmers and the Mon(s) which were based on ancient Indian letters. The letters were created by the Sukhothai Dynasty's King Ramkhamhaeng the Great. The Thai language is very similar to that of Laos. Therefore, it is possible for those who speak and write in Lao to communicate with those who speak and write in Thai. Both alphabets have phonemic letters in which consonants and vowels are combined to form letters and sounds.

Indonesian : Nowadays, Indonesians use the Latin alphabet to write the Indonesian alphabet. The national language Bahasa Indonesia is easily written with the Latin alphabet. Jawi script and other letters which were influenced by the Arabic alphabet can sometimes be seen in signs and temples. Jawi script is called the "Arab Malay letter." Bahasa Indonesia is often used as a second or third language in countries such as Malaysia, Singapore, and Brunei.

4. Arabic Alphabet

Regarding the Arabic alphabet, they say that "God drew a line while man marked a point on it," which distinctly expresses the characteristic of the Arabic alphabet. This sentence articulates the divinity of the letters well. The Islam's Koran is believed to have completely recorded the one and only god, Allah's revelation using the Arabic alphabet. As the Koran is considered to contain God's commandments, the Arabic alphabet is worshipped as well. In the Arabian region, the Arabic alphabet is not used solely for recording speech. Arabian calligraphy, which emphasizes the beauty of the letters, has done much to maintain their presence.

5. India's Hindi Letters

For hundreds of the languages of the ethnic minority groups in India, writing is not yet used. In these regions oral traditions are generally preferred. For a long time, in India's Brahman, writing was considered inferior to speech. Therefore, until the 8th century BC, writing was not used in the Indian continent. However, as letter usage spread across various languages, writing systems were used for great literature. India is one of the places in the world with the most diverse and rich literary traditions. According to an Indian scholar, nowadays, a new letter system appears every three months. There are currently 3,372 languages in India. Hindi and English are the official languages.

Development of the Internet and Switch to Digital Letters

Through the invention of the woodblock printing process in the 8th century and the movable type printing process in the 11th century in China, the letters were more widely used. After that, Johannes Gutenberg invented the printing press, which allowed massive production in publication. Various fonts were developed to help people to read more easily. Also, letters were developed to become artistic as well.

With the Information Age of the 21st century, letters came into a new period. Letters changed from simply being printed on paper or copperplates to being displayed digitally. As the spread of letters becomes more rapid, it is now possible for thousands of people to see one another's writings simultaneously.

The development of the Internet, ironically enough, emphasized the importance of writing. In the past, people communicated by telephones or by meeting in person. Now, however, many aspects of communication are done through writing on the Internet. Correspondence between individuals and the transfer of work materials in an office setting are done mostly through e-mails. There are also many people who write their thoughts down on their blogs or homepages. Furthermore, through websites, Facebook, Twitter, and other tools, information can be spread at the speed of light.

Understanding a Nation's Culture and History Through Its Writing System

To preserve speech and to pass it on, humanity invented letters. Civilizations could be developed through letters, in which knowledge could be preserved, accumulated, and transferred. As a result, not only was remote communication possible but also the build-up of historical consciousness by establishing the prospect of social consensus.

The rise and fall of letters were indicators of power in ancient societies. The Scythia did not leave behind any documents or records because they did not have a writing system. As can be seen from this case, nations that did not have a writing system were quickly forgotten. However, with letters, even minority ethnic groups can be remembered through their great written works.

Language is like music while letters are like pictures. Language is like time while the letter is like space. If music and pictures, time and space come together, writing becomes humanity's culture itself. Through freedom of expression, language and letters create a consensus in society and an identity for that society. Moreover, they are important elements for peaceful coexistence. Letters were invented to preserve and pass on speech. Letters are the site where the humanity's soul and knowledge are accumulated.

Kim Kwang-Hyun
Chief, Publication and Public Relations Team, APECIU

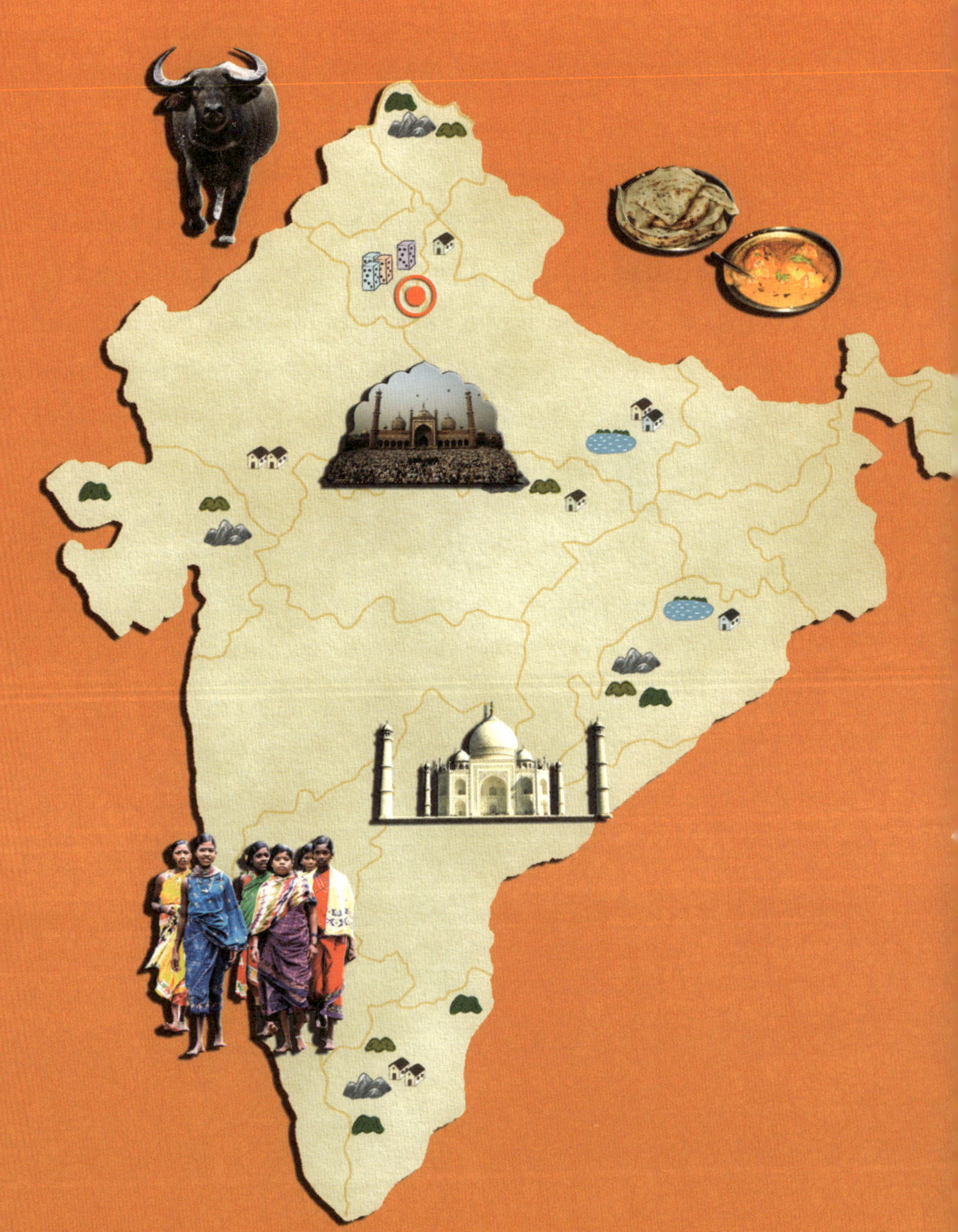

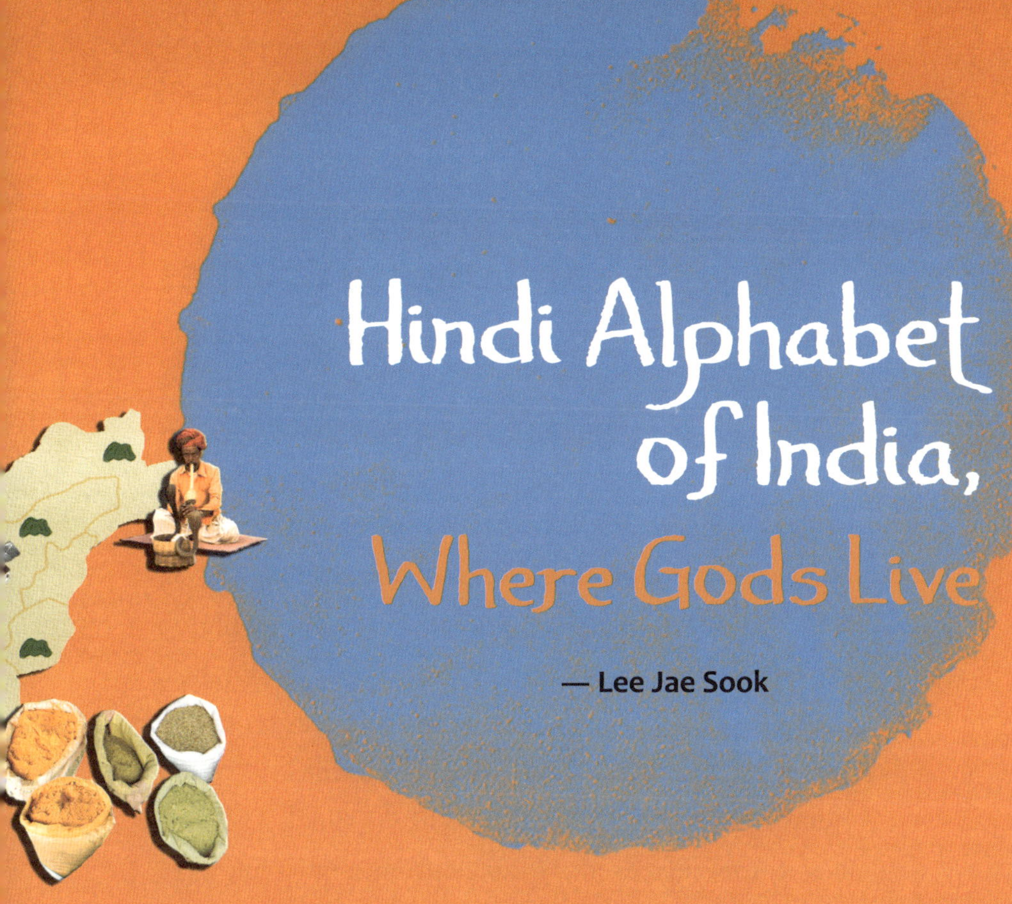

Hindi Alphabet of India, Where Gods Live

— Lee Jae Sook

एक साथ

India has 22 Official Languages and Diverse Cultures

With a population of 1.2 billion, the second largest in the world, the country's territory is the seventh largest in the world. In this manner, with 22 Indian official languages, English, and many other languages not yet listed in the Constitution, India has a multi-language environment. More local languages, which are not included in these languages, are used in everyday life. In this way, being spoken 22 Indian official languages, English, and many other languages which are not listed yet in the Constitution, India has multi-language environment.

Among them, the first official language is Hindi. Although English is commonly used, Hindi is prominently found in stamps, currency, transportation, communication, and other things that represent India. Hindi has practical use in the fields of administration, education, and broadcasting for the central government and ten northern Indian states. In 18 other states and 7 union territories, regional languages of each state are used, while Hindi and English are used additionally.

When we travel to India, we can easily notice signs using different letters in each region. Not all of these Indian languages use the same letters. There are also many cases where the English alphabet is used. However, from their many different languages all used in certain ways, we can say that they are very proud of their diverse culture.

Though India is one country, the people in India have coexisted having many languages and different cultures. They have lived together in this country for a long time with many religions, such as Hinduism, Islam, Sikhism, Buddhism, and Christianity. In India, religion and language are closely affiliated because religion has played a large role in life in India. This might explain why people with the same religion usually share the same language.

About 80% of the Indian people follow Hinduism, the

traffic signs written in Hindi and English

representative religion for Indo-European language users of northern India as well as for Dravidian language speakers of southern India. Hinduism is a religion that many people of northern and southern India believe in, and loosely links the many cultures of India together. Not all Hindus use Hindi, but many people have respect for and pride in Sanskrit, the classical language of Hinduism. Because Hindi is the closest modern Indian language to Sanskrit, educated Hindus tend to speak Hindi regardless of his or her mother tongue.

The second influential religion is Islam. Muslims usually use Urdu language, which derived from Persian letters. Even though the letters are different, Urdu is similar to Hindi in terms of speaking.

Sikhism is a religion that stemmed from Hinduism and Islam in the northern Indian region of Punjab in the 15th century. The family name shared by most Sikh people is Singh, meaning "lion." They are known as brave people who fought against the Mughal oppression, and later, British colonialism. They speak Punjabi, which is little similar to Hindi. Many people speak both languages.

In addition, even though the number of believers is small, there are Christianity, and also Zoroastrianism which is called Parsi in India. Christianity entered southern India very long ago. Just like the other religions of India, it can be seen through villages and communities using the same language. Indian regions with few upper classes of Hinduism had many people converting from Hinduism and Islam into Christianity. Moreover, because Portugal had colonized Goa (Western India) and France had colonized Pondicherry (Eastern India), the population of Christians was especially high in these regions. Zoroastrianism had also spread out in specific regions of central and northern India, such as Maharashtra and Gujarat. They speak the Gujarati language with a Parsi dialect and English. They have a strong fellowship and a rich economic power.

The Indian flag has various colors and a wheel symbol to express this diversity in India. The colors orange, white, and green adjacent to one another symbolize the diversity of cultures. The blue wheel in the center symbolizes King Ashoka, the most famous emperor of India. King Ashoka, who made Buddhism the state religion, used this symbol to embrace the people of many cultures.

Indian flag

Hindi and Devanagari Script

The name of the language "Hindi" came from the Sanskrit word "Sindhu," which refers to ancient name of the Indus River, called the Sind River, in Punjab, northern India. Sindhu was also the name of the surrounding area. Because the river has played a core role and was a symbol in ancient civilization, we can understand how the region was named after the river.

Then, how did Sindhu become Hindu? The [s] sound changed to an [h] sound. Changing [s] sound to [h] and to [i] is common in Indo-Aryan languages, where Hindi is included. We can see this change in Asura, meaning "demon," in which it was Ahura in the ancient neighboring language of Persian. Sindh River was gradually called Hind, and using the suffix "-i," which means language of surrounding region, it became Hindi. Also, the reason that India is called such in English is because when the Greeks encountered India long ago, the [h] sound of [hind] was pronounced weakly to become Indikka, or India. Hindi, meaning "the language of this region" became the most widely used language (about 400 million people estimated) among many included in the four different language families (Indo-European language, Dravidian language, Sino-Tibetan language, and Austro-Asiatic language) in India.

There are people who sometimes say that Hindi is the same language as Hindustani and Urdu, but this is because there were not distinct classifications as there are today. In the Middle Ages, Khari boli, which is like a relative to these languages used in the central and northern region of India, was mixed and used with many other language names. These languages today are actually different languages, because they differ in letters and words used according to regional characteristics. Urdu, where the Persian alphabet and words are greatly used, is regarded as one of the 22 official languages, including Hindi.

The oldest form of Hindi is Sanskrit. This language is also the oldest among Indo-European languages, which includes English, French, German, and most European languages. Linguists were able to examine the inherent characteristics of Hindustani, Persian, Arabic, and European languages through Sanskrit. The oldest form of Sanskrit was found on the incantation of ancestral rites in *Rig Veda* (12th century BC), and was used to record many Indian classics, such as *Upanishad, Mahabharata, Ramayana, Bhagavadgītā*, including book of myths, various scriptures, poetical works, plays, novels, and Mahayana Buddhism scriptures. It is not known exactly when these letters first started to be recorded. However, we can estimate from the epitaph of King Ashoka in the 3rd century BC, and the abundant traditional texts mentioned that this letter system was used long before Christ, since Sanskrit became known to all regions of Asia through Buddhism.

In early Buddhism, Sanskrit, which emphasizes strict grammar and phonological rules, was a language only for the nobles and priests. Therefore, Buddhist scriptures were written in Prakrit, mostly in Pali, which was the spoken language of that time, and common people didn't need to learn Sanskrit. In later Buddhism, scriptures were again written in Sanskrit. It was during later Buddhism when many scriptures were spread to China, Korea, and Japan. We can say that through scriptures written in two languages, ancient types of Hindi spread to all regions where Buddhism had diffused.

Hindi was developed from languages of abundant tradition and classics, and became the representative language of India today, embracing the historical inheritance of the country. For Hindi to be the means of expression for various Indian cultures, the Constitution of India (Article 351) defines the obligation for the central government to develop, expand, propagate the Hindi language, and states that, to interrupt an influx from foreign words such as English and to enrich Hindi words, they need to be retained first from Sanskrit and next from languages in each region.

Then, shall we take a closer look at Hindi language? The Indian language can be divided into two origins, the Aryan and the Dravidian. With the Deccan Plateau in the middle of Indian Peninsula, the people of Aryan origin live in the north and the people of Dravidian origin live in the south. Accordingly, along with Hindi, the languages of Aryan origin are used in the north, while the languages of Dravidian origin, including the Tamil language, are used in the south. Up to 74% of the population uses the languages of Aryan origin, which means that two third of the population uses Hindi or languages of Hindi-similar origin.

When looking at their letters, we find that Devanagari, Gurmukhi (Punjabi), Bengali, Gujarati, Oriya, and others all developed from Brahmi letters. The letters on the stone pillar recording King Ashoka's imperial order in the 3rd century BC were Brahmi letters, the oldest in Indian writing system history. Languages of Dravidian origin, including Telugu, Kannada, and Malayalam, use letters transformed from the Tamil letters, but the Tamil language itself originates from Brahmi letters. Therefore, we can say that Indian letters developed mostly from Brahmi letters. All these letters are phonetic letters, which are recorded as they sound through a combination of vowels and consonants. Usually, vowels have 15 to 16 letters, and consonants have 40 letters, which can express various sounds.

Devanagari, in particular, is known as the script for Sanskrit, the old form of Hindi. Aside from some letters that are not used today, most Devanagari letters are still used in Hindi.

Hindi uses the phonetic alphabet of Devanagari, which is composed of 11 vowels and 35 consonants. A "vowel + consonant" completes one basic syllable. Vowels are divided into short vowels and long vowels. Also, there is the diphthong, in which two vowels are pronounced in white-hot succession. For example, the basic vowel [a] and the long [a-] are used separately in letters, and it is as the case for [i], [i-] and [wu], [wu-]. Also, [o] is separated with the diphthong [au], and [e] is separated with the diphthong [ei].

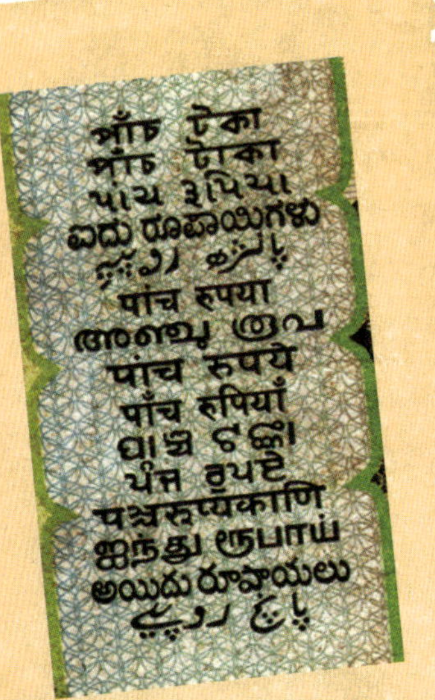

various official letters of India written on a five-rupee bill

There are 35 consonants, which can express many different sounds. Tense sounds such as [kk], [tt] and strong sounds such as [k], [t] can be written separately. Unvoiced sounds not vibrating the vocal cords, voiced sounds vibrating the vocal cords, unaspirated sounds made by not inserting breathing

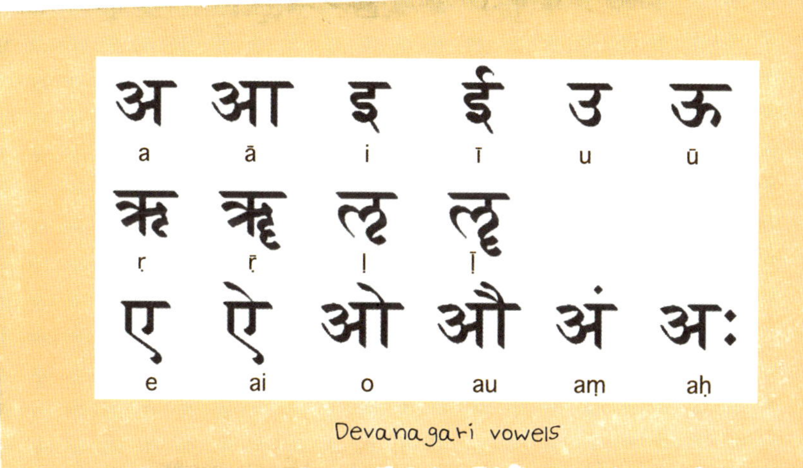

Devanagari vowels

sounds, and aspirated sounds made with rough breathing sound are all distinguished. Uniquely, retroflex sounds (tongue rolling sounds), which are made by rolling the tip of the tongue up on the palate and pressing, distinguish Indian language from other languages in Indo-European languages.

When we look at the system of consonants by introducing five letters on the first line of consonants, we can understand in greater detail about the sounds of Devanagari. Firstly, the first and second letters are voiceless sounds, third and fourth letters are voiced sounds, fifth letter is nasal sound and all letters are guttural sounds made from the throat. The first two letters are tense sounds (voiceless unaspirated sound) with voiceless sound,

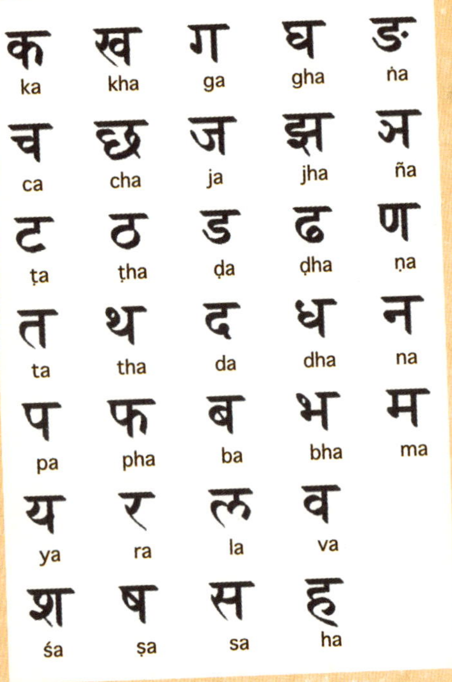

Devanagari consonants

and aspirated sound of "h" is included in k [kk] to be distinguished as a strong sound of kh [k] two letters of voiced sounds are also distinguished based on whether they are an aspirated sound or not. The nasal sound is a throat sound, therefore it sounds like [eong]. These compositions all apply the same to 25 letters. Also, there are four sibilants made of sounds such as [y], [r], [l], [v], and [swit] which are somewhat like semi-vowels. These 35 consonant sounds can express more sounds than English or many other languages.

Hindi numerals of India are the numerals in the name of "Arabic numerals" which had been spread worldwide by Arabian merchants. Since they spread through Arabian merchants, they are known as Arabic numerals. However, originally, they were

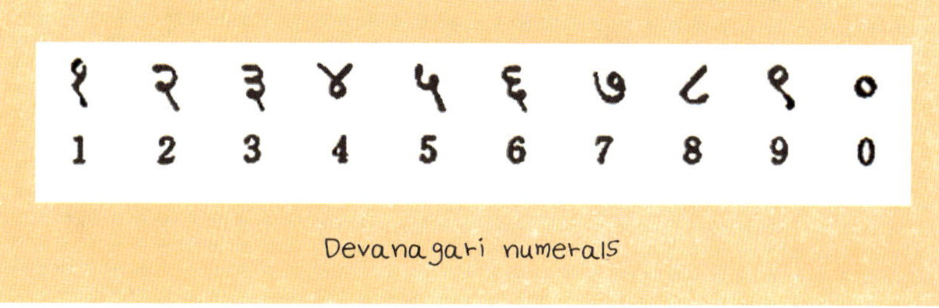

Devanagari numerals

considered Hindi numerals.

Two Roots of Indian Letters
: Indus Civilization and Aryan Civilization

Indian culture today is said to have diversity and unity. This is a result of two different civilizations' meeting and blending in each region. The cultures are diverse today because they came from two different origins. One is the Indus civilization on the Indus River Valley, and the other is the Aryan civilization, which came to India from the north to conquer the Indus civilization. Indian letters also came from these two roots. First of all, we will see how these two civilizations formed and developed, and how they blended together.

An ancient culture of India is well known through Indus civilization showing waterway technology of various waterways.

The trace of the oldest water and sewage facility in the world makes us imagine their lifestyle. The Indus civilization began in 3000 BC, 5,000 years ago from today. Historical sites of cities such as Harappa and Mohenjodaro started in the basin of the Indus River, originating from the Himalayas and flowing down to several locations. They are found near the Indus River, which soaked the land of India. After the first discovery in early 1850s, remains were found in hundreds of sites until today. From this, we can assume that the size of the Indus civilization was very large and consisted of many cities.

We can imagine, as thousands and hundreds of years pass, how the river changed its flow or dried out to no longer be a river. Most places where the Indus River used to flow are no longer river, but with the artifacts, traces of it being a river remain. Most excavations have been in the territory of Pakistan, which became a separate nation from India in 1947. Therefore, the Indian and Pakistani governments are mutually operating Indus civilization discovery and exploration projects. Recently, many historic sites were discovered in the Indian states of Gujarat and Rajasthan. When we estimate the size of the territory by gathering remains of the city together with the same civilization characteristics, it seems to be larger than the Pakistan of today, and shows signs of having operated a trade network with Mesopotamia, which was astonishing for its size.

The well-organized streets, shapes of houses, wells, and waterways including sewers are unique to the Indus civilization. After archaeologists discovered the remains, they said that there were not any big difficulties in distinguishing cities of the same civilization through their geological time zones and their characteristics. This civilization, existing in the Bronze Age, was a hierarchical society with a top to bottom structure. It had an amazing facility to bring water from the river to use in the city, and discharged the used water outside the city through the sewer. The public bath in the city remains of Mohenjodaro was 83 square meters, and the trace of a dock to anchor ships in Lothal show that it was the oldest in the world.

Did the people who lived here also worship god? We are getting to know more about them through many artifacts including round-shaped seals. Most of all, to pray for fecundity and abundance, they especially worshipped goddesses. In this agricultural society, it is probably because bearing many children for labor was important. Also, there are many artifacts carved like animals, such as cows, bulls, and snakes. It may point to the animal worship we easily find in India today. Also, the most popular symbol in India today is Shiva, the god of destruction, and the seals of people sitting in yoga asana were found among these artifacts. Goddesses, animal worship, yoga, and others can be easily found in today's India.

letters of the Indus civilization

These pictures here are seals, both discovered on the historic sites of the Indus River Valley. A human figure is engraved on the seals; these two character seals show a yoga posture. Considering that they were wearing a sharp head ornament similar to a crown and feature engraved letters, the figures probably represent a god or important character close to god.

Today, people conclude that this character was an early figure of the Shiva. Also, the letters shown here was the expression of that content. As we can see frequently in letters of ancient civilization, was it trying to deliver a message by imitating some shape? Even though we can't know the exact meaning, because it seems to be using some symbols to express a certain meaning, we think that this is

human figure seals in yoga posture

the root of Indian letters. Doesn't the letter shape somewhat resemble Devanagari, the Hindi letters of today?

In about 1500 BC, the large Indus civilization suddenly disappeared. Instead, outsiders occupied the same region. The curiosity of how the Indus civilization, which continued for 2,000 years, disappeared has not been solved yet. At this moment, we only know that between 2000 BC and 1500 BC, when Aryans had come in, there was not a large population in cities such as Mohenjodaro, and that they were already destroyed. Maybe the river was completely dried up and people could not continue to live, thus had to move along the river. Otherwise, perhaps the water not only dried up, but changed to a desert such as that which exists today, and a large-scale migration may have occurred. This region is now almost a desert, not suitable for people to live. Then, shall we find out who came into the location that the Indus civilization used to be in?

Between 2000 BC and 1500 BC, the people who came into the Indus River Valley were none other than the Aryans. After settling in the northwestern region of the Indian continent, they gradually crossed the Indus River to spread along the river to the east and south. They possessed wheels and ironware, which were the newest technologies at the time. They forced the natives who were probably descendants of Indus civilization, to move far below the Deccan Plateau. This was a major incident in history of Indian culture.

Aryans showed up not only in India. The oldest trace of Aryan civilization was found in the grassland region between the Caspian Sea and the Aral Sea. Some people think that the people who lived in the Eurasian plains long before were the first Aryans. Aryans who stayed here or somewhere else started to migrate and divided into two factions, settling in several regions.

One group spread to most European regions of today, while others headed to Persia and to Indian regions. Actually, linguists were already aware of these facts. They found out that the languages used in North India and in Europe today were passed on by Aryans who spread to different regions after 2000 BC.

Aryans were nomads who moved with livestock to find grassland. When the population of people and their livestock exceeded what they could subsist on from the grassland or when they fell behind in competition to other nomads, they had to travel long distances. As they moved for hundreds or thousands of years, some Aryans with ironware culture came to the Indian continent through the Indus River Valley and settled down.

As Aryans moved through the rivers of India and settled in the northeastern region at large, they built a new civilization. They performed rites to gods with *Veda* scriptures; the title means "all knowledge of the world." Just like how gods control nature, they took over not only the Indus River Valley, but also the Valley of the Ganges River. This was why the civilization was called Veda civilization.

Veda is a scripture. It includes details of Aryans. They called themselves Aryans, and of other natives with different skin tone or appearance, called non-Aryans or Dasa. We can see that Aryans believed they were nobler than people who were not Aryans. They had the attitude of a conqueror.

The most terrible ethnic chauvinism in world history was made while imitating the attitudes of the Aryans. Adolf Hitler, who commanded the notorious bigotry and racism of Nazis in the 1930s, said that they were the descendants of Aryans. In order to claim that they were the most prominent people in the world, he used the symbol of sun god, one of the Veda gods, in the Nazi symbol.

Aryans worshiped many forces of nature as gods, and prayed for their safety and happiness. They showed similar parts to gods that are shown in Greek and Roman mythology. For example, the god of lightning and thunder, Indra, has as similar weapon and power as the god Zeus. For the god of wind, Vayu, the god of the sea Samudra, the god of fire Agni, and other gods, the people performed ancestral rites. They prayed to gods of nature, who had powers of blessing humans but also regarded with fear.

Today, how can we know the activities of gods' fighting on chariots? It is because we can see the praise poetry of *Veda* written in the oldest language of Indian Sanskrit. *Veda* includes not only praises to gods, but also contains a lot of knowledge in astronomy, mathematics, geometry, architecture, phonology, grammar, and etymology. This abundant knowledge was used in practice to perform ancestral rites to all gods. Shouldn't they set a good day to perform ancestral rites to gods? This is why skies were watched. Constellations needed to be observed to avoid days of thunderous rain or days of drought. Also, even though gods cannot be seen, they are the subjects receiving ancestral rites. Gods were methods of expressing unseen forces

god of fire, Agni

god of thunder and lightning, Indra

of the nature. From this point, came the mathematical concept of numeral 0. Thanks to the Aryans who first used it, we were able to easily distinguish the difference of 1, 10, and 100. Because concepts of measurement, direction, size, and balance were necessary to build the altar for rites, geometry also developed. For sounds from people's mouths to be precise when praising for the happiness of gods, phonology studying short, long, high, and low sounds developed. Also, because the words had to make sense for gods and people to understand, grammar was also needed. For descendants to also understand the contents of the praise, the origin of the word was revealed, and to explain why those meanings derived, etymology also developed. Seeing that all these developments were for rites for gods, we can see how much effort Aryans put into rites.

The "Indian culture" that we call today is made up of a combination of two roots, the Indus civilization and the Aryan civilization. The same goes for the languages and letters of India. Though Aryans had the ironware culture and chariots with wheels, and took over northern region of India, but it can be contrary for culture. As Aryans settled down and adapted to the environment, there were many cases of assimilation and adaptation to the cultures of natives who originally lived there. This is the reason why it became the culture of the Indo-Aryans, distinct from the European-Aryans.

In Sanskrit, the language of the *Veda*, numerous Dravidian words assimilated. Retroflex (tongue rolling sound) in the Hindi consonant flowed into Sanskrit at this time. In the languages of southern India, a more divergent retroflex from Hindi is used.

Aryans who settled in nothern India appropriated these native elements to their *Veda* and built their unique perspective of the world and ways of living. Indra, the god of gods in Aryans' eyes, Agni, the god of fire, Vayu, the god of wind lost power through time. In a later myth, these gods lowered their heads to Vishnu and Shiva. Now, the new world of gods had begun. Brahma, Vishnu, and Shiva each symbolized the universal energies of creation, maintenance, and destruction. After a trial of strength, it became Trinitarianism in Hinduism. Among the three gods, we can say that Brahma and Vishnu started from the *Veda* civilization, while Shiva is a god who has his origin in the Indus civilization. Aside from gods, many goddesses appeared as well. We can find the origin of goddesses from the matriarchal society of Indus civilization.

The History of Indian Letters

Devanagari script, which was originated from Brahmi letters, is the matrix of most letters used in India, Nepal, and Southeast Asia. According to the Kutila epitaph, Brahmi letters transformed into the letters similar as today's in the 9th century passing through the Gupta letters (AD 350-500), the Sharda letters (AD 500-800), and the Siddham letters (AD 800-1000).

In the beginning, this letter system was only called Nagari, meaning "city" which may clearly show that it symbolized a cultural, hierarchical value of the city, not the rural area. The reason that "god (related) · sacred" was added to be known as "Devanagari" was because the letters were established as a sacred language to record teaching of cultural value or scriptures. Along with "sacred city," this letter also became a subject of worship, and had mysterious symbolisms surrounding it becoming a scripture.

Evidence of letters being used in India was clearly found in the Brahmi letters of King Ashoka's epitaph in the 3rd century BC, and based on this, letters had developed into phonographs at the time. It was also popularized through usage in the King's imperial order along with it becoming the symbol of the Maurya Kingdom.

The Brahmi letters, which were the origin of Hindi letters, were used from the 5th century BC to the AD 4th century, and the Devanagari script of Hindi was used from the 9th to 10th centuries.

The letters of the seal that were found in the remains of the cities of the Indus civilization, which was the ancient civilization of India from 3000 BC to 1500 BC, were the Sendau letters. Through the relationship between the Brahmi and Sendau alphabets is not clear, it is believed that both had influenced many languages of southern India. In southern India, the Paschimi (5th-9th century), the Madhya Pradesh (5th-9th century), the Telugu-Canari (5th-10th century), the Grant (13th century), the Kalinga (7th-12th century), and the Tamil (5th-6th century) alphabets were used.

Among the southern Indian languages, the Tamil alphabet today was directly inherited from the Tamil alphabet from the 14th century. In addition, the ancient Tamil alphabet had also developed into Singhali, Baladivi (Maldive Islands), Siro Malawari (Siria Malawaru), Hindesiyai (Indonesia), Champa (Champa, Cambodia), Khmer (Cambodia), Barmi (Myanmar), Shan (Thai), Philipiney (Philippines), and other alphabets to influence most of Southeast Asian languages' writing systems of today.

India is an expansive country with diverse cultures. In the

Contents engraved in the stone pillar of King Ashoka (268-232 BC)

"I, Ashoka, now found enlightenment and to be a happy man, will respect Buddha's teaching of the Dharma and all noble teachers' lesson and religion, and for Dharma, meaning fairness and peace, to spread to all people, I will do what I can for them to live in peace. As a father loving his son, I do love my people."

past, the Indian Peninsula rarely fell under one country, like the India of today. Historically, the only kingdom in which one king ruled most of the land was the Maurya Kingdom, which lasted for 150 years from the 4th century BC to the 2nd century BC.

In particular, the name Ashoka, who was the 3rd king of the Maurya Kingdom, is more well-known than the name of the kingdom itself. Ashoka was the king with the most powerful royal authority in the history of India. Chandragupta, the grandfather of King Ashoka, had built the Maurya Kingdom by overtaking in all directions of the Indian Peninsula. The capital, Pātaliputra, was a large city famous for its beautiful silks, spices, and teas, which drew in a number of merchants from Persia and Greece. It is said that King Bindusara, the father of Ashoka, had many sons, and had intended for another prince to become

"Ah, is this victory? Were all the victories I have won in the battlefield like this? Everywhere I see dead bodies bleeding and other dead bodies on top of them... they are all dead, but why do I hear these screaming? Is it a wailing sound? My victory tore other kingdoms like mine to pieces and did it bring wailings of wives who lost their husbands, and children who lost their fathers, and parents who lost their children?"

his successor. As Ashoka personally excelled in important wars which lead to victories, however, many people believed that he would be suitable as the king. As we can commonly see in ancient kingdoms, when the king has many sons, as in India, they are often born from different queens and battle for the throne. Otherwise, they would be exiled or killed.

Ashoka prevailed in this cutthroat competition and became the king. For ten years, he continued to war to broaden his land. It is said that in the famous Kalinga War, however, he was deeply shocked by the horrific sight of the war.

King Ashoka, who indulged in war even before becoming an adult, realized the reason he was suffering from bigger anxieties and nightmares despite numerous victories. It was due to the shock from the battlefield. To calm his mind, he sought out the teachings of Buddha. He deeply regretted the slaughter of wars and confessed that he was a weak man suffering nightmares after the happiness of each victory. By listening to Buddha's teaching everyday to calm his mind, King Ashoka wanted to apologize to and compensate for the numerous people in his kingdom who had lost their family or had been hurt. When Ashoka went with Buddhist monks around his kingdom, including the sacred place of Buddha, he shed tears of repentance.

"By seeing people's lives so closely, my heart aches with regret. I have brought wars to make orphans and for families to lose their children. It is my sin that makes people suffer greatly. I want to compensate for the debt that I owe to my people."

Ashoka promised that Dharma, the law of fairness taught by Buddha, will be applied to the people.

To perpetuate the teachings of Buddha, King Ashoka built many towers, including the Great Tower of Sanchi. Also in Budh Gaya, where Buddha found enlightenment, the large Mahabodhi Temple was built for many monks to reside. As this big temple

"I say to my ministers, after listening carefully to Buddha's teaching, I now think that this is the way for my people. Therefore, from now on, I shall not rule my nation at my will; I shall decide and practice all matters according to Dharma. First of all, a Director General for Dharma will be appointed and sent to all cities and villages. The Director General for Dharma will check how my people live and report to me without omission."

was built, people could always go to the temple to listen to Buddha's teaching.

Also, in many cities such as Lumbini, Sarnath, and Budh Gaya, stone pillars displaying the intention of King Ashoka were built. On the pillar, which was very high for everyone to see from a distance, was engraved, "Every life is precious, and each should be treated with justice and mercy, and all people and religion should be accepted generously." Because there were several languages in the large kingdom, each intrinsic letter and language was used for people using different languages.

These 80 stone pillars were built over 15 meters high. Usually, there would be an animal statue at the top of each pillar and the imperial order of the king engraved on the bottom. After King Ashoka died, the Maurya Kingdom disappeared in vain

Brahmi letters

after 50 years. But through the engraved messages found on the stone pillars, King Ashoka is forever remembered for generations to come. The four lion statues engraved with letters also became the national symbol of India today, and are used in many places including moneybills. The wheel ectype that represents the wheels of Dharma symbolizes Dharma's law of fairness, and became the symbol of India's spirit.

Conflicts and Efforts of India Regarding Languages and Letters

About 5% of Indians use English at a native level, and we can readily see them using English with other Indian languages. Speaking English and switching to Hindi depending on the subject or mood, or talking in Hindi and suddenly speaking in English, is a scene easily observed in the big cities of India.

When the British started ruling India, the British wanted some Indians to think like the British and have Indians to do their work for them. They thought that this would be possible by making many Indians think and speak in perfect English. When young Indian people with a thirst for learning believed that receiving education would be impossible without learning English while seeing Christian missionaries building schools in small villages and teaching. So, the British established a university in India where students could study and think and speak in English. This university was established to socialize Indians into those who would decide and act in the values of the British. To write the Hindi letters of Devanagari in the English Roman alphabet, many guidelines were made. Studies were done to research how to express all the sounds of Devanagari, which has more letters than the English alphabet. Indian students believed that studying in Great Britain was an important gateway to finishing the best education. The British thought that this would complete the process of transforming Indians into British people.

After several decades passed with the completion of the best British education, however, Indians did not change as the British had predicted. The British thought that when there were more Indians thinking in English like them, English would change the languages of India. However, instead of Indian letters and languages disappearing because of English, they were more actively used due to introduction of English literature and science. Even to people who cooperated with the British, English did not completely become a native language.

The reason for this failure of expectations was because Indians had originally lived in an environment of many languages. In other words, because many languages were used in India at the same time for many years, Indians, who were educated in English for many decades, thought of English as merely an additional language, and did not feel any inconvenience in using many languages.

Eventually, the British could not change the Indians through English and gave up their language policy. Instead, they instilled the policy of alienating Hindus from Islam, which triggered the debate of the Hindi and Urdu languages, which represent the two religions respectively. These two languages each used the Indian Devanagari letters and the Kharoshti letters belonging to Persian letters developed in the 13th century. In speech, however, the two languages are nearly indistinguishable, and are spoken without much problem. The East India Company of the British put the Urdu language, which was only used by a small number of people, and Hindi in the same level and changed the administrative language of some regions in North India to the Urdu language to instigate conflict between the two parties. Therefore, there were more movements to make Devanagari, which most people used, and Hindi, which uses these letters, as the official script and language of India. The Urdu speakers who opposed this actually caused conflicts between Hindi and Islam, leading to religious disputes and even bloodshed. Hindi and Urdu clearly displayed their religions

commemorative stamp of Gandhi

letters on the upper left and right are each Hindi and Urdu, meaning "father of nation"

and cultural identities by borrowing more words from Sanskrit and Persian respectively. As the turmoil continued, Mahatma Gandhi insisted to combine the two languages under the name Hindustani and to use both alphabets freely. As the usage of Hindi and Urdu was permitted in schools of India, young Indians had to experience a language conflict for the same job.

In the 19th and the early 20th centuries, there were internal conflicts regarding language. In this regards, many organizations like the Nagari Pracharini Sabha (Baranas, 1893), Hindi Sahitya Sammelan (Alahābād, 1910), Dakshina Bharat Hindi Prachar Sabha (South India, 1918), Rashtra Bhasha Prachar Samiti (Delhi, 1926), and Nagari Letters Spread Committee wanted Hindi using Devanagari script to be the only official language. They nearly accomplished their purpose through their actions. Muslims organizations, such as Anjuman Taraqqi-e-Urdu, resisted these organizations for Urdu users' rights and interests, leading the conflicts to persist. Eventually there was criticism that the language conflict between Hindi and Urdu would forever divide India into two parts, never to be united again.

Mahatma Gandhi, who is called the "father of independence," used Gujarati as his native language. However, he asserted that the language of independent India should be Hindi. He pointed out Hindi as the language that will guarantee the intellectual and cultural homogeneity of India as well as the language that shares and communicates the soul of Indian culture throughout India. He emphasized that Hindi is easy to learn and diffuse. However, there are quite a number of people who questioned why India could not unify the language. Many people said that in order for education and the administration to be effective in a country, unification of the language is the most pertinent action.

However, in India, the language problem is not that simple. Languages are not just dialects and because they have hundreds or thousands of years of history and foster their own regional culture of literature, thought, art, and religion, so users of these languages regard their language the same way they do culture. If another language other than their own becomes the official language, their culture would disappear immediately. This is why they have to resist. But if English is to become the official language, the entire culture of India would be greatly damaged and no one would want this to occur in India. Actually, to solve this complicated language problem in India, the government made great efforts after their independence. The Official Language Commission has been operating since 1955. Their task is to investigate and report official language problems every ten years to the National Assembly.

As a result of this organization's activity, there was a

regulation that all administrations of the government are to be written in Hindi through the Constitution Article 343 in 1960. In South India, especially in Tamil Nadu, the emotional turmoil brought on by the belief that the Central Government was forcing Hindi upon the people brought about riots. At that time, Prime Minister Nehru said that if people want, English can be supplementarily used, but anti-Hindi sentiments in the southern Indian region affected northern India's Hindi strengthening movement once again. Affirmative and dissenting opinions were divided regarding the notion of Hindi as an official language all across India, and its political impact was staggering. As a result, in 1963, the Central Government gave up on the Hindi strengthening policy of using English until 1965, and had

signpost of historic site
written in Oriya, Hindi, and English

to continue a stance of using Hindi with English. Therefore, important national administrations such as politics, military, diplomacy, and finance of today's India had to use Hindi centrally in Delhi. But the government is continuing to use English as a supplement with state (local) government for smooth communication.

Hindi, being the official language of the central government, is a language that government employees from all regions use. Therefore, users of Hindi in public fields are steadily increasing. Few give up their native language, but many multilingual users use two or three languages at the same time. Generally, people use their native language, Hindi, and English freely. Also, Indian cinema, the fruit of pop culture, generally uses Hindi the most. After receiving good news from spectators, movies made in each region are now dubbed in Hindi in order to expand to other regions. Even though some don't speak Hindi as a native language, most of them can hear and understand Hindi used in everyday life.

The social consensus has yet been made for Hindi to become the official language because the big obstacle is ironically "cultural pride." Since India is a multicultural society, when a proposal to have one official language arises, the prides of each culture begin to compete. They worry that if Hindi becomes the official language, non-Hindi users would become second-tier people. Even in the same Hindi temple, South India's priests who do not know Hindi or Sanskrit change the Hindi scriptures into their own language or read in their original scripture language. In Tamil Nadu, oppositions do not solely exist. Krishna Swami Ayar established the South India Hindi Propagation Organization in 1918 and is still operating. A contest was held in 1975. Every year, Indians from abroad come to this World Hindi Contest to find their roots. In the present circumstance, because they must realistically have a connective and official language, Hindi, which most people use, is set as first official language by the constitution, and English is set as a supportive official language for communication.

From Letters in Traditional Culture to Modern Artistic Characters

As we can see in many artifacts of India, letters were used in buildings or symbols in India from a long time ago. By using rock or metal, intaglio letter designs were engraved on the walls of huge buildings, and the "Om" letter, which is regarded as a symbol of Hinduism, has hundreds or more years of history.

"om" letter symbol

The oldest letters found in India is the epitaph of King Ashoka made approximately during the 3rd century BC (265-238 BC). In ancient India, letters are engraved into fumigated palm tree leaves. This old tradition dating back 2,000 years was made known to us through stone pillars, not palm tree leaves. These palm tree leaves endured for 400 years through the process of fumigation (exposed in hot smoke or insecticide, sterilized), but could not endure the effect of stones. However, these fumigated leaves played an important role in handwriting development due to its smooth surface. This handwriting (character style) tradition of letter engraving spread to many other regions in South Asia and contributed to the development of letters, handwriting, and painting.

Cases of applying beautiful handwriting to designs continued in present-day folk traditions. Even today during festivals, Indian people make colorful letters and patterns using colorful grains from the front of their houses or from their gardens. In the decoration of women's bodies through *henna*, which uses natural dye as body art for occasions such as weddings, we see many patterns and letters in the designs. We can also find character decorations on the designs of scarves and in clothing that feature various decorations.

In this manner, in India, letters are traditional elements intrinsically embedded within the lives and daily culture of Indian people. If you visit any city in India, you can see character decoration on store signs, book covers, movie posters, concerts, plays, dances, performance posters, election advertisements, religious assembly advertisements, and other media. Actually, it is more difficult to find them without any character decorations at all. In particular, the glamorous artistic letters used in the designs of wedding invitations amaze us through their exquisite

rural bus in India

poster advertising to eat milk and egg

and unique methods, as do logo designs using calligraphy. Art using specific font protected by copyright enables us to realize that letters are not solely limited to words.

The history of Indian letters presents the culture of India well. Indian letters were created with infinite imagination through the artistic minds of Indian people and developed through various means. Not merely simple letters, they are an artistic tool that holds many stories, and still play an important role today. After suffering under colonialism and confronting many cultures of the West, Indians assimilated new ideas on top of their own. Therefore, Indian letters and cultures were able to retain their native identities. The absorption of other cultures in developing their own allowed a big advantage for Indian culture to prevail.

Today, we have moved from a culture of valuing only our inherent identity to understanding other intrinsic identities through valuing tolerance. For a long time, Indian culture, adapting different cultures to live together in an environment, experimented with a spirit of tolerating differences. For example, Hinduism acknowledges not one god, but many gods, and India has 22 official languages. If we admit the differences between one another and learn from them, this will propel us to the future.

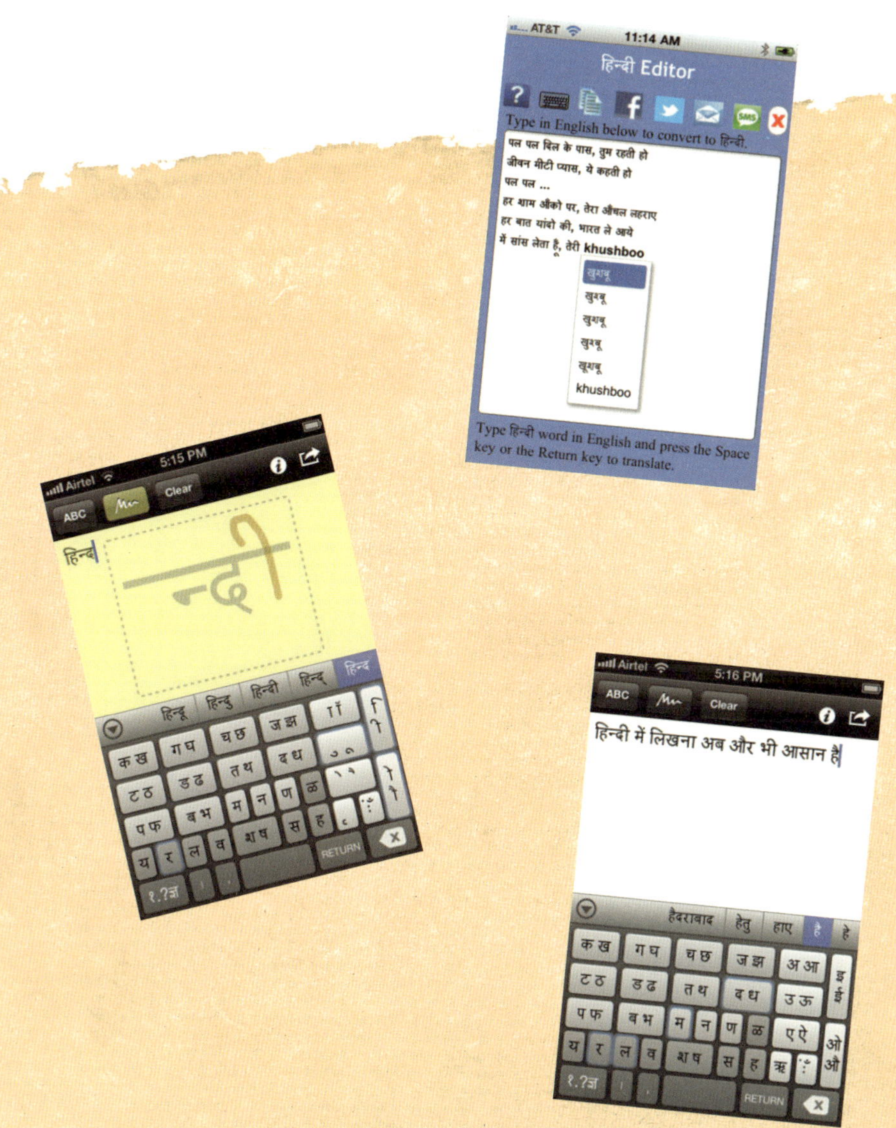

Devanagari keypads

معا

The Mysterious and Beautiful Alphabet of Arabic

— Kong Ji-Hyun

The Arabic Alphabet, the Most Widely Used during the Middle Ages

The Arabic alphabet is the letters used to write Arabic, Persian, and Urdu, which is currently used in Asia and Africa.

Countries Using Arabic Alphabet

- Officially used at a lower level in countries such as China and India as well as in Malaysia where it is acknowledged as substitute letters
- Officially used in countries along with other letters
- Countries in which it is used as the only alphabet, but other letters are acknowledged as the national language or regional language
- Countries in which it is the only official alphabet

The Arabic alphabet was widely used in the Middle Ages when the Arab·Islam Empire was prosperous and Islam was spreading. This is because the people who did not have the letters to write their language used the Arabic alphabet to design their native language writing system. The Arabic alphabet was used as their second language, religious language, or their only experienced alphabet. Therefore, Arabic alphabet became the most used letters in the Middle Ages. In Spain, some documents were written using the Arabic alphabet up until the 16th century.

As the Arab·Islam Empire weakened, however, regions using Arabic alphabet also became smaller. Entering the 20th century, the Arabic alphabet was replaced by the Latin alphabet in the Balkans, southern Africa, and Southeast Asia. Also, the Arabic alphabet, which was also used in some regions of Soviet Russia, was replaced by the Latin alphabet and again changed to the Cyrillic alphabet not long after. In 1928, as part of the Westernization reformation, Turkey changed their writing letters from the Arabic to the Latin alphabet.

Most languages included in the Iranian language family, the Indian·Aryan of Pakistan, and the Muslims of India still use the Arabic alphabet. However, the Arabic alphabet written on Bangla in Bangladesh changed to the Bengali alphabet.

Today, besides the 22 Member States of the Arab League,

Afghanistan, Pakistan, Iran, Israel, and China use the Arabic alphabet to record their official language or one of their official languages. Unlike the Arabic language included in Semitic languages, because the Iranian language, included in the Indo-European language family, is written using the Arabic alphabet, people often confuse Iran as a country that uses the Arabic language. Currently, the Arabic alphabet is the most widely used alphabet in the world next to the Latin alphabet.

Actually, because the Arabic alphabet and Latin alphabet are connected to the Phoenician alphabet, which was used in about 1000 BC, we can say that the ancestors of two languages are the same. The Phoenician alphabet consists of the letters used by the Phoenicians, ocean traders centrally located in the ancient Mediterranean world, to record the Phoenician language. The Phoenician alphabet is regarded as the ancestor of the Arabic, Greek, Hebrew, Latin, and Cyrillic alphabets. There are more proofs that Arabic and Latin alphabets have been developed from the same root. We can see the names of the alphabet letters and their order are very much similar.

Arabic Alphabet Originated from Nabatean Alphabet

Due to the nomadic life and oral cultural tradition of the Arabs, the Arabic alphabet developed slowly compared to those of other civilizations. In Mecca and other places where commerce had developed at that time, documents were used to record commercial trades and a primitive Arabic alphabet was thought to have existed in the period before Islam.

It seems that the primitive Arabic alphabet adopted the Nabateans' Nabatean alphabet. After that, it was used, modified, and developed to the next level. The Nabateans were people performing vigorous intermediary commerce and caravan trade from the 6th century BC to the AD 2nd century in northwest Arabia and Syria to accumulate wealth and prosperity. The Nabatean Kingdom conquered North Arabia and South Syria areas in

ancient remains of Petra

the 1st century BC and established the capital on what is Petra of Jordan today. The ancient remains of Petra became famous through the film series *Indiana Jones*. In 2007, it was selected as one of the new Seven Wonders of the World.

The Nabateans were influenced by the Aramaic and their Aramaic alphabet, which was the official language at the time. The Aramaic alphabet has a direct link to the Phoenician alphabet and became the prototype for many Semitic alphabets. The Nabateans developed and used their own alphabet, the Nabatean alphabet. Just like Arabic today, it was written from right to left. The Nabatean culture deeply influences the Arabian Peninsula at the time and also greatly affected the development of the early Arabic alphabet.

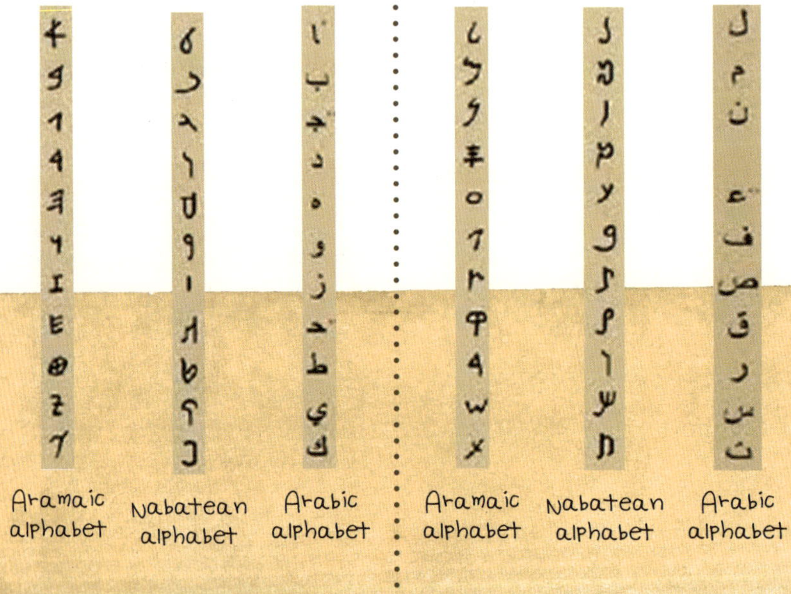

Aramaic alphabet
Nabatean alphabet
Arabic alphabet
Aramaic alphabet
Nabatean alphabet
Arabic alphabet

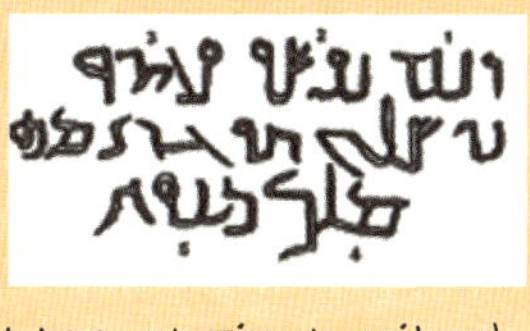

Umm al-Jimal epitaph

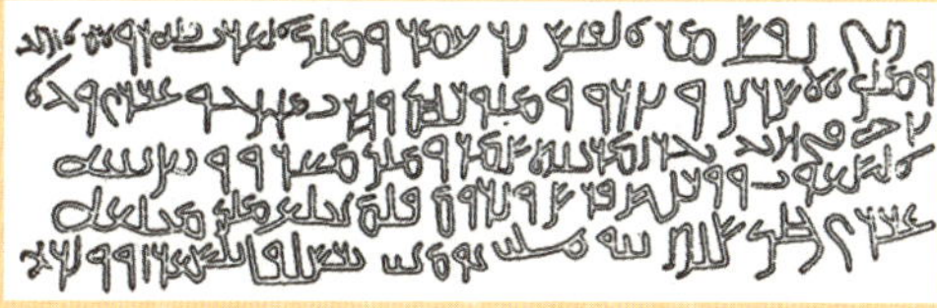

Namaran epitaph

The ancient epitaph of the Arabic alphabet showed its origin in the Nabatean epitaph Umm al-Jimal (AD 250), and Namaran (AD 328), which were found in the tombs of Imru' al-Qais, a poet before the Islam age.

The oldest record of the Arabic alphabet is the epitaph discovered in the Zabad region. The Zabad epitaph, which is estimated to have been built in AD 512, was written in three alphabets: Arabic, Greek, and Syrian.

Also, another Nabatean epitaph found in the Umm al-Jimal is assumed to date back to the 6th century, and the alphabet used in this epitaph is similar to Arabic alphabet used by the Hira and Anbar tribes in the northern Arabian Peninsula.

Zabad epitaph

The Arabic Alphabet Used by Adam

Most Arabs·Muslims believe that the Arabic alphabet was a gift from God (Allah) to humans. It is said that Adam first wrote Arabic alphabet on clay and Ismael used the alphabet after the Great Flood. Muslim scholars claim that the Arabic language was the mother of all languages and was the language that Allah taught Adam in heaven. As Adam disobeyed Allah's words, however, Allah took the Arabic language away and taught other languages instead. Therefore, the Arabs believe that all humans of the world will again communicate using the Arabic language in heaven.

The sanctity of the Arabic language and its alphabet stemmed from the fact that it was used as a way to deliver and record the Koran. In 612 in the Gregorian calendar, the night between the 26th and the 27th of the Ramadan month is regarded as the "Night of Power" to all Muslims because the Koran was first revealed to the prophet Muhammad on this very night. The first verse of the revelation begins like this: "Read in the name of your Lord who created man from a clot. Read, for your Lord is Most Bountiful, who teaches by the pen, teaches man that which he knew not." Among Arabs, this verse is regarded to emphasize the holiness of the Arabic and its alphabet and also the importance of learning.

Some Egyptian scholars claim that the Arabic alphabet borrowed the form and pronunciation of the hieroglyphics of ancient Egypt. For example, they say that the Arabic consonant of ط [ṭ] imitated the shape of in Egyptian hieroglyphic and with this consonant the Arabic noun طائر means "bird." Another example is the Arabic consonant خ [kh], which imitated the shape of in Egyptian hieroglyphic, and the Arabic noun خروف using this consonant means "sheep." Likewise, the Arabic consonant ر [r] imitated the Egyptian hieroglyphic and the Arabic word ريح used this word to mean "wind." Doctor Ossama Alsaadawi of Egypt provided the following chart showing the letters of the Arabic alphabet borrowed from

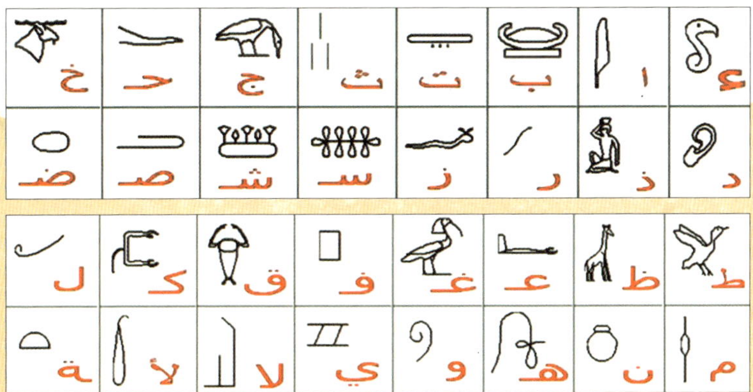

Arabic alphabets borrowed from Egyptian hieroglyphics

Egyptian hieroglyphics.

Today, the Arabic language is used as follows on mobile phones and keyboards.

Arabic mobile keypad and computer keyboard

From the early 1970s, as the Arab countries' voice and influence in international society grew, the Arabic language was used as an official and diplomatic language in various international organizations. Furthermore, in Arabic countries including Saudi Arabia and the United Arab Emirates, an enormous amount of crude oil is produced, greatly affecting the world economy. Consequently, the Arabic language is used as an important trade language in the international oil resource market. Because of these political, diplomatic, economic, and religious importance of it being the language of the Koran, futurologists predict that along with English, Spanish, and Chinese, Arabic will be a language that will remain on Earth even after 2,000 years.

The Arabic Language Written from Right to Left

Like other Semitic languages, the Arabic language is written from right to left. With 22 consonants changed only in form from the Semitic language and six consonants added to express the unique sounds of the Arabic language, the Arabic alphabet is composed of a total 28 consonants.

When we look at the Arabic alphabet in detail, there are many similar consonants. Thus, small dots are added to the top, bottom, and middle of letters to distinguish them. For example, the Arabic letter of ب having [b] phonetic value and ت having [t] phonetic value are the same in the form of ٮ, but the letter of [b] phonetic value has a small dot on the bottom, and letter with [t] phonetic value has two small dots on top. These small dots were designed when recording the Koran in the early Islam age in the 7th century.

In fact, when recording the Koran in the beginning, 15 alphabets were presented and 28 phonemes were being used. For example, the letter ب expressed different phonetic value of [b], [n], [t], and [th]. Muslim historians claim that in the early Islam age, this wasn't any problem for the Arabs. However, as Arabic and the Koran began to spread to non-Arabic Muslims, there were confusions and improper usages. Also, Arabs felt obligated

خ [x]	ح [ħ]	ج [ʤ]	ث [θ]	ت [t]	ب [b]	أ [a:, æ:]
ك [k]	ظ [zˤ, ðˤ]	ط [tˤ]	ز [z]	ر [r]	ذ [ð]	د [d]
غ [ɣ]	ع [ʕ]	ض [m]	ص [sˤ, ts]	ن [n]	م [m]	ل [l]
ي [j]	و [w]	ه [h]	ش [ʃ]	س [s]	ق [q]	ف [f]

to pass the Koran to next generations accurately. Therefore, they felt the need to elaborate on the Arabic alphabet. Eventually, the Arabs solved these confusions using the method of putting small dots in different spots and having different number of dots. In other words, with the basic form of ٮ, one dot below ب makes the [b] sound, one dot above ن makes the [n] sound, and two dots on top ت makes the [t] sound.

The Arabic language has a total eight vowels; three monophthongs of [a], [u], [i] and three long vowels of [a], [u], [i] and two diphthongs of [ai] and [au]. Actually, in the early Islam age, the Arabic language did not have a monophthong notation system. Originally, the Semitic language had a characteristic of marking only the consonant, while the Arabic language, which was a relatively new language among Semitic languages, followed this characteristic. But the archives without vowels bring confusion in communicating exact meaning and understanding. In particular, in the manuscript of the Koran recorded in its early stage, there were often cases of the main verses being recited incorrectly because vowels were not marked. To solve these problems, the Arab scholar Abu Aswad ad-Duwali designed a vowel notation system using these distinction dots in the mid 7th century. He informed his clerks to mark the distinction dots according to his mouth shape when reading the Koran. To

monophthong	َ	ِ	ُ
Phonetic value	[a]	[i]	[u]

distinguish the vowels, if his mouth opens to pronounce the [a] vowel, the dot is marked on top of the letter; if the mouth splits to pronounce the [i] vowel, it is marked on the bottom of the letter; and if his mouth is rounded to pronounce the [u] vowel, it is marked on the side of the letter. Through the constant efforts of many scholars, the vowel notation system became more systematic, and in the late 8th century, the vowel symbols that people are using today were finally established.

Since Arabic alphabet system has been developed gradually

1 أ	2 ب	3 ج	4 د	5 ه	6 و	7 ز	8 ح	9 ط
10 ي	20 ك	30 ل	40 م	50 ن	60 س	70 ع	80 ف	90 ص
100 ق	200 ر	300 ش	400 ت	500 ث	600 خ	700 ذ	800 ض	900 ظ
1000 غ								

yet substantially during the 7th and 8th century, the phoneme of each consonant could be distinguished with a system to notate the monophthong, and develop into complete alphabet system.

Also, before numerals came from India, the Arabic alphabet was used in substitution for numerals. For example, the consonant أ was 1, ب for 2, and ج for 3.

Arabic Numerals and Arabic-Indic Numerals

Today, many Arabs use Arabic-Indic numerals (Indian numerals), not Arabic numerals (Hindu numerals), which we use currently. Arabic numerals originated from the numeric system designed by Indian mathematicians in the year 500. The reason the system was known as "Arabic numerals" in the West, is that Arabs in Northern Africa spread the Hindu numerals to Europe in the 10th century. Europeans did not know that numerals were designed in ancient India, and because they learned the numeric system from the Arabs, they referred to this system as "Arabic numerals."

Also, Arabic-Indic numerals originated from India as well, and Arabs call the numerals "Indian numerals." Today, countries

Arabic numerals (Hindu numerals)	0	1	2	3	4	5	6	7	8	9
Arabic-Indic numerals (Indian numerals)	٠	١	٢	٣	٤	٥	٦	٧	٨	٩

in the Maghrib region, west of Egypt, use Arabic numerals. But the eastern regions of Egypt on the Arabian Peninsula and Arabic countries nearby use Indian numerals (Arabic-Indic numerals).

The Alphabet of the Middle Age Is Maintained

The Arabic alphabet has a unique characteristic of not marking the monophthong within words. Also, one consonant has several types of being independent, placed in the front, middle, and back of words, and several dots are also marked at the top or bottom of the letter. The Arabic alphabet, which is the alphabet to record the Koran, is thought to be the perfect letters having religious and aesthetic importance to Arabs·Muslims. Thus, the Arabic alphabet system established in the Middle Ages is still used without any modern change or modification.

In the modern era, as a flexible method to express modern thinking or to develop a symbol of political-economic revival, various efforts by the Arabs were taken to reform the Arabic language. Among them, some reformers claim that the Arabic alphabet needs to be reformed to modernize the Arabic world.

There were several proposals and disputes concerning the Arabic alphabet reformation. However, all reformation and changing attempt failed because most Arabs·Muslims consider Arabic alphabet as sacred letters, all reformation and changing attempt failed. Public opinion about the alphabet reformation raised many disputes, but ended without any practical solution.

For the Arabic alphabet reformation, some scholars claimed to replace the Arabic alphabet with the Latin alphabet, as Turkey had done in the 1920s. But these claims were not accepted by most scholars and were even considered to be an act of heresy. Arabs·Muslim scholars claim that because the Arabic language is a line of Semitic language, it cannot be easily adjusted to become another language system. Also, they say that converting the Arabic alphabet to the Latin alphabet is inappropriate because it violates the spirit of the language, and there is no benefit aside from convenience for non-Arabic people to speak Arabic. Moreover, they insist that if the Latin alphabet is used, the Arabic language will be damaged due to the abuse of foreign words.

In addition, Arabic scholars say that if Arabic alphabet is substituted by the Latin alphabet, the base of the Arabic language, which is the pivotal for many Arabic countries, will weaken and be divided into several linguistic groups. It is because the language notation system not only preserves the meaning of its language, but also the national spirit of the people speaking it. Moreover, the point is that Latin alphabets cannot express certain unique pronunciations possible only in the Arabic language. Unlike Turkish, there are enormous amount of literature recorded in the Arabic alphabet accumulated for more than 13 centuries. On the basis of Arabic alphabet's aesthetic beauty in handwriting art, Arabs today have a dominant stance that the Arabic alphabet must be maintained at its current state.

Some futurologists predict that after 2,000 years, among many languages used worldwide today, only the four languages of English, Spanish, Arabic, and Chinese will remain, and the rest will be used as a regional dialect or will disappear entirely. This exemplifies the value and importance of the Arabic language and alphabet.

Artistic Sublimation of the Arabic Alphabet

The Arabic alphabet, in which the shape of letters changes when it comes in front, middle, and back of one word, has an excellent design element and artistic function of the letter itself. The form of early Arabic handwriting was simple, but as decorations were added, it developed beautifully. Through calligraphy using Arabic alphabet, Arabs maximized their artistic ability to express the Arabic alphabet beautifully and brilliantly.

Among the Arabic handwritings, there are the Kufi script, the Naskh script, the Thuluth script, the Ruq' script, the Divani script, the Farisi script, and the Maghribi script to name a few. The Kufi script is the oldest, which was used starting from the end of the 7th century. The Kufi script had a bold, solemn style, appropriate for engraving the words of coins, or on the wall of a temple or an epitaph. Afterwards, in the Abbas Dynasty, the Kufi script developed to a beautiful style and was used as handwriting for decoration. It is said that the Kufi script was mainly used until the 11th century to transcribe the Koran. The Naskh script, which was used from AD 1000, is a cursive style, mainly used on paper for ordinary purposes. The Naskh script was used widely as publishing·printing script and today,

Kufi Script

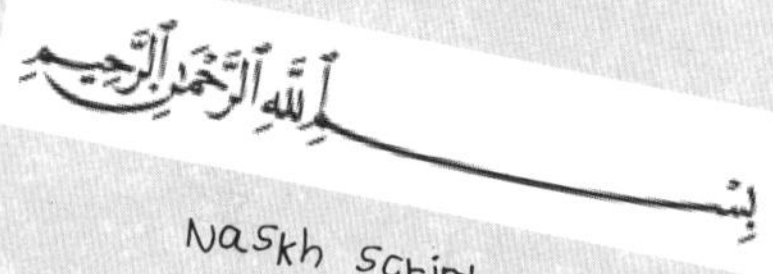

Naskh Script

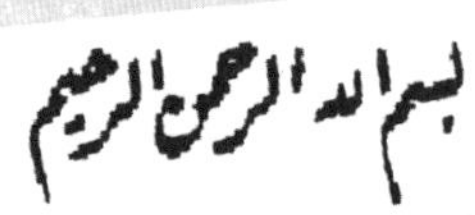

Thuluth Script

Ruq' Script

Divani Script

Farisi Script

Maghribi Script

various Arabic scripts meaning "in the name of Allah, the merciful and benevolent" it is mainly used for books, newspapers, magazines, and other print media. The Thuluth script, which is a rather decorative style of Naskh script, is a style that is long lengthwise. It was mainly used in the Mamuluk Dynasty in the 14th-15th centuries and developed into a more polished script during the Ottoman Turks Dynasty. It is mostly used for titles of books or articles. Also, during the Ottoman Turks Dynasty, a cursive style of the Ruq' script was designed for fast writing and is still widely used in the Arabic world as a cursive script today. The Divani script also developed in the Ottoman Turks Dynasty, used mainly for official documents issued by the palace such as proclamation of sultan, etc. The Farisi script originated in the east of Iran, derived from the script when Arabs wrote Persian through borrowing the Arabic alphabet. Lastly, the Maghribi script was a widely used script in northern Africa and southern part of Spain, Andalusia region. It is similar to the Kufi script.

Islam prohibits the depiction of people's faces because it is considered part of idolatry. Therefore, even the portrait of Prophet Muhammad, who is a respectable figure for all Muslims, had not been shown to this day. It is said that they feared that people of the following generations will worship Muhammad instead of God, so there are no existing portraits of Muhammad. Instead, calligraphy using the Arabic alphabet became works of

figures made of Arabic alphabet

vases decorated with Arabic alphabet

structure decorated with Arabic alphabet

art in the Arabic·Islamic world.

Arabic handwriting was unique in combining extreme regularity, glamour, and freedom, which helped to create the traditional Islamic atmosphere. Therefore, Arabic handwriting was used in Islam temples and on the walls of structures, and was also used to decorate pottery and crafted work. For example, it was decorated in a frieze style on door frames and domed backgrounds of structures and on all types of ornaments such as vases and plates. The texts used on these decorative tablets were mostly verses of the Koran. It is believed that the various, beautiful decorations of Arabic handwritings have embodied the artistic Arabian world.

ร่วมกัน

Easy When You Know It,

Thai Letters

— Kim Hongkoo

Thai, with Their Own Unique Alphabet

Thai (Pasa Thai) is the official language of Thailand and the language of the Thai people, who are the majority of the population. Thai belongs to the Tai language group of Tai-Kadai language family. The people using the languages of this group live in Thailand, southwestern China, northern Vietnam, Laos, northern Myanmar, and northern India. Thai is the most important language among the Tai language group, with 67 million people of Thailand using it as an official language.

The standard Thai language is based on the capital Bangkok and the nearby central dialects. In other areas, different dialects are used respectively. For example, the Isan dialect, a variant of the Thai and Lao languages, is used in the Isan area on the northeastern side of Thailand. In the north, where the old Chiang Mai Kingdom was based, the northern dialect is used. Meanwhile, in the south, the southern dialect is used.

Besides this, many other languages not related to Thai are used in Thailand. The Thai hill tribes, who live on the borders of Thailand, Laos, and Myanmar, use their own languages. On the border areas of Thailand and Cambodia, the Cambodian language is used, while in the central Supanburi area, the Mon-

July 29th, National Thai Language Day

Khmer language known as Suoyi or Guoyi is used.

In Thailand, various dialects and languages of other ethnic groups different from the standard languages are mixed and used. However, most people are able to use the standard language because of the widespread usage in schools and in media.

The Thai language originated from the Khmer alphabet (ancient form of current Cambodian alphabet), which was modeled after the alphabet used in Ancient India. It was created by King Ramkhamhaeng the Great (1278-1298) of the Sukhothai Dynasty (1238-1438) in 1283. The first Thai alphabet can be found on the epitaph of King Ramkhamhaeng the Great. Through many centuries, the Thai alphabet has changed its shape. At the time of creation, the alphabet was somewhat different from the Thai alphabet in today in terms of arrangement method and style. More letters and two intonation signs were later added, and the vowel was changed to be freely positioned above, below, to the left, and to the right of the consonant, where it once positioned only to the left or to the right. The Thai alphabet in use today was revised during the reign of King Rama I (1782-1809).

History of Thailand and Birth of Thai Alphabet

The Thai people, who use the Thai language, come from Mongolian ancestry. The general theory is that they lived across the northwestern part of China near Altai mountain range and passed through the upper regions of the Yellow River to move south to the Valley of the Yangtze River. The Thai people who lived in the Valley of the Yangtze River were divided into several villages: Mung, Lung, Pa, and Ailau. They gradually established a unified nation. However, due to frequent invasions from China, they moved south until Sinulo built the Nanzhao Kingdom in the Yunnan province in AD 651. At the time, the language used in the Nanzhao Kingdom was included in the Tai language group of Tai-Kadai languages. Tai is a language used in the bow-shaped regions of Hainan to Yunnan in China, and also in Thailand, Laos, Myanmar's Shan state, and the Guangxi region of today.

Kublai Khan of the Mongol Empire had conquered the Nanzhao Kingdom in 1253, leading the Nanzhao people to split into three paths, moving south towards Southeast Asia. The people who moved to the Salween River south of Myanmar were called Shan or Thai-yai, and some of them continued to move west to build the Ahom Kingdom on the eastern region of the Assam in India. The Tai moved east to settle in the Valley of the Mekong River, with some moving to Tongking, the northern part of Vietnam, and to Laos. Another group moved to the Valley of the Chao Phraya River, and they are the direct ancestors of the Thai people today, called Thai Noi.

Before the Thai people moved from South China to the Thailand of today, this region was occupied by the Mon and Khmer. The Mons built the Dvaravati Kingdom (6th-11th century) and the Hariphunchai Kingdom (7th-13th century), but were overtaken by the Ankor Kingdom (9th- 15th century) of the Khmer. In the glory days of the Ankor Kingdom, they expanded their land from the center of Cambodia to the end of the Malay Peninsula and to northern Thailand and Laos on the northern side.

In the northern regions of Thailand in the early 13th

century, many small kingdoms, in the form of city-states, were rivals. Among the small kingdoms, the Lat Kingdom and the Bangyang Kingdom formed an alliance to eliminate the Ankor Kingdom, who were ruling the Sukhothai region, and later built the Sukhothai Kingdom (1238-1438). The first king was King Sri Intratit and afterwards, nine kings ruled the Sukhothai Kingdom for 200 years.

The Sukhothai Kingdom had their golden days during the reign of the third king, Ramkhamhaeng the Great. In 1283, King Ramkhamhaeng the Great invented the Thai alphabet based on the Khmer alphabet, which originated from South India. In the early Sukhothai Kingdom, the alphabet of the Mons was used. But there were inconveniences in writing Thai words and making Thai intonations using the Mons alphabet. Considering such inconveniences, the king drew from the Khmer alphabet to invent the Thai alphabet. It was during this time that the Thai culture began to establish its form. Wide use of the Thai language in nearby regions marked the success of that language. The Thai alphabet contributed to the creation and spread of Thai culture. It was used not just in literary works, but also in legislations and history records. Thai people believed that the invention of the Thai alphabet by King Ramkhamhaeng the Great was a decisive victory in securing the country's status as an independent country

Statue of
King Ramkhamhaeng the Great

and inspiring national consciousness of the Thai people.

The invention of the Thai alphabet by King Ramkhamhaeng the Great is recorded in the epitaph documenting his historical achievement. However, there were some questions later surrounding the discovery of the epitaph for King Ramkhamhaeng the Great. The person who found this epitaph was Prince Mongkut (later King Rama IV). He claimed that before becoming a king, in 1833, when he was a monk, he was inspecting the old ruins of the castle of the Sukhothai Kingdom and found the epitaph of King Ramkhamhaeng the Great.

When we look at the epitaph of King Ramkhamhaeng the Great, it is written, "Before, there was no Thai alphabet, and in 1826 after Buddha (1283), King Ramkhamhaeng the Great, concerned over this, wrote the Thai alphabet." This was seen as King Ramkhamhaeng the Great's invention of the Thai alphabet. Recently, however, there were some claims that the Thai alphabet was actually made after this period. Political scientists claim that this epitaph was made in order to establish legitimacy to survive the imperialist invasion and to maintain the country's independence. Linguists point out that this epitaph does not correspond with the Sukhothai period in terms of the letters and styles used, and there are parts that lack in unity of person.

During these disputes, in 1989, Princess Kalayani Wattana, sister of King Bhumibol (1946-present), ordered for the analysis of this epitaph in comparison with other epitaphs thought to be from the same period. The analysis concluded that it was made in the same period. Nevertheless, this dispute still continues today.

contents on epitaph of King Ramkhamhaeng the Great

epitaph of King Ramkhamhaeng the Great

The Alphabet and Intonation of the Thai Language

Consonants

There are 44 consonants in the Thai language, but two of them are not currently used. There are 21 different pronunciations for the consonants. Because some consonants have the same sound, each consonant has one representative noun for easy memorization (e.g., *a* for *apple*, *b* for *bat*). In fact, the representative noun is not pronounced when reading the actual word. To pronounce the consonant, a อ [eo] of vowel is used. For example, ก is pronounced กอ [kkeo].

Table of Consonants

No.	Consonant	Pronunciation	Example	Pronunciation	Definition
1	ก	kkeo	ไก่	kài	egg
2	ข	keo	ไข่	kài	egg
3	ค	keo	ควาย	kwa̅-i	water buffalo
4	ฆ	keo	ระฆัง	lákang̅	bell
5	ง	eungeo	งู	eungū-	snake
6	จ	jjeo	จาน	jja̅-n	plate

No.	Consonant	Pronunciation	Example	Pronunciation	Definition
7	ฉ	cheo	ฉิ่ง	chìng	jing (instument)
8	ช	cheo	ช้าง	chá-ng	elephant
9	ซ	sseo	โซ่	ssô-	chain
10	ฌ	cheo	เฌอ	cheū-eo-	tree name
11	ญ	yeo	หญิง	ǐng	woman
12	ฎ	deo	ชฎา	chádā-	dance
13	ฏ	tteo	ปฏัก	ppàttàk	spear, pole
14	ฐ	teo	ฐาน	tǎ-n	pedestal, platform
15	ฑ	teo	มนโฑ	mōntō-	woman's name
16	ฒ	teo	ผู้เฒ่า	pû-tâo	old man
17	ณ	neo	เณร	nē-n	sramaera monk
18	ด	deo	เด็ก	dèk	child
19	ต	tteo	เต่า	ttào	turtle
20	ถ	teo	ถุง	tǔng	bag, sack
21	ท	teo	ทหาร	táhǎ-n	soldier
22	ธ	teo	ธง	tōng	flag, flagpole
23	น	neo	หนู	nǔ-	mouse
24	บ	beo	ใบไม้	bāimái	leaf

No.	Consonant	Pronunciation	Example	Pronunciation	Definition
25	ป	ppeo	ปลา	ppeūlla	fish
26	ผ	peo	ผึ้ง	peûng	bee
27	ฝ	hwo	ฝา	hwǎ-	cap, cork
28	พ	peo	พาน	pā-n	tray
29	ฟ	hwo	ฟัน	hwān	tooth
30	ภ	peo	สำเภา	sǎmpāo	sailing ship
31	ม	meo	ม้า	má-	horse
32	ย	yeo	ยักษ์	yák	goblin
33	ร	reo	เรือ	reū-a	ship
34	ล	reo	ลิง	rīng	monkey
35	ว	wo	แหวน	waě-n	ring
36	ศ	sseo	ศาลา	sša-rā	pavillon
37	ษ	sseo	ฤาษี	rēu-sši	virtuous man, ascetic
38	ส	sseo	เสือ	sseǔ-a	tiger
39	ห	heo	หีบ	hì-b	box
40	ฬ	reo	จุฬา	jjùllā-	name of kite
41	อ	eo	อ่าง	à-ng	basin
42	ฮ	heo	นกฮูก	nókhû-g	owl

Certain consonants sound completely different in its final form depending on the initial consonant of the word. For example, ญ [yeo]'s initial consonant is [j] and ล [reo]'s initial consonant is [l], but the final sound is [n]. For example, the name of the current King of Thailand (ภูมิพล , Bhumibol) is read "phumiphon," not "bhumibol."

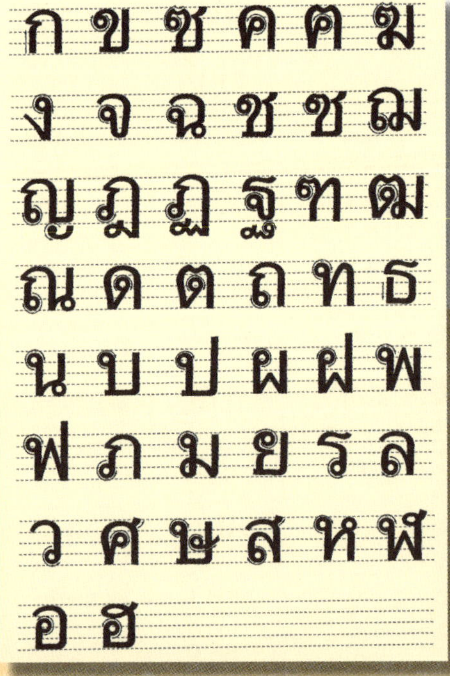

method of writing Thai consonants

Vowels

The vowels of the Thai language are marked above, below, to the left, or to the right of the consonant. Unlike the consonants, the vowels do not have names. There are thirty-two vowels, which are divided into eighteen monophthongs, six diphthongs, and eight syllable vowels. Each group is divided into monophthongs and long vowels.

Monophthongs (18)

Single vowels			Long vowels		
-ะ	a	จะ	-า	a-	นา
-ิ	i	ต	-ี	i-	ดี
-ึ	eu	ถึง	-ื	eu-	มือ
-ุ	u	ลุง	-ู	u-	ดู
เ-ะ	e	เตะ	เ-	e-	เท
แ-ะ	ae	และ	เ-ะ	ae-	แบบ
เ-ะ	eueo	เลอะ	เ-อ	eueo-	เธอ
โ-ะ	o	โกะ	โ-	o-	โต
เ-าะ	eo	เกาะ	-อ	eo-	คอ

Diphthongs (6)

Single vowels			Long vowels		
เ-ียะ	iya	เกียะ	เ-ีย	i-ya	เสียง
เ-ือะ	eua	เกือะ	เ-ือ	eu-a	เมือง
-ัวะ	ueo	กัวะ	-ัว	u-eo	วัว

Syllable Vowels (8)

Single vowels			Long vowels		
ฤ(รึ)	reu	ฤดู	ฤๅ ฦๅ	reu-	ฤๅชา
ฦ(ลึ)	reu				
-ำ	am	คำ			
ใ-	ai	ใจ			
ไ-	ai	ไว			
เ-า	ao	เบา			

* "–" is the place the consonant is located.

In other words, these are seen as vowels made of one syllable. ฤ [reu], ฤๅ [reu-], ฦ [reu], ฦๅ [reu-] are used in the Pali language of India and in loanword of Sanskrit, but ฦ , ฦๅ are not used today, and ฤ is used most often. For example, the word ฤดู *(reudu)* is seen as one syllable of ฤ and ร+ึ, so ฤดู is seen as made of two syllables.

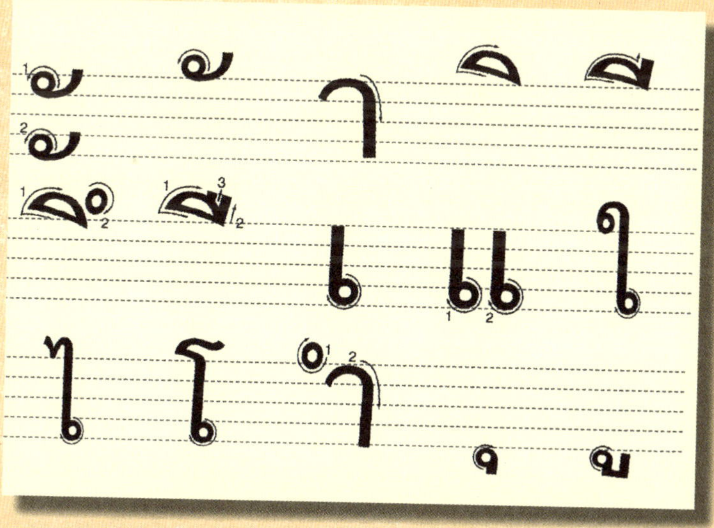

method of writing Thai vowels

Numerals

In Thailand, Arabic numerals are used, but the following unique numerals of Thailand are used more widely.

Numerals

๑ (neung)	๒ (sseong)	๓ (ssam)	๔ (ssi)	๕ (ha)	๖ (hok)	๗ (jjet)	๘ (ppaet)	๙ (kkao)	๐ (ssip)
1	2	3	4	5	6	7	8	9	0

Intonation

Thai is a tone language. There are specific intonations for each syllable. Even if it is a syllable or word with the same consonant and vowel, if the intonation is different, it is considered a word with a different meaning. Therefore, it is highly important to pronounce with the exact intonation.

For example, according to the high and low of the sound, the word ขาว (*kau*) can be "rice," "news," or an adjective of "white." In other words, the definition can be changed according to the high and low tone of the sound.

There are four intonation symbols in the Thai language, but five intonations are pronounced when reading. It is because the basic articulation of even tones and consonants do not have intonation symbols. In addition, not all consonants have five intonations. The intonations of the Thai language are divided into concrete intonation, which use four intonation symbols to express the intonation and intangible intonation, where the intonation is determined according to the initial consonant, rhythm of the vowel, and type of the final consonant without the intonation symbol. The four intonation symbols are ่ ้ ๊ ๋ .

The Thai Language Reflects the Unique Culture of Thailand

The Thai language and alphabet played an important role in forming the culture of Thailand. Because the Thai language is closely linked to the living culture, we can see the people's habits through the language. There are no special distinctions in the language used by men and women aside from *krap* and *ka*. *Krap* **ครับ** which comes at the end of the sentence is used by men, while *ka* **ค่ะ** is used by women. They seem to speak informally even with elders and seniors, but in actuality, Thai people are very careful when speaking. Difficult honorific words must be used especially if in conversation with royal parties. Special words are also used with Buddhist monks.

Greetings

When someone clasps both hands to their chest and politely says, "**สวัสดี ค่ะ** (*Ssawatdi ka*)" or "**สวัสดี ครับ** (*Ssawatdi krap*)," you may answer "Ssawatdi ka" or "Ssawatdi krap" with your hands together as well. This is a common greeting used for hello or goodbye.

greeting

When you meet someone who you have not seen for a while, the person might say "**สบายดีไหมคะ** (*Ssabai di mai ka*: How have you been?)." Then you can answer by saying "**สบายดีใคะ** (*Ssabai di ka*: Yes, I have been well)." The purpose of this greeting is to be courteous. "**ไปไหน** (*Ppai nai*: Where are you going?)" is also used as a greeting. Therefore you can also answer "**ไปธุระ**

(*Ppai tura*: I have some matters…)," but sometimes they can ask you where you are really going. Therefore, it must be used on the right occasion.

Mai ppaen rai (ไม่เป็นไร)

ขอบคุณค่ะ (*Keop kun ka*) is thank you and **ไม่เป็นไร** (*Mai ppaen rai*) is you're welcome (I'm okay, don't worry). We can even say that the Thai culture is "*Mai ppaen rai* culture" since the use of this word is diverse and it can sometimes be difficult for people in other cultures to understand. For example, if someone is late to an appointment or accidentally spills water on you, you may say "Mai ppaen rai" to them.

Names and nicknames

The order of Thai names is same as that of English; the family name comes after the first name. The family names are often long and difficult, almost impossible to memorize at once. The reason is because most originated from Pali and Sanskrit. When you call someone at work using their long family name, most of the time, others cannot identify that person because people don't usually refer to others by their family name. It is because they use first names or *cheuren* (**ชื่อเล่น**, nickname) in everyday life. Therefore, there are cases in which even old friends don't know each other's full names. Many animal names are used for *cheuren*. Initially, *ppu* (crab), *ppeulla* (fish), *nok* (bird), *kkung* (shrimp), *mi* (bear), *sseu-eo* (tiger), *ssing* (lion) were mostly used, but as Western culture was introduced, words like *jjo* (joy), *ni-u* (new), *kkem* (game), *jjet* (jet), and others were in greater use.

Most notable Thai people we know are referred to by their first names. The former prime minister of Thailand, Yingluck's full name is Yingluck Shinawatra (**ยิ่งลักษณ์ชินวัตร**). "Yingluck" is her first name and "Shinawatra" is her family name, but people mostly refer to her as Prime Minister Yingluck or Ppu (crab) in *cheuren*.

Honorifics

In Thailand, where the king and Buddhism are the pinnacles of the nation, honorifics (lionization), which reflect these social aspects, are well developed in the language. Honorifics are used for the king, royal family, and monks. For the honorifics, special types of words are used for the noun and the verb. For royal family honorifics, special words of Sanskrit, Khmer, ancient Thai, and other languages are used. For example, a normal person's eye is called *tta* **ตา**, but a royal family's eye is called *peuranet*. The verb "eat," which we use with friends, is *kkin* **กิน**, but to Buddhist monks, it is *chan* **ฉัน** and to the royal family, it is *ssawoi* **เสวย**.

religious mendicancy

Various foreign languages

The words of the Thai language can be divided into those from the native language, loanwords that originated from the ancient languages of Pali, Sanskrit, and Khmer, and other loanwords originating from Western languages (mainly English). The words of the original Thai language are made of monosyllables, with many basic words used in everyday life. Words of Thai language from Pali and Sanskrit were assimilated as Buddhism was introduced. Khmer words are mainly court languages. Recently, many Western language words, mostly from English, have been absorbed. As they were integrated into the Thai phoneme system and changed their sounds, there were considerable deviations from the original words.

Thai Language
Similar to Lao Language

The Thai language and alphabet are similar to the official language of Laos, Passa Lao. Most privileged elite in Laos can read and write the Thai language. More than half of Thai words, grammar, intonation, and vowels are similar to those of the Lao language. According to the language group classification, the Lao language is also included in the Tai-Kadai family. Because they are considered of the same linguistic regional variety, people using the Lao language and Thai use the partial mutual understanding of both languages to communicate some ideas. Also, because most people of Laos learn the Thai language from media, they can become more fluent. On the other hand, for most people in central and southern parts of Thailand, there are definitely difficulties in understanding the Lao language.

The Lao language is composed of 26 basic consonants, 28 basic vowels, 4 intonation symbols, and 6 special consonants. The 28 vowels are composed of 12 monophthongs, 12 long vowels, and 4 complex vowels. The Lao language is a tone language, made up of 6 sounds. Like the Thai language, the Lao language is written from left to right. The vowel is located above, below, to the left, and to the right of the consonant.

Various Forms of Thai Alphabet

Thai alphabet in pictures

To easily learn the Thai language, Thai children use the picture cards as shown below.

Picture cards

Various letter styles

Writing styles of the Thai language can be largely divided into the following four types.

โรงเรียนแม่ใจวิทยาคม	letter style used in textbooks
โรงเรียนแม่ใจวิทยาคม	letter style used in King's order, constitution
โรงเรียนแม่ใจวิทยาคม	letter style written quickly and easily with fountain pens, ballpoint pens, brushes
โรงเรียนแม่ใจวิทยาคม	lletter style mostly seen in advertisements and on book titles

Handwriting can be divided into three types according to size and proportion.

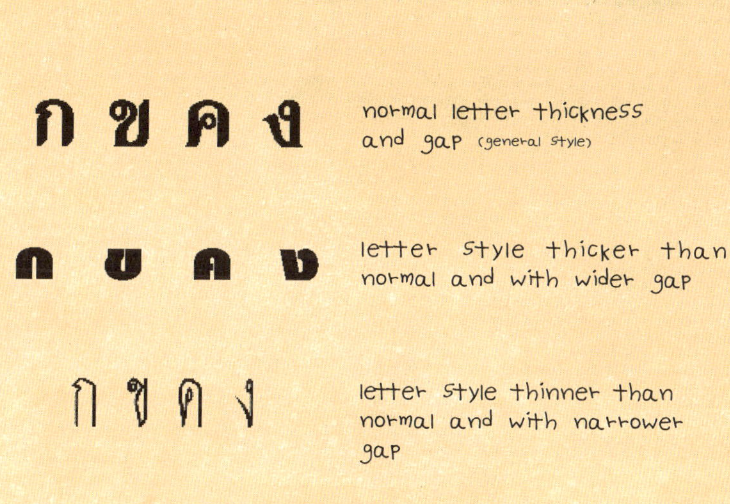

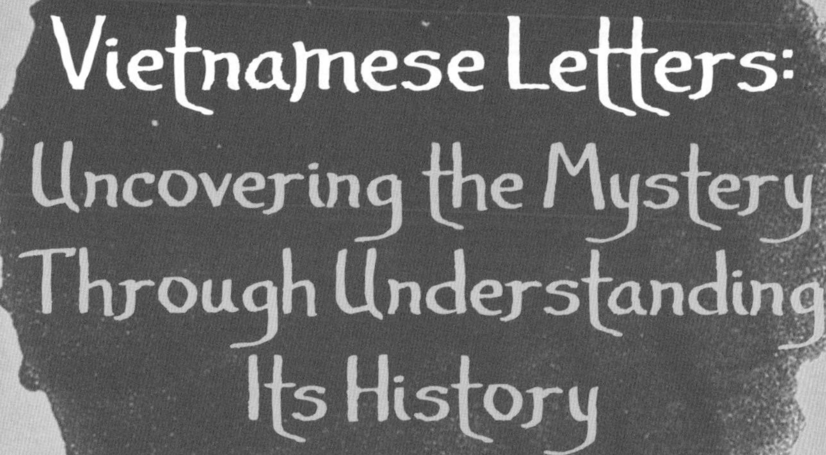

Vietnamese Letters: Uncovering the Mystery Through Understanding Its History

— Ahn Kyong Hwan

cùng nhau

Vietnamese Letters Originated from Latin Alphabet

Vietnam is located in Southeast Asia far from the Western world. So isn't it strange that Vietnamese letters have the same origin as the Western Latin alphabet? The Vietnamese people have different looks from Western people and have a totally different culture as well. To say that the alphabets from two totally different locations have the same origin will sound quite fascinating. However, once you learn more about Vietnamese history, you will quickly understand, saying, "Oh, so that's what happened!"

For a long period from 111 BC to AD 938, Vietnam was under the colonial rule of China. As a result, Vietnam was only permitted to use Chinese characters. After their independence, the script called Chu Nom, in part, played a significant role in Vietnam's writing system even though it was not widely used throughout the country. In 1498 Portuguese explorer Vasco da Gama discovered a route to India. Afterwards merchants and Roman Catholic priests from Europe began to visit Southeast Asia. In particular, priests were sent to Vietnam at the start of the 16th century. Out of the Catholic priests, those from Portugal made up the largest number. These priests wrote early Vietnamese using Latin alphabet, Portuguese, and Greek letters.

Bishop Alexandre de Rhodes

Bishop Pigneau de Behaine

In particular, the Vietnamese alphabet being used today first appeared when Bishop Alexandre de Rhodes (1591-1660) from Avignon, France, published the *Vietnamese-Portuguese-Latin Dictionary* in 1651 in Rome. Also, it is said that in 1772, French Bishop Pigneau de Behaine tried to prepare a Vietnamese-Latin dictionary composed of 4,843 words but was unable to publish his work. Adding upon the dictionary that Pigneau de Behaine tried to publish, French Bishop Taberd added 116 words to the dictionary and published it as *Vietnamese-Latin, Latin-*

Vietnamese Dictionary in India. Therefore, 1838 is considered the year when the modern Vietnamese script was born. Bishop Alexandre de Rhodes became a very important figure in the history of Vietnamese letters, as he was the one to introduce the Latin alphabet to Vietnam. The Vietnamese alphabet and Latin alphabet are nearly the same. Since the letters and the order are the same, it can be presumed that the Vietnamese alphabet and Latin alphabet share the same origins.

The Vietnamese alphabet has 12 vowels and 17 consonants which creates a total of 29 letters.

A Ă Â B C D Đ E Ê G H I K L M
N O Ô Ơ P Q R S T U Ư V X Y

Looking at the 29 letters of the Vietnamese alphabet, there are letters that exist in Latin alphabet but aren't in the Vietnamese's. They include F, J, W, and Z. Also, there are letters that exist in the Vietnamese alphabet but are not found in the Latin. They are Ă, Â, Đ, Ê, Ô, Ơ, and Ư. Of course there are differences in the pronunciation as well. The letters not only have different pronunciations, but are completely different in terms of words and meanings.

Comparison of the Vietnamese and Latin Alphabets

Latin alphabet	Vietnamese alphabet	Vietnamese pronunciation
A	A	a
	Ă	a
	Â	eo
B	B	beo
C	C	kkeo
D	D	jeo
	Đ	deo
E	E	ae
	Ê	e
F	–	-
G	G	geo
H	H	heo
I	I	i (eong-an)
J	–	-
K	K	kka
L	L	reo

Latin alphabet	Vietnamese alphabet	Vietnamese pronunciation
M	M	meo
N	N	neo
O	O	o
	Ô	o
	Ơ	eo
P	Ơ	ppe
Q	Q	kkui
R	R	reo
S	S	seo
T	T	tteo
U	U	u
	Ư	eu
V	V	beo
W	–	-
X	X	sseo
Y	Y	i (jai)
Z	–	-

Vietnam's Letters
: Used by All 54 Vietnamese Ethnic Groups

As a multiracial country, Vietnam is made up of 54 different ethnic groups. The Kinh constitute the largest ethnic group, making up 88% of the population. Besides the Kinh, there are 53 minority ethnic groups, amounting to nine million people. Most of the minor ethnic groups live in mountainous regions or highlands. They make a living through hunting and slash-and-burn farming. Every ethnic group also has its own indigenous traditional culture and language.

In Vietnam there are a total of five language systems, there are many different languages depending on the regions and ethnic groups. As a result, the education of the Vietnamese language, the country's official language, is very important. Wouldn't it be very troublesome if you met a person from the same country but you couldn't communicate with that person? People cannot communicate

children of a minority ethnic group

with one another, there would be conflicts over small or insignificant matters, making it quite difficult for the people of the country to be united as one. This is why the Vietnamese government is putting effort into teaching the Vietnamese language to minority ethnic groups. Since mountainous regions have only small populations and are far from one another, it is very difficult and dangerous for children from minority ethnic groups to go to school. So, many young people are selected and sent to each household to teach the children. Through this system, the illiteracy rate is lower compared to that of other countries, even though not many Vietnamese people live in lightly populated regions. The teachers' efforts in visiting each house and teaching the children have resulted in people from minority ethnic groups being able to speak two languages. Therefore, there are almost no communication problems among the Vietnamese people.

Truong Sa Archipelagoes introduction program

cover from the booklet introducing the Truong Sa Archipelagoes

History of Vietnam's Writing System

Hung Vuong period: a nation without letters

Vietnam boasts a very long history. The Hung Vuong period began in 2879 BC. The kingdom that Hung Vuong ruled during Hong Bang period was called Van Lang. Since this period occurred during the Bronze and Iron Ages, it began with the tribal state period. Although the Vietnamese language existed in this period, they did not have a writing system for people to use. So you could say it was frustrating. Usually if a language exists, we imagine that there must be some type of script. However, other than rock and cave paintings, no evidence has yet been found to prove that a writing system existed in ancient Vietnam. You could probably say that most of the human civilizations at

cover of Vietnam's greatest literature masterpiece *Truyenkieu*

that time were also in a similar situation, as they had no way to write other than rock and cave paintings.

Usage of Chinese characters

After the kingdom of Van Lang during the Hung Vuong period came the kingdom of Au Lac, which lasted from 257 to 207 BC. Au Lac was overthrown by the kingdom of Nam Viet which was later conquered by the Han Empire's Wudi (武帝). For 11 centuries from 111 BC to AD 938, Vietnam was dominated by China. The period in which Vietnam was colonized by the Chinese empires was called the North Occupation Period, the period in which Vietnam was part of the north. As Vietnam was continuously occupied by the powerful Chinese empires for 11 centuries, the Vietnamese could not do anything to develop their own script. So it's no surprise that the Vietnamese had no choice but to write with Chinese characters. Until the 20th century, the history of Vietnam was written completely in Chinese characters. During the Chinese domination, Chinese characters were used for official documents as well as textbooks used by students. Therefore, it is said that the Vietnamese have called Chinese characters "our letters." We could say that it is a nation's sorrow that they would call another country's letters as "our letters."

Chu Nom's birth during the independent period

Chu Nom is Vietnam's native alphabet, created after the Chinese colonial domination ended in 938 when Vietnam was able to achieve independence. Afterwards, as the Vietnamese gradually built up their independence, they came to realize that they needed a native writing system, resulting in the Chu Nom script. The Vietnamese people called Chu Nom, meaning "the script of the south," their national language. This was because Vietnam was south of China and so the letters were southern letters. In other words, it meant "our letter."

There are many possible explanations as to when Chu Nom first appeared. Most scholars say that it originated in the 8th to the 9th century during the Chinese colonization period and was established after Vietnam gained independence between the 10th to 12th centuries. Chu Nom was then developed in the beginning of the 13th century and used until the early 20th century. The establishment of Chu Nom occurred during the reign of Ly Thai To, who founded the Ly Dynasty in 1009 and moved the capital to Thang Long (present-day Hanoi). During the fourth king Ly Nhan Tong's reign in 1075, the high-level state examination system was established. Thus, the Ly Dynasty could be considered the kingdom that revived Vietnam's legitimacy.

Hanoi's 1000 Year Anniversary Memorial

In analyzing the form of Chu Nom, we see that it is a modification of Chinese characters. Therefore, the characters of Chu Nom cannot be found in a dictionary of Chinese characters, and even if such characters are used, they are done so for different meanings. Chinese and Chu Nom characters that were alike and had the same meanings made up a very small percentage of Chu Nom.

Comparison Between Vietnamese Letters and Chinese Characters

Chinese characters	Chu Nom	Vietnamese letters	Meaning (pronunciation)
火	焒	lửa	fire (reu-eo)
水	渃	nưôc	water (neu-eok)
一	沒	môt	one (mot)
母	媄	mẹ	mother (mae)
导	碍	ngại	interfere (eung-ai)

For example, during the Chinese colonial domination period there was no character to write "lửa (*reu-eo*)" which meant "fire" in Vietnamese. So the Chinese character of 火 (fire) was used. After the appearance of Chu Nom, the Chinese character for fire 火 was combined with the Vietnamese "lửa" with the similarly sounding 呂 (*ryeo*) to create 焒 which was pronounced *reu-eo*.

Creation of the Present-Day Vietnamese Alphabet

In Vietnam, Chu Nom was used after independence from China. Although Chu Nom usage was not widespread, it had the status of being Vietnam's writing system and was continuously developed. When Vasco da Gama discovered a route to India in 1498, merchants from Europe and Roman Catholic priests with the purpose of spreading Christianity began to enter the Asia. In particular, Roman Catholic priests from Europe were sent to Vietnam in the beginning of the 16th century. The highest number of priests was sent in the 17th century and later, from 1645 to 1788, 145 Jesuit priests from 17 countries were sent to Vietnam. The number does not include the 31 priests of Vietnam, only counting those from foreign countries. Out of the priests were seventy-four from Portugal, thirty from Italy, ten from Germany, eight from Japan, five from France, four from Spain, two each from China, Macao, Poland, one each from Switzerland, Czechoslovakia, Hungary, and other countries. The priests spread Christianity in Vietnam.

Before the Roman Catholic priests arrived in Vietnam, Chinese characters were widespread, but Chu Nom was still in use as well. When Roman Catholicism and Protestantism arrived in Vietnam in sequence, priest and pastors had to learn Vietnamese for their sermons or had no choice but to make records using their own letters. Out of all the priests in Vietnam, those from Portugal, the most numerous in Vietnam, used Portuguese and Greek letters to record Vietnamese. This was the early stage of the development of the Vietnamese letters we see today.

With these efforts, Bishop Alexandre de Rhodes published the *Vietnamese-Portugal-Latin Dictionary* in Rome in 1651. This dictionary became an important turning point in the history of the Vietnamese language. This dictionary was Vietnam's first grammar book, which included definition for words, marks for intonation and categories for parts of speech. It is regarded as the initial form of the present-day Vietnamese alphabet. Bishop Alexandre de Rhodes first came to Vietnam in 1624. In order to make the dictionary, he studied Vietnamese for 12 years with the local Vietnamese priests.

Adoption of the Latin Alphabet

The 19th century was a period when the Western powers' ambition to invade and colonize various Asian nations resulted in constant wars. The Western powers used their forces to fight for colonies in order to reap the benefits for their own countries. Minh Mang, the second emperor of Nguyen Dynasty, was especially hostile to the West. In 1825, he banned Roman Catholicism, and in 1833, he had eight missionaries and Vietnamese converts executed. In 1836, by royal decree the killing of a missionary was not considered to be murder while those who hid missionary were given capital punishment. In 1847, the third Nguyen Dynasty's emperor Thieu Tri ordered that all Europeans be captured and executed. This resulted in an incident in the port city of Da Nang in which two French warships had arrived and demanded religious freedom in the country. The two French ships sunk two Vietnamese ships in the incident. The fourth Nguyen emperor, Tu Duc, increased persecution against missionaries in 1848 and 1851. Up until 1860, 25 European missionaries, 300 Vietnamese priests, and 20,000 Vietnamese converts were executed. In reaction to this, France sent warships to Da Nang and demanded that those responsible be punished. However, they were refused. The French warships bombarded the fortress at Da Nang and left in August of 1856. In July 1858, a fleet of 14 French and Spanish allied ships carrying 3,000 troops entered and bombarded Da Nang. They then captured the Anhai and Tonhai fortresses. This started the French colonization of Vietnam, which ended in 1954 when the French was defeated at the battle of Dien Bien Phu. On April 6, 1878, the French colonial government passed legislation stipulating that starting January 1, 1882, all official documents as well as school textbooks could only use the Latin alphabet to write Vietnamese. Through the French colonial government, adoption of the Latin alphabet officially began. In addition, the high-level official examination system was abolished in northern Vietnam in 1915 and in central Vietnam in 1919, which led to the gradual disappearance in the usage of Chinese characters and Chu Nom.

Some foreigners say that Vietnamese is a difficult language to learn while other foreigners say that Vietnamese is very easy. Why do some find Vietnamese easy to learn while others say it is hard? Those who think that Vietnamese is difficult to learn say that Vietnamese is hard to pronounce due to the usage of intonation. On the other hand, those who say that Vietnamese is easy to learn say that its grammar is simple unlike English or French, and that there are few exceptions to the basic rules. Since Vietnamese grammar isn't complicated, it can be picked up just by reading along and shadowing the speech. It is a language that doesn't require too much thought, but relies more on intuition.

Then, shall we look at some features of the language? Firstly, Vietnam and Indonesia are the two countries where the Latin alphabet is used outside of nations that use English as an official language, such as India, Malaysia, and Singapore. Vietnamese letters are based on their sounds, which differ from hieroglyphics like Chinese characters. It is somewhat strange to see a nation that has used Chinese characters and Chu Nom, based on Chinese characters, now use a Latin alphabet.

Vietnamese which uses Latin alphabet

a bishop house marker at the Phat Diem Cathedral

Secondly, the Vietnamese language is monosyllabic, meaning that each pronunciation and each syllable holds a meaning. For example, the English word *mother* is made up of two syllables. However, the same Vietnamese word for mother consists of just one syllable, "mẹ" (pronounced *mae*). Recently, with the introduction of words from polysyllable languages such as English, French, and other foreign languages, the words are modified into Vietnamese as monosyllables or two syllables. For these reasons, Vietnamese words are easy to remember and easy to learn unlike English or French, which require one to memorize long words.

Thirdly, the form of Vietnamese words does not change. The forms of English, French, and other languages are subject to change. What is a form? Is it the form of speaking? Is it the look? Is it the shape? That is right. Don't we change our clothes according to the season? When the season changes the temperature changes as well, so people have to change their outfit accordingly to live. On the other hand, the Vietnamese people live in a country where it is always hot. So there is presumably no reason for the Vietnamese to change their clothes. That is maybe why the form of the language doesn't change. For example, there is an original form of English word *go*. The word *go* can be changed into various forms such as *gone*, *went*, *going*, *goes*, and others. Just as people change their clothes according to the passage of time like the change of form of words, this sort of change occurs with tense. However, in Vietnamese, the basic form of the word never changes. Vietnam is a unique nation which never changes but has the talent to use others to look as if it changed. In the same way, the language matches with the changes in tense.

Finally, out of the various features of the Vietnamese language, the most important one is that there are six types of intonation. Intonation can be defined as the rise and fall of the voice and the use of inflections in speech. The meaning of a spoken word changes according to the intonations. Even if letters and words are the same, the meaning can radically differ according to how one uses inflections. Since the meaning changes with the pronunciation, it is essential for a person to accurately pronounce the tone in order to be understood. For example, when Vietnamese people say, "Xin chào" to each other it means "Hello." When they say "chào," the word has an inflection, which symbolizes that the word should be spoken with a low tone. If a person mispronounces the word and instead

Vietnamese with its intonations

cover of President Ho Chi Min's introduction booklet

Hanoi TV's "The Regained Smile" special performance

uses a high voice, then it has a totally different meaning. If a person pronounces "cháo" with a high voice at the vowel, then the word means "rice porridge." The person would then be speaking nonsense as a result. That's why when foreigners talk to Vietnamese people, it's said that many funny incidents occur.

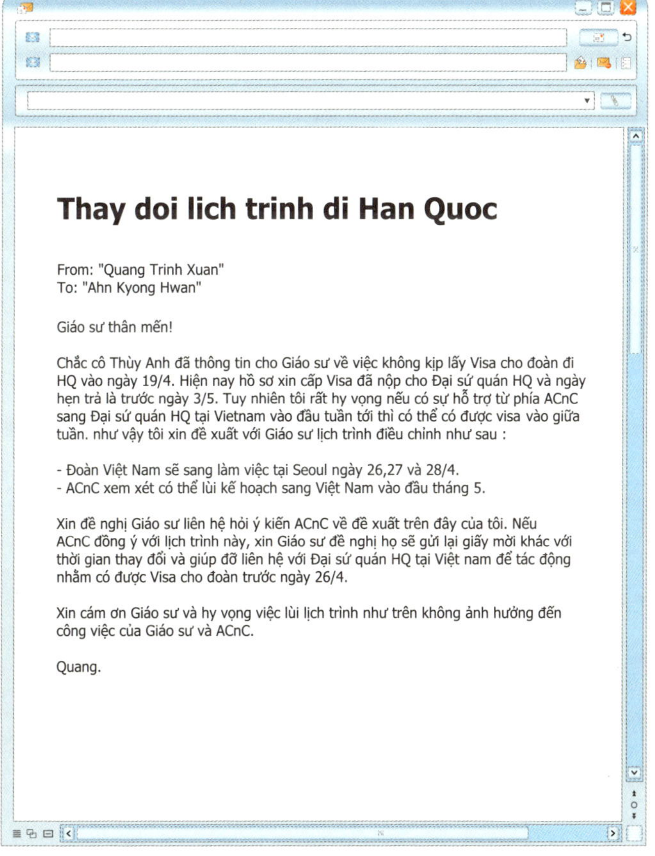

Thay doi lich trinh di Han Quoc

From: "Quang Trinh Xuan"
To: "Ahn Kyong Hwan"

Giáo sư thân mến!

Chắc cô Thùy Anh đã thông tin cho Giáo sư về việc không kịp lấy Visa cho đoàn đi HQ vào ngày 19/4. Hiện nay hồ sơ xin cấp Visa đã nộp cho Đại sứ quán HQ và ngày hẹn trả là trước ngày 3/5. Tuy nhiên tôi rất hy vọng nếu có sự hỗ trợ từ phía ACnC sang Đại sứ quán HQ tại Vietnam vào đầu tuần tới thì có thể có được visa vào giữa tuần. như vậy tôi xin đề xuất với Giáo sư lịch trình điều chỉnh như sau :

- Đoàn Việt Nam sẽ sang làm việc tại Seoul ngày 26,27 và 28/4.
- ACnC xem xét có thể lùi kế hoạch sang Việt Nam vào đầu tháng 5.

Xin đề nghị Giáo sư liên hệ hỏi ý kiến ACnC về đề xuất trên đây của tôi. Nếu ACnC đồng ý với lịch trình này, xin Giáo sư đề nghị họ sẽ gửi lại giấy mời khác với thời gian thay đổi và giúp đỡ liên hệ với Đại sứ quán HQ tại Việt nam để tác động nhằm có được Visa cho đoàn trước ngày 26/4.

Xin cám ơn Giáo sư và hy vọng việc lùi lịch trình như trên không ảnh hưởng đến công việc của Giáo sư và ACnC.

Quang.

e-mail written in vietnamese letters

Bersama

The Easiest to Learn: Indonesia's Language and Letters

— Shin Yoon Hwan

The Indonesian Language, Written in the Latin Alphabet

Indonesians use the Latin alphabet to write their national and official language, Bahasa Indonesia. The Latin alphabet is also used for writing English. It is the most popular writing system as it is used around the world to express different languages in written form. The Korean experience of inventing its own writing system, Hangul, is an extremely rare case in the history of humanity. Most languages use the writing system of other languages either as it is or in a modified form. Indonesian is a case in point.

The Latin alphabet used in Bahasa Indonesia has 26 letters like in English, and the pronunciation of each letter is

Immigration (Imigrasi) at an Indonesian airport

Indonesian Alphabet

Aa	Bb	Cc	Dd	Ee	Ff	Gg	Hh	Ii	Jj	Kk	Ll	Mm
a	be	ce	de	e	ef	ge	ha	i	je	ka	el	em
Nn	**Oo**	**Pp**	**Qq**	**Rr**	**Ss**	**Tt**	**Uu**	**Vv**	**Ww**	**Xx**	**Yy**	**Zz**
en	o	pe	ki	er	es	te	u	fe	we	eks	ye	zet

also similar to that of English. Indonesians give names to and pronounce the 26 letters of their alphabet, such as A [a:], B [be], and C [tse:], in a similar way to the English A [eI], B [bi:], and C [si:]. The Indonesian variations in the name and pronunciation of the letters were introduced by Dutch colonial administrators and scholars. They either replaced the old Indian- and Arabic-influenced scripts with the Latin (Dutch) alphabet or employed the latter for the first time in expressing various local and regional languages including Malay, from which the modern Indonesian language has evolved. As the phonetic values of the Indonesian language differ from Dutch, however, there are differences between the two in some of their names and pronunciations; most notably, "c, k, p, q, t" are not pronounced as the aspirated English "c, k, p, k, t" but as unaspirated fortes like in Latin languages.

As mentioned earlier, many languages including Indonesian use the Latin alphabet either "as it is" or "in a modified form." The Latin alphabet used in the Indonesian language has only 26 letters as in English, and no modifications are made in the letters, which makes it even easier for English speakers to pronounce Indonesian words. Vietnamese, another Southeast Asian official language, borrowed the Latin alphabet but added diacritics and tone marks on vowels to represent Vietnamese phonetic values better. The Indonesian language, however, does not use such symbols so that reading all letters can be learned with little practice. Simplicity, clarity, and consistency are evident not only in reading the language but also in its grammar, vocabulary, pronunciation and speech. That is why it is often called "the easiest language to learn in the world."

Malay, the Origin of Bahasa Indonesia

Clues to why independent Indonesia chose to use the Latin alphabet instead of already established Indian- or Arabic-influenced scripts can be found in the historical and political circumstances surrounding the birth of the new nation and state called Indonesia and the complicated language environment in which hundreds of mutually unintelligible vernaculars and dialects divided the inchoate nation. Such unusual circumstances and environment led to Malay, the native language of the ethnic Malay minority and the most popular *lingua franca* of traditional Southeast Asia, being renamed as Bahasa Indonesia and recognized as the national language of the newly born Republic of Indonesia, where the number of native languages spoken was somewhere between 150 and as many as 700, depending on how you define language. Therefore, it was not easy for the newly independent Indonesia to decide on its national language.

When new nations came into being in Asia and Africa after World War II, it was the trend that they declared the colonizer's national language as one of their official languages, the only official language, or even their national language. In Southeast Asia, the Philippines and Singapore designated English as one of their official languages, and, decades later, East Timor declared one of its official languages to be the colonial Portuguese, in addition to an aboriginal language Tetum, while

part of *Hikayat Abdullah*, a book written in the Jawi script excluding the then virtual *lingua franca* Indonesian from the same status.

Indonesia's experience with her national language was more an exception than a rule. Indonesians who took pride in their "Revolutionary War" (1945-1949) against the Dutch who returned after World War II walked a glorious nationalist path. They chose as their only national language Bahasa Indonesia, a formalized and standardized variant of the Malay language, not the colonial Dutch language. Malay was the mother tongue of the ethnic minority Malay who accounted for less than 10% of Indonesia's total population. The Indonesians named their national language Bahasa Indonesia in order to pronounce it in the national language of Indonesia where hundreds of different regional languages and dialects are spoken in different geographical areas. Then a question can be raised: Why did Indonesia not choose any other language than Malay, a minority language, as the source of her national language?

There are at least two reasons, which are interrelated, why Malay faced no objections when it was first recognized in 1928 as the "unifying language (*satu Bahasa*)" for nationalism and, later in the wake of independence, renamed as Bahasa Indonesia and elevated to the status of the national language of independent Indonesia.

First of all, Malay was functioning as the most important *lingua franca* not only in the Indonesian archipelago but throughout Southeast Asia. In fact, its role as an international language in the region can be traced back hundreds of years to the classical era. In official and commercial contacts across different linguistic groups, diplomats, military leaders, and merchants preferred to use Malay as the medium of communication. The reason, in turn, why Malay enjoyed such privilege is its easiness to learn as was already pointed out.

It is interesting to compare Southeast Asia and Northeast Asia from the perspective of what languages played the role of *lingua franca* historically, and how. The popularity and significance of Malay in the former makes a fine contrast with those of Chinese in the latter. Malay was used more widely and commonly in Southeast Asia's coastal areas where commercial and religious activities flourished than was the Chinese language in Northeast Asia of which the use was more or less confined within official and elite contacts. More importantly, Malay took the forms of both oral and written language whereas Chinese was largely used in its written form, *hanzi*. Thus, the size of the native population who could express themselves in written Chinese was limited to the small elite or literati classes in neighboring countries beyond the border of the Chinese empire whereas nonnative Malay speakers encompassed various types of sojourners and migrants that travelled and settled in most urban areas in Southeast Asia.

Malay from *Lingua Franca* to Official Language

Various factors from politics, trade and religion came into play before the Malay language spread beyond the small Malay-speaking regions to be understood in the entire Malay Peninsula and the coastal towns of the Indonesian archipelago as well as many other parts of Southeast Asia and eventually grew to be the *lingua franca* of archipelagic Southeast Asia. In the period prior to the 15th century which historians call "the classical age," two kingdoms vied to become powerful and prosperous empires in Southeast Asia. One of the two was the kingdom of Srivijaya that had under its sphere of influence the islands of Southeast Asia, stretching from the Malay Peninsula to the Outer Islands of East Indonesia. This kingdom was more like an inter-island network of commercial activities and agricultural production than a hierarchically administered political system, with the capital established in Palembang, located in the south of the

sign "Prioritize Malay Language" written both in the Jawi script and the Latin alphabet

largest island Sumatra. Epitaphs found in the old sites of Srivijaya are engraved with the Malay language using the Indian Pallava script. Such historical and archeological evidence shows that Malay played the role as an official language in the governing of the vast territory of Srivijaya.

Views diverge on the political nature of this kingdom, but it is largely agreed that Srivijaya either included most coastal cities on the Malay Peninsula and the islands of Indonesia or at least formed loose networks with them. The mainstay of those networks was maritime trade, supported by Buddhism which Srivijaya embraced from India and made a state religion. Srivijaya served as a center for spreading Buddhism to the entire Southeast Asian region and, possibly, Northeast Asia as well. Temples and Buddhist schools abounded in the kingdom, the capital of which once accommodated more than one thousand monks from all over Asia on their way to and back from India to learn Sanskrit or translate Sanskrit scriptures into their native languages. Some records of their voyage are still available, which tell stories about monks, in particular monks from the Tang Dynasty of China and the Silla Kingdom of Korea. One of them was Hyecho, a Buddhist monk from Silla, who wrote the famous *Wang O Cheonchukguk Jeon* (*Memoir of the Pilgrimage to the Five Kingdoms of India*). Srivijaya appeared around the 7th century and existed until the 13th century while claiming to be the political, economic and religious center in the archipelagic Southeast Asia. Over this long period, the Malay language played a key role in connecting and binding the vast territory and its diverse peoples to the center as well as to their neighbors.

After Srivijaya collapsed in the 15th century, the Malay language maintained its important role as a *lingua franca* in this region. As trade increased and Islam spread in the early modern period, the Malay language also advanced from the Malay-speaking Riau Archipelago to play the role of *lingua franca* in multi-ethnic cities and towns in coastal areas

"mental health" says an Indonesian sign written in the Latin alphabet in Indonesia and some parts of Southeast Asia. The kingdom of Melaka, one of the most powerful and prosperous polities during the 15th century that opened the "Age of Commerce" (Reid 1990) in Southeast Asia, adopted Malay as its official language, and other traditional kingdoms which were to be Islamized soon afterward, also took Malay as their official language. Not only Southeast Asians but also traders and priests who traveled a long distance from the Middle East and India learned the Malay language when they engaged in opening up trade routes and preaching Islam. How popular the Malay language was and how easy it was to learn for foreigners is demonstrated by the historical fact that even the colonial officials from the British Empire and the Netherlands learned Malay to rule the colony instead of forcing the indigenous subjects to learn English or Dutch.

The advantage of easy learning, a long tradition as *lingua franca*, and geographical expansion in tandem with the growth of trade and the spread of Islam combined to lead to the elevation of the Malay language to the status of official language in four Southeast Asian countries, namely Indonesia, Malaysia, Brunei, and Singapore, after they gained independence. When Indonesia, the most populous country with a vast territory, declared Bahasa Indonesia to be its national language, Bahasa Indonesia was adopted *in toto* from Malay so that Indonesians would have little difficulty in communicating with other Malay-speaking people. Bahasa Malaysia, as the national and official language of Malaysia is called now, was still called Bahasa Melayu, or the Malay language, until a few years ago. Unlike the Indonesian language that hundreds of ethnic groups learn to use as their second language, Malay is the mother tongue of the majority of Malaysians. Among minority groups in Malaysia, the ethnic Chinese whose first settlement in the Malay Peninsula can be traced well back to the pre-colonial era, the descendants of Indians who migrated from South India during the colonial period, and the indigenous Orang Asli from East Malaysia, better known by the colonial name Borneo, all have their own first language from birth and start to learn the official language of Malaysia as they grow up.

Evolution of Indonesian Spelling Systems

Let me go back to the story of the Indonesian language. The idea that Indonesian based on Malay should become the national language was conceived by the nationalist youth as early as the 1920s. Nationalism arose at the end of the 19th century among

Islamic leaders, Western-educated intellectuals, and those traditional elites who detested the Dutch rule. These nationalist leaders of diverse backgrounds realized that a new nation would need a common language to communicate and help integrate hundreds of ethnic groups into one people and that they should reject Dutch, the language of colonial suppression and exploitation. Javanese, the language of the largest ethnic group in Indonesia, was also declined as a candidate for the reason that it would be too difficult to learn and that it could reinforce the Javanese numerical dominance. Thus, it was natural and fortunate that the Malay-based national language Bahasa Indonesia was easily agreed upon without strong opposition or serious conflicts of any kind.

On October 28, 1928, young nationalists who gathered at the Second Youth Congress produced the Sumpah Pemuda (Youth

students in Indonesia

Pledge) made of three articles, the last of which reads: "We the sons and daughters of Indonesia, uphold the language of unity, Indonesian (*Kami poetra dan poetri Indonesia, mendjoendjoeng bahasa persatoean, bahasa Indonesia*)."

Seventeen years later, Sukarno and Hatta proclaimed the independence of Indonesia and its constitution. The process of drafting a new constitution required negotiations and compromises, especially regarding the provisions on religion, but it took no efforts to include Article 36 stipulating that "the national language shall be Indonesian (*Bahasa Negara ialah Bahasa Indonesia*)." By the time Indonesia declared independence, Bahasa Indonesia had already become established as the "one and only language (*satu Bahasa*)" or the "language of unity (*Bahasa persatuan*)." For the seven decades since then, Indonesians have come through incessant hardships of wars, poverty, massacres, economic crises, ethnic and religious conflicts, and political turmoil. Indonesian observers agree that without their national language, Bahasa Indonesia, their new nation would not have been built and their new state would not have grown into what it is now.

Although Indonesians are proud of their national language, history shows that the first person to standardize its spelling rules was ironically a Dutch linguist, Charles Adriaan van Ophuijsen.

Following official recognition in 1901 by the Dutch colonial government, the Van Ophuijsen Spelling System came into wide use in indigenous society, thereby contributing substantially to the growth and development of the Malay literature in its early period. In 1947, two years after the declaration of independence, the Minister of Education Soewandi announced that the new Ejaan Republik (Republican Spelling System) would replace the van Ophuijsen system. Ejaan Republik is in fact not a serious replacement but a minor modification of the half-a-century-old system. Named after Minister Soewandi, Ejaan Republik is also called Ejaan Soewandi (Ejaan Spelling System).

As the Republican Spelling System, like its predecessor Van Ophuijsen Spelling System, followed the Dutch orthography it looked awkward to and confused the post-colonial speakers and readers of Indonesian who were accustomed to the English style of the Latin alphabet. Equally important, Indonesia's second spelling system was still quite different from the way in which the Malaysians spelled and read Malay words, that is, the English orthography. To approximate the two different orthographies, scholars and officials from Indonesia and Malaysia initiated and made efforts to construct a unified spelling system, with partial success. The outcome from those efforts was Ejaan Yang Disempurnakan (EYD: Perfected Spelling System or Enhanced

Indonesian Spelling System) in Indonesia and Ejaan Rumi Baharu (New Rumi Spelling) in Malaysia. These two systems allowed the citizens of the two countries to pronounce the same letter with the same pronunciation but left intact the two different spellings for the same word. EYD is still in effect in Indonesia.

The simultaneous revision of the spelling system in both countries made writing and reading easier not only for publications in one's own country but also for those in the other

Changes in the Indonesian Spelling System

Van Ophuijsen Spelling System (1901)	Republican Spelling System (1947)	Perfected Spelling System (EYD, 1972)	Examples of changes (1901→1947→1972 to today)
oe	u	u	soekarno → sukarno → sukarno
tj	tj	c	atjeh → atjeh → aceh
dj	dj	j	djawa → djawa → jawa
j	j	y	ajam → ajam → ayam
nj	nj	ny	njonja → njonja → nyonya
sj	sj	sy	sjair → sjair → syair
ch	ch	kh	achir → achir → akhir
' (glottal stop)	k	k	bapa' → bapak → bapak
(repetition)	2	(repetition)	bermain-main → ber-main2 → bermain-main

a sign says "Hygiene is the key to health, diligence to fortune, faith to happiness"

country. Books published in Malay or Indonesian now cross the border and find their markets in four countries. Studies show that Indonesian and Malay enjoy at least 80% lexical similarities. When you learn one language, you will get to know two.

It cannot be ignored, however, that there still exist nearly 20% lexical differences between the two languages. The differences are often found in basic words needed for everyday life, so that mutual miscommunication and misunderstanding could be bigger and more serious than imagined. Let me give only several examples: "room" (*kamar* vs. *bilik*), "restroom" (*wese* vs. *tandas*), "automobile" (*mobil* vs. *kreta*), "delicious" (*enak* vs. *sedap*), and "look" (*lihat* vs. *tengok*). As Malaysia and Indonesia were long colonized by England and the Netherlands respectively, differences are also found in vocabulary and in pronunciation of loanwords. To unify their official languages or at least narrow down the differences, the two countries in 1972 set up the Majlis

Bahasa Brunei-Indonesia-Malaysia (MABBIM: Language Council of Brunei-Indonesia-Malaysia). When Brunei declared independence from the United Kingdom, it also joined MABBIM. It has since developed into a regional organization that carries out various activities and, recently, has been taking more aggressive actions to promote Malay-Indonesian. Singapore, too, participates in MABBIM as an observer.

Traditional Script 1: Jawi Script for Islam

If the Latin alphabet began to be used only from the early 20th century onward, what scripts were used in previous times? What about hundreds of regional languages? Do or did traditional alphabets or scripts exist to write Malay and any regional languages?

One of these "traditional" or old scripts is the Jawi script, also called Arab Malay script. You would often encounter signs and nameplates for streets, places, and buildings with Arabic and Arabic-like letters written in parallel under or above Latin letters, if you traveled around provincial towns and historical sites in Indonesia and especially Malaysia. As the name Arab

Malay script implies, it was adopted from the Arabic alphabet which Persians brought to Southeast Asians together with Islam in the early 14th century. When the original Arabic letters were introduced, some of them were modified and new ones were added to reflect the peculiarities of local phonetics.

Southeast Asians who converted to Islam began to write their language in the Jawi script. It was none other than the Malay language which found Jawi to be the most useful in doing international trade with the Arabic world and spreading Islam in local society. This is why the ethnic group as well as the language Malay began to be identified with Islam. In Malaysia today, the one who professes Islam is accepted as Malay, and an ethnic Malay is automatically assumed to be Muslim. Back in the early Melakan period, the Malay people could not speak the spoken language of Arabic but still wished to write in the sacred script, Arabic, which gave birth to the slightly modified version Jawi. Malay literature written in the Jawi script flourished well into the late colonial period and spread all over Islamic Southeast Asia.

Islamic kingdoms that emerged in the Malay Peninsula and the Indonesian Archipelago during the early modern period (15th-17th centuries) facilitated the dawning of the "Age of Commerce" and the dissemination of the Jawi script as well as the Malay language. Melaka, Johor, and Pattani of the Malay

Peninsula, Aceh of Sumatra, Ternate of Maluku Islands, Brunei of Borneo, and Sulu of the southernmost Philippines were among the most powerful and prosperous kingdoms. In these kingdoms, the Jawi script was used widely for laws, documents, diplomatic letters, and literature and also became quite popular among commoners. In some areas where the Malay language was not much used, Jawi script was borrowed to write their dialects, Acehnese, Minangkabauan, Banjarese, and Javanese being good examples. This trend continued until the early 20th century when the nationalist movement began to gain momentum in the Netherlands Indies.

In Indonesia, the Jawi script experienced an unexpected and rapid decline after World War II and colonialism came to end. The use of Jawi as a script to write Malay and regional languages was challenged by the Latin alphabet, which earned the status

epitaph in Jawi script

Jawi Script

ز zai z [z, dʒ]	ر ra r [r]	ذ dzal dz [dz]	د dal d [d]	خ kha kh [x, k]	چ cha ch [h]	ح ha h [tʃ]	ج jim j [dʒ]	ث tha th [s]
ت ta t [t]	ب ba b [b]	ا alif - [Ø]	ق qaf q [k]	ڤ pa p [p]	ف fa f [f, p]	ڠ nga ng [ŋ]	غ ghain gh [ɣ, r]	ع ain - [Ø]
ظ dzo dz [z]	ط tho th [t]	ض dhad dh [z, dʒ]	ص shad s [s]	ش shin sh [ʃ, s]	س sin s [s]	ڽ nya ny [ɲ]	ي ya y [j]	ء hamzah - -
لا lam alif la [la]	ه ha h [h]	ۏ va v [v]	و wau w [w]	ن nun n [n]	م mim m [m]	ل lam l [l]	ݢ gaf g [g]	ک kaf k [k]

of the official script from the Indonesian government. As Indonesians got accustomed to the simple and easy Latin script, Jawi quickly lost its ground and popularity. In contrast, Malaysia and Brunei, which declared Islam to be their state religion, adopted the Jawi script as an official script along with the Latin alphabet. In the latter two countries, Jawi was taught and used selectively for Islam-related subjects in schools, but its fate as a dying script was much the same as in Indonesia. It was a curious twist of history that the Jawi script somehow flourished under the colonial rule but struggled to survive under new independent governments.

The use of the Jawi script has continued to decrease since independence. This tendency can be seen not only in Indonesia and Singapore where Jawi has been neglected by the government, but also in Malaysia and Brunei, where Jawi has been recognized as one of the official scripts. Muslim dominant states of Malaysia in the north and Johor, the ethnic Malay dominant province Riau of Indonesia, and Pattani of southern Thailand where the Muslim minority fight Buddhist Thais for their identity are among the few regions where the Jawi script has been in use. Yet these areas have not escaped from the decreasing trend, either; today, Jawi is found only in a limited number of religious and cultural publications, magazines, and newspapers. Those who maintain fluency in reading and writing are also rare. The Jawi script appears doomed to fade away.

Traditional Script 2: Kawi and Java Scripts for Dialects

Now let me go back even further in the past. What letters or alphabets had been available before the Arabic script spread to Southeast Asia and was modified into the Jawi script to express the Malay language? When you have learned about this older "classical" period, you will be able to understand the entire history of the Indonesian alphabet.

ancient kawi alphabet

As mentioned earlier, the classical period is when Indian Civilization spread to most of the areas which constitute

Southeast Asia today. The historian George Cœdès named Southeast Asia of that time as "Indianized Southeast Asia." Indian scripts were on the endless list of cultural items that traveled from India to Indianized Southeast Asia. Those scripts popular in South India were introduced to Southeast Asia thanks to their geographical proximity. Except for the Chinese characters in Vietnam, Jawi in Muslim regions, and the Latin script in the contemporary Archipelagic Southeast Asia and Vietnam, it would not be an exaggeration to generalize that all the scripts used in the past and present Southeast Asia are of the South Indian origin, particularly from the Pallava script, the letters of

Javanese alphabet (top) and Balinese alphabet (bottom)

the Brahman caste in the Pallava Kingdom that existed in South India from the 2nd to 9th century. Old Malay that connected different provinces in the kingdom of Srivijaya was written in the Pallava alphabet. Srivijaya that built a great empire in insular Southeast Asia and was a rival of the kingdom of Angkor (Khmer) in the continental part of the region contributed to the spread not only of the Malay language but also of the Pallava alphabet in the classical age.

Srivijaya was followed by a series of Javanese kingdoms that emerged and disappeared in the center of today's Indonesia, which played the leading role in indigenizing and transmitting the Pallava script to peripheral regions and other kingdoms in Southeast Asia. Javanese imported the Pallava alphabet in the 4th century and modified it to reflect their own phonetic values. The Kawi or Old Javanese alphabet gradually evolved and finally became established as a new system in the 8th century. The word Kawi looks and sounds similar to Jawi, causing confusion. But we now understand that the two alphabets have no relations at all, and have completely different origins.

From the 10th century, the Kawi alphabet was recognized as the alphabet of the Javanese language and spread to other islands of Southeast Asia. Kawi became a standard and universal alphabet system to write most local languages or dialects of insular Southeast Asia. Among them were Balinese, Macassarese, Buginese, and Batak, to name only a few. Some languages from the Philippines such as Tagalog and Mangyan also adopted Kawi, demonstrating the power and popularity of the Kawi alphabet. If we consider the fact that such major ethnic groups of continental Southeast Asia as Mons, Khmers, Chams, Rannas, Burmans, Thais, and Laos also developed their own alphabet system from the Southeast Asian letters, the Pallava script can aptly be called the Latin alphabet of Southeast and South Asia, including India itself.

The Kawi alphabet prevalent on many islands of Indonesia in the precolonial era took up the current form in the 17th century. The Javanese alphabet established then is now called Carakan, Hanacaraka, or Dentawiyanjana. It was also about this time when Islamization took place in Java with the polities, ruling elites, and people all converting to Islam. The conversion,

Sign plate in a Hindu temple written both in the Balinese and Latin alphabets

however, failed to replace the Kawi script, which had originated from Hindu India, with the Jawi script or other Arabic-based scripts. Kawi remained firmly as the alphabet for the Javanese language for quite a long time to come.

In the meantime, the Jawi script spread, along with Islam, only to those regions where the ethnic Malay ruled as well as those coastal towns which were frequented by Muslim traders. In Java, where a strong cultural tradition of Hindu-Buddhism remained deep and intact even after Islamic conversion, Jawi was used in a limited circle and fashion, mostly in mosques and Islamic schools for religious purposes. The Islamized royal courts and literate classes continued to use the Kawi script until the end of the 19th century, when the Latin alphabet began to threaten both Kawi and Jawi. Bali, which stood aside from the tide of Islamization, had cherished and stuck to the slightly different Balinese version of the Kawi alphabet more faithfully than Java.

The Kawi script that had survived the strong tide of Islamization was to face an overpowering force from the mid-19th century onward. It was the Latin alphabet that Dutch scholars and indigenous nationalists found to be useful and promoted as an alternative writing system to replace the complicated Jawi and Kawi. It slowly penetrated into the domain of the two established scripts and soon found its momentum in the early 20th century as the Van Ophuijsen Spelling System was well accepted and as Indonesian nationalists turned to this simple and easy system to write their "language for unity." The decisive blow to Kawi, and Jawi for that matter, came from the independent government of Indonesia when it declared the Latin alphabet to be the official script. Today the Kawi script barely keeps its head above water thanks to its use in the areas of classical literature and fine arts. With a professed aim of preserving the regional languages and traditional alphabets, the elementary schools and some middle schools in Java still have the Javanese language in the curriculum that allocates a few

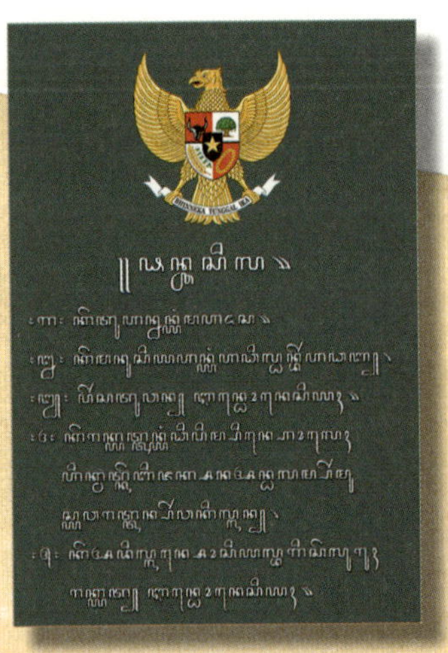

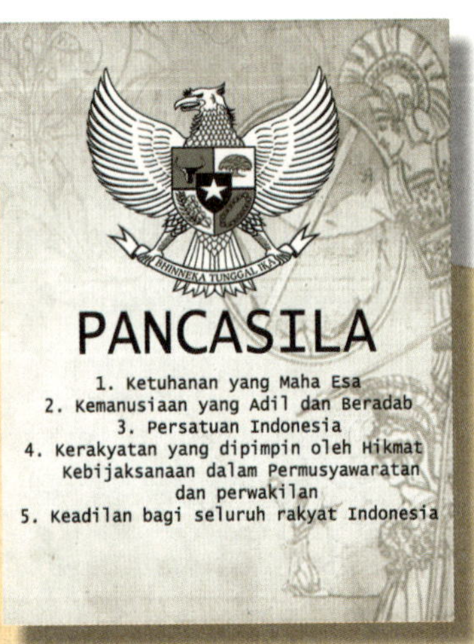

Indonesia's state philosophy, Pancasila, written in Kawi (left) and Latin (right) scripts

hours to teach Kawi, but with its real effects in doubt. As the script is completely out of everyday use, it is no longer easy to meet a Javanese who can read or write Kawi fluently.

To conclude, ordinary Indonesians no longer use other scripts than the Latin alphabet to write the national language Bahasa Indonesia and hundreds of regional languages. The Indic Kawi and the Arabic Jawi could be exceptions but have been losing their appeal to ordinary Indonesians. They are used only in the religious, literary, and cultural realms. Even these practices are confined geographically to such areas with a strong cultural or religious tradition as Bali, Yogyakrata, Riau and Aceh. Malaysia, with Islam as the state religion and with the Jawi script as an alternative script to Latin, has the more visible presence of Jawi overall. Jawi in Brunei enjoys even stronger support from the government. Yet the popularity of the traditional scripts by no means lives up to the efforts and expectation of the government and religious community to revive its past glory. The reality is that both Jawi and Kawi have been struggling desperately to survive, let alone revive to their past usage. Bahasa Indonesia written in the Latin script, on the contrary, has developed into a much easier-to-learn language than old Malay in Jawi, playing an important role in building the Indonesian identity and rising to become the fastest growing major language in the world.

Хамтдаа

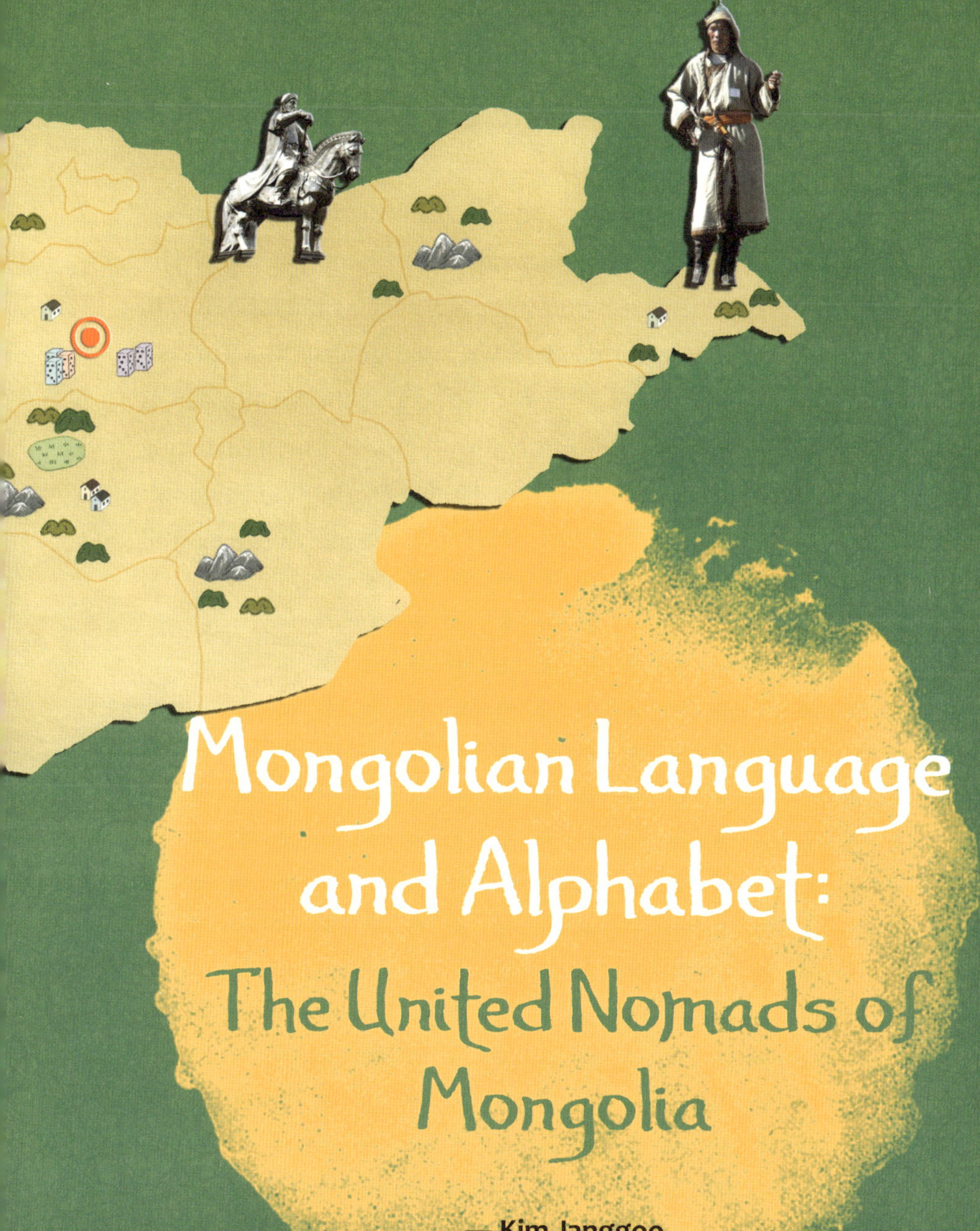

Mongolian Language and Alphabet: The United Nomads of Mongolia

— Kim Janggoo

Languages of Altaic Lineage

There are many languages and letters in the world. Letters are notation systems invented to write the relevant languages. The Latin alphabet, used to write languages such as English, French, and German, is even used to write languages like Turkish and Vietnamese, as well. The Cyrillic alphabet in Russian is mainly used in countries of the former Soviet Union including Uzbekistan, Kazakhstan, and Mongolia. During the period of socialism, Mongolia and Russia (former Soviet Union) exchanged support and influenced one another. Because the Cyrillic Mongolian alphabet was most similar to the Russian alphabet, it seemed that anyone who could read Russian could also read Mongolian. Of course, even though Russians could read Cyrillic, the meaning could not be understood because the alphabet was used to express the Mongolian language.

The Mongolian language, along with the Turkic and Tungus languages, belongs to Altaic lineages. Some scholars say that in a broad sense, Korean and Japanese are also included in Altaic lineages. Of course, there are also scholars with opposing opinions.

Areas that use Mongolian language in the world are Mongolia, China (Neimenggu, some parts of northeast China, part of Xinjiang Uygur), and Russia (Buryat Republic, Kalmyk Republic) among others. However, the status of the Mongolian language in these three countries is overtly different.

Alphabet from the West, Mongol Bichig

The background behind the Uigur Mongol Bichig

Genghis Khan, who united Mongol grasslands, knew the utility of alphabet very well. Therefore, during the Naimans conquest in 1206, he informed Tata Tunga, his captive, to make the Mongolian alphabet and to teach his sons and daughters. This Mongolian alphabet used the Uigur alphabet to write the Mongolian language. Uigur alphabet was also borrowed from the Sogdian alphabet, which originated from the Aramaic alphabet of the far west. This is the reason the Mongolian alphabet is called Uigur Mongol Bichig (Uigur Mongolian alphabet). The famous documentation of the Mongol Bichig lies in the Genghis Khan Memorial stone.

We need to consider why the Mongolians or the nomads did not use Chinese characters. Many Asian countries like Korea, Japan, and Vietnam adopted Chinese characters in the early days as tools to communicate. Probably one of the reasons

Genghis Khan Memorial Stone

also called Yisungge Monument (approximate 1224-1225)

* Contents of the epitaph:

Činggis qan-i Sartaγul irge daγuliju baγuju qamuγ Mongγol ulus-un noyad-i Buqa sočiqai-tur quriγsan-dur Yisüngge ontudurun γurban jaγud γučin tabun aldas-tur ontutulaγa.

After the people of Sartaul surrendered to Genghis Khan, all the kings and dukes of Mongolia gathered to Buka-Sochikai, and (in the archery competition) Yisungge shot the longest 335 aldas (1 alda is distance of arms spread wide, total about 536m).

1 2 3 4 5 6 7 8 9 10

upper row

1. nige 2. qoyar 3. γurba 4. dörbe 5. tabu 6. jirγuγa 7. doluγa 8. nayima 9. yisü 10. arba

lower row

10. arba 20. qori 30. γuči 40. döči 50. tabi 60. jira 70. dala 80. naya 90. yire 100. jaγu

traditional Mongolian numeral writing passed down from Tibet

No.	Mongol Bichig			Sound Change & Alphabet Change			
	initial consonants	medial (vowel)	final consonants	(sound change)	(alphabet change) initial consonant	medial	final consonants
01	ᠠ	ᠠ	ᠠ	a | e	' '	'	/ | (-)/ |\
02	ᠢ	ᠢ	ᠢ	i	'i	i	k
03	ᠣ	ᠣ	ᠣ	o | u	' w	w	b
04	ᠥ	ᠥ	ᠥ	ö | ü	' wi	w	b
05	ᠨ	ᠨ	ᠨ	n	n	n | '	n- | \
06		ᠩ	ᠩ	ng	-	'k	'i /
07	ᠬ	ᠬ	-	q	q	' '	-
08	ᠭ	ᠭ	ᠭ	γ	γ	γ | ' '	γ | ' \
09	ᠪ	ᠪ	ᠪ	b	b	b	b | w /
10	ᠫ	ᠫ	ᠫ	p	p	p	p
11	ᠰ	ᠰ	ᠰ	s	s	s	s | \
12	ᠱ	ᠱ	-	š	š	š	-
13	ᠳ	ᠳ	ᠳ	d	t	d | w '	d | w \
14	ᠲ	ᠲ	-	t	t	d	-
15	ᠯ	ᠯ	ᠯ	l	l	l	l
16	ᠮ	ᠮ	ᠮ	m	m	m	m
17	ᠴ	ᠴ	-	č	č	č	-
18	ᠵ	ᠵ	-	j	i	j	-
19	ᠶ	ᠶ	ᠶ	y	i | y	i | y	k
20	ᠺ	ᠺ	-	k	k	k	-
21	ᠭ	ᠭ	ᠭ	g	k	k	i /
22	ᠷ	ᠷ	ᠷ	r	r	r	r
23	ᠸ	ᠸ	-	v (w)	v	v	-
24	ᠾ	ᠾ	-	h	'h	h	-

Mongol Bichig matrix

When we look on the left side of the chart, the form used in the initial consonant, the medial, and the final consonant are all different. The right side is Mongol Bichig alphabet changed in sound and alphabet to the Latin alphabet.

was that Chinese characters were made by the Han tribe, who were settlers, and to the nomads, these characters were seen as difficult symbols and pictures that they could not understand. Also, to the nomads of North Asia, China was regarded solely as a country fighting for economic benefit. In regards to moral culture, nomads in the Mongol grasslands looked up to the west (including West Asia, India, and Tibet).

Among the historical books of Mongolia, in *Secret History of Mongolia* written in the 13th century, the copy written in the original Mongolian language was not passed down, but only the copy using the phonetic Chinese characters remains. Though written in Chinese characters, it was read in Mongolian.

In Mongolia, the Cyrillic alphabet has been in use since 1941 and the Mongol Bichig has been officially disused since 1946. Mongolia is using the Cyrillic Mongolian alphabet borrowed from the Russian alphabet. But in Neimenggu of China, Mongol Bichig is still officially used to this day.

Also in Mongolia, after the democratic movement progressed during the 1990s, there were movements to revive Mongol Bichig. However, they did not succeed due to several problems. But recently in 2010s, many efforts have been put into changing and publishing historical books or classical works originally written in Mongol Bichig to Cyrillic Mongolian.

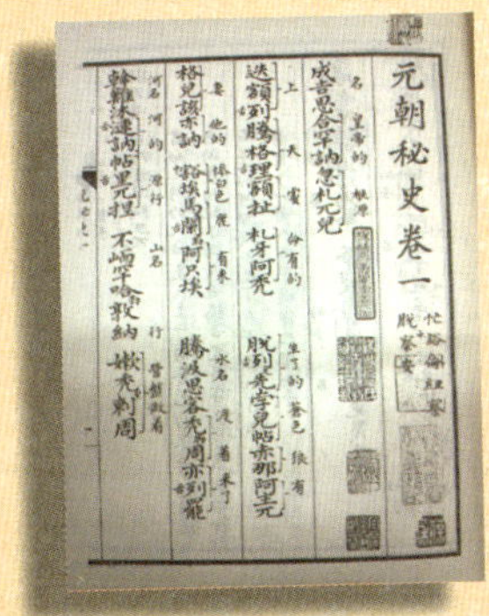

first chapter of
Secret History of Mongolia

Mongol Bichig book cover
published in Inner Mongolia

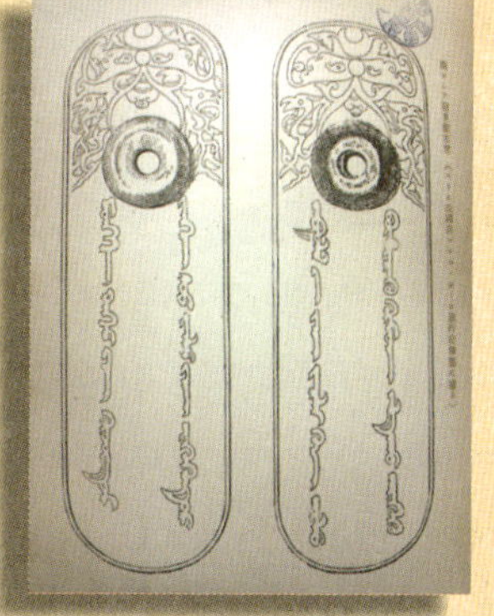

Mongol Bichig scripture

left
möngke tngri-yin küčün-dür yeke suu jali-yin ibegen-dür
Receiving protection of great gospel by the power of eternal Heaven

right
abdulla-yin jrliy kün ülü büsirekü kümün aldaqu ükükü
Those who do not follow the holy doctrine of Abdulla Khan shall be put to death

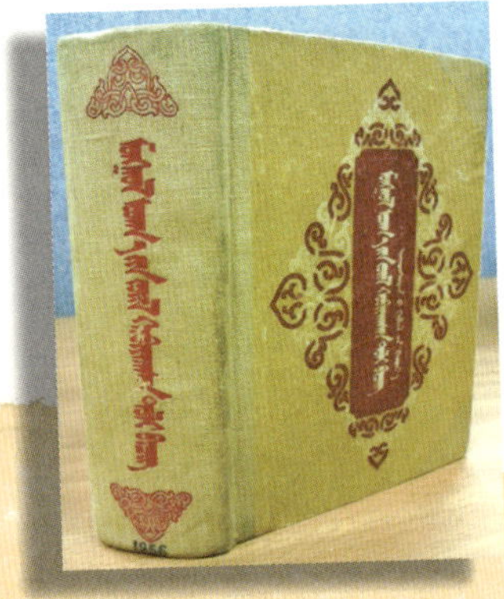

cover of Mongol Bichig book Mongolian Alphabet Classification Dictionary

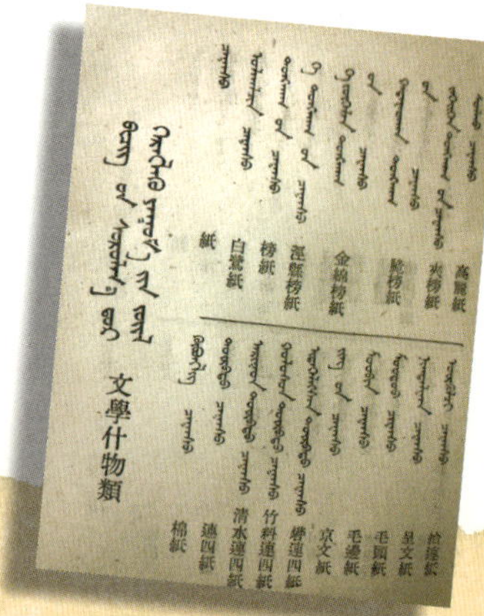

文學什物類

毛頭紙

毛邊紙

京文紙

竹料連四紙

清水連四紙

棉紙

contents of Mongolian Alphabet Classification Dictionary

Mongol Bichig in Mongol Ulaanbaatar Genghis Khan (činggis qaγan) International Airport

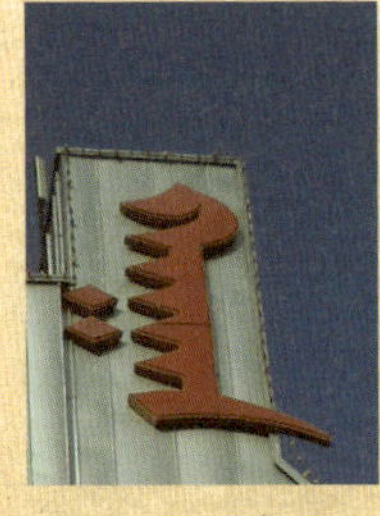

činggis (Genghis) qaγan (Khan)

Karakorum Museum (Cyrillic alphabet), kharkhorum muzei

Karakorum Museum (Mongol Bichig), ɣar-a ɣorum muzei

"Mongol (Mongɣol)" written in Mongol Bichig

Mongolian alphabet engraved in bronze kettle

book cover in Mongol Bichig

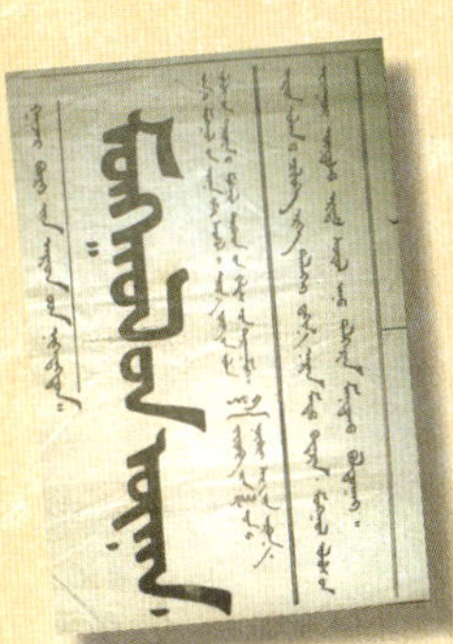

the first newspaper in Mongol

modern Mongol book cover (1937)

Magazine named *Shine Toli* (New Mirror) published every two months by the Institute of Science in Mongolian People's Republic.

The Mongolian Language Written in Many Alphabets

The Phags-pa alphabet (Square alphabet)

Kublai, the grandson of Genghis Khan, wanted to create an alphabet to write all the languages of the lands that the Mongols ruled. Therefore, in 1269, he ordered Phags-pa, a scholar from Tibet, to create a new alphabet. Phags-pa slightly modified the Tibetan alphabet to create the new alphabet, the Phags-pa alphabet. Because of its square shape, it is also called the Square alphabet (Durbeljin Usek). Because writing system using the alphabet was too difficult, it was only used in some official documents or on epitaphs and stamps. Instead, the Uigur Mongol alphabet was widely used.

Phags-pa alphabet stamps

Phags-pa alphabet scripture – from left, Persia, Phags-pa, (Uigur) Mongol Bichig

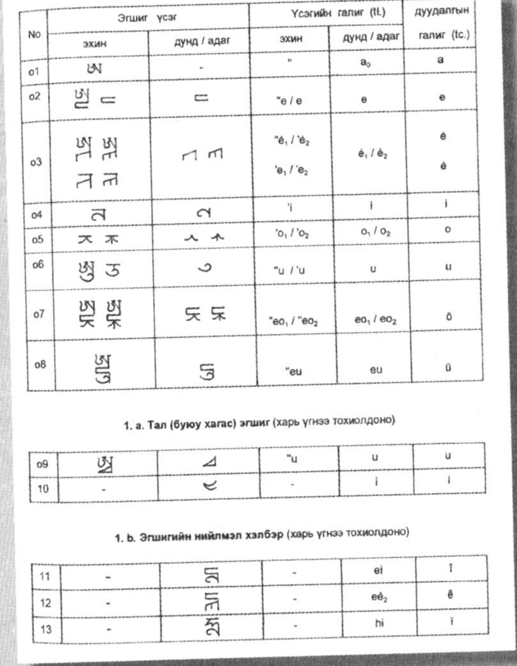

No	Эгшиг үсэг		Үсэгийн галиг (tl.)		дуудлагын галиг (tc.)
	эхин	дунд / адаг	эхин	дунд / адаг	
o1	[illegible]	-	"	a_0	a
o2	[illegible]	[illegible]	"e / e	e	e
o3	[illegible]	[illegible]	"$ė_1$ / '$ė_2$ 'e_1 / 'e_2	$ė_1$ / $ė_2$	ė ė
o4	[illegible]	[illegible]	'i	i	i
o5	[illegible]	[illegible]	'o_1 / 'o_2	o_1 / o_2	o
o6	[illegible]	[illegible]	"u / 'u	u	u
o7	[illegible]	[illegible]	"eo_1 / "eo_2	eo_1 / eo_2	ö
o8	[illegible]	[illegible]	"eu	eu	ü

1. a. Тал (буюу хагас) эгшиг (харь үгнээ тохиолдоно)

o9	[illegible]	[illegible]	"u	u	u
10	-	[illegible]	-	i	i

1. b. Эгшигийн нийлмэл хэлбэр (харь үгнээ тохиолдоно)

11	-	[illegible]	-	ei	î
12	-	[illegible]	-	e$ė_2$	ê
13	-	[illegible]	-	hi	ï

Vowels of Phags-pa alphabet

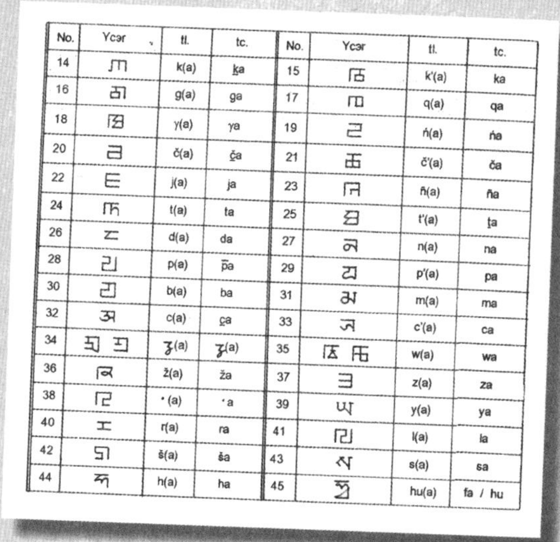

No.	Үсэг	tl.	tc.	No.	Үсэг	tl.	tc.
14	[illegible]	k(a)	k̲a	15	[illegible]	k'(a)	ka
16	[illegible]	g(a)	ga	17	[illegible]	q(a)	qa
18	[illegible]	γ(a)	γa	19	[illegible]	ń(a)	ńa
20	[illegible]	č(a)	č̲a	21	[illegible]	č'(a)	ča
22	[illegible]	j(a)	ja	23	[illegible]	ñ(a)	ña
24	[illegible]	t(a)	ta	25	[illegible]	t'(a)	t̲a
26	[illegible]	d(a)	da	27	[illegible]	n(a)	na
28	[illegible]	p(a)	p̄a	29	[illegible]	p'(a)	pa
30	[illegible]	b(a)	ba	31	[illegible]	m(a)	ma
32	[illegible]	c(a)	c̦a	33	[illegible]	c'(a)	ca
34	[illegible]	ʒ(a)	ʒ(a)	35	[illegible]	w(a)	wa
36	[illegible]	ž(a)	ža	37	[illegible]	z(a)	za
38	[illegible]	·(a)	·a	39	[illegible]	y(a)	ya
40	[illegible]	r(a)	ra	41	[illegible]	l(a)	la
42	[illegible]	š(a)	ša	43	[illegible]	s(a)	sa
44	[illegible]	h(a)	ha	45	[illegible]	hu(a)	fa / hu

Consonants of Phags-pa alphabet

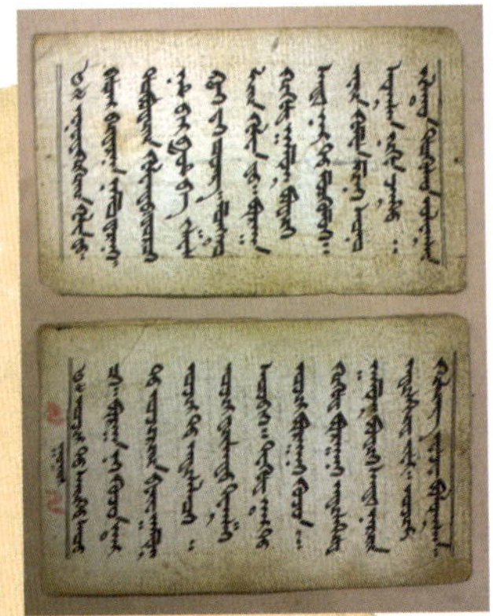

part of a scripture written in Tod alphabet

national flag of Mongolia

On the left, the first letter of Soyombo alphabet is drawn in. "Soyombo" symbolizes freedom and independence of Mongolia, the flame is prosperity of the Mongolia race, the sun and the moon below the flame are the people's lives and glory, the inverted triangle means that enemy will be defeated. The fish design symbolizing *yin* and *yang* means they will be careful of foreign invasion, and the rectangular pillar on each side means rampart.

Tod (Oirat) alphabet

The Tod alphabet was created in 1648 at West Mongol by Jaya Fanditha, a monk from Oirat, who slightly modified the existing Mongolian alphabet. This alphabet has the benefit of distinguishing O and Ö, U and Ü, D and T in writing, which is not distinguished in Mongol Bichig. This alphabet is still used by the Oirat people living in Xinjiang Uygur in China.

Soyombo alphabet

The Soyombo alphabet was created in 1686 at Khalkha Mongol (Outer Mongolia) by the religious leader Bogd Gegeen Javzan Damba. This alphabet was created on the basis of Lantsa alphabet from India. Because of its strong fanciness, it is used for some covers of religious scriptures or as a symbol. On the Mongolian national flag, the first letter of Soyombo alphabet is included.

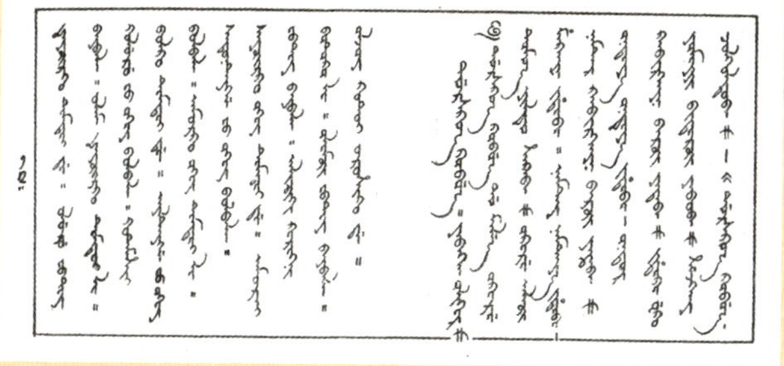

Vagindra alphabet scripture published in 1907

Vagindra alphabet

The Vagindra alphabet was created by the monk of Bouriate, Agvan Dorjieff. Among the Mongolian languages, this alphabet was made by slightly modifying the Mongol Bichig to fluently articulate the Bouriate dialect.

Latin Mongol alphabet

After becoming free from the Qing Dynasty, Mongolia built their modern country and abandoned the Mongol Bichig alphabet they were using. In the 1930s, they tried to write the Mongolian language using the Latin alphabet. However, due to interference by the pro-Soviet Union power and the enforcement of the Cyrillic alphabet, this attempt ended up in failure.

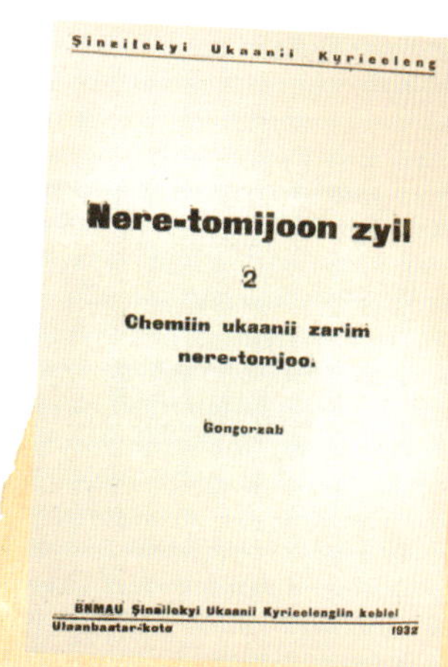

Şinzilekyi Ukaanii Kyrieeleng

Nere-tomijoon zyil

2

Chemiin ukaanii zarim nere-tomjoo.

Gongorzab

BNMAU Şinzilekyi Ukaanii Kyrieelengiin kebiel
Ulaanbaatar-koto 1932

book cover
in Mongol Latin alphabet

Borrowing the Russian Cyrillic Alphabet

The Russian Cyrillic Mongol alphabet was created by Soviet Union forces, made to write the Mongolian language in the Russian Cyrillic alphabet. Because it was difficult to write the vowels of the Mongolian language using the existing Russian, Ө and Y were added. Long vowels were originally written by putting a line on top of the letter, but later, the vowel was written twice. After 1941, most published books and official documents were officially written in this alphabet.

Shall we take a brief look into the background of the Mongolian People's Republic's adoption of the Russian Cyrillic alphabet? In March 1940, the Mongolian People's Revolutionary

А а	Ж ж	Н н	У у	Щ щ
Б б	З з	О о	Ү ү	ъ
В в	И и	Ө ө	Ф ф	ы
Г г	Й й	П п	Х х	ь
Д д	К к	Р р	Ц ц	Э э
Е е	Л л	С с	Ч ч	Ю ю
Ё ё	М м	Т т	Ш ш	Я я

Russian Cyrillic Mongol alphabet
(current official alphabet of Mongolia)

Party opened the 10th party meeting to approve the new doctrine. In this meeting, they confirmed that the goal of fostering a "democratic revolution" in Mongolia was already accomplished, and furthermore, it was converting to "socialistic revolution" stage. Therefore, it stated that the government was obligated to provide free medical services and education for the people of Mongolia. According to this, to reduce the rate of illiteracy, the Russian Cyrillic alphabet, easy to learn and write, was adopted in 1941. Afterwards, in all areas of Mongolia, alphabet clubs and organizations were created in each *som* (town) and *bak* (smaller town). The government was also obligated to send teachers to educate workers and people in factories and government offices. Then there was a movement calling for each

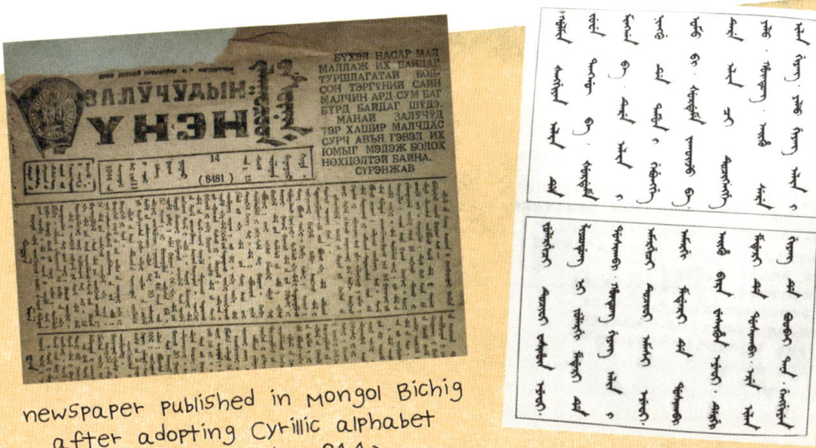
ЗАЛУЧУУДЫН ҮНЭН

14

(8481)

БҮХЭЛ НАСАР МАЛ МАЛЛАЖ ИХ БАЙДАГ ТУРШЛАГАТАЙ БОЛСОН ТЭРГҮҮНИЙ САЙН МАЛЧИН АРД СУМ БАГ БҮРД БАЙДАГ ШҮҮДЭ. МАНАЙ ЗАЛУЧУУД ТЭР ХАШИР МАЛЧДАС СУРЧ АВЪЯ ГЭВЭЛ ИХ ЮМЫГ МЭДЭЖ БОЛОХ НӨХЦӨЛТЭЙ БАЙНА.

СҮРЭНЖАВ

newspaper published in Mongol Bichig after adopting Cyrillic alphabet (February 11th, 1944)

Manchurian alphabet (borrowed from Mongolian alphabet)

person who had learned how to write using the alphabet to teach three other people. After these preparations, the Cyrillic alphabet started to be used in national official documents in 1946. Surprisingly only after ten years in 1956, 90.5% of the population ages 13 to 45 were able to read. To this day, Mongol Bichig is not officially used, and only Cyrillic alphabet is used.

Art Expressed in the Mongolian Alphabet

Today, the majority of the Mongolian population does not know how to use the Uigur Mongol alphabet. After 1946, they concluded that the tradition was merely the fancy feudal system

kümün, meaning person written in Mongol Bichig

mori, meaning horse as decorative letter written artistically in Mongol Bichig

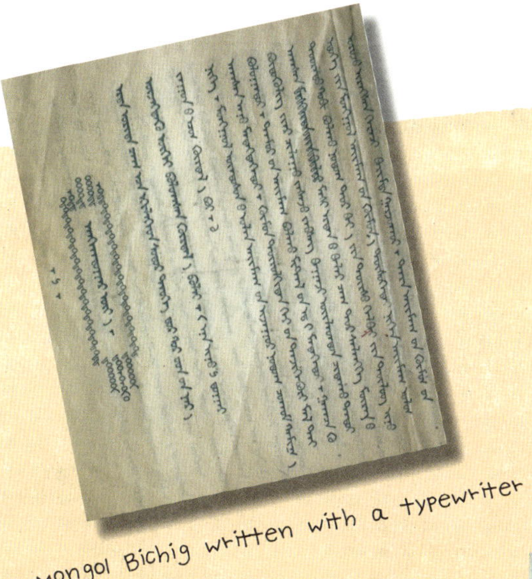

Mongol Bichig written with a typewriter

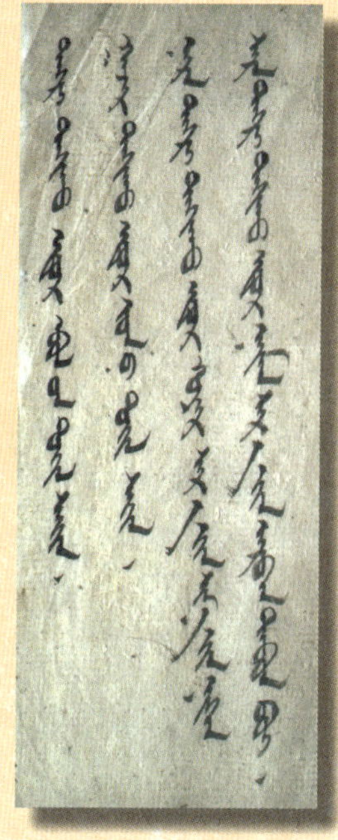

handwriting written in Mongol Bichig

* Contents:

tngri takiqu edür ebül-ün toyil sayin

A good day to perform ancestral rites to the sky is on the winter solstice

γajar takiqu edür jun-u toyil sayin

And a good day to perform ancestral rites to the land is on the summer solstice

Naran tngri takiqu edür qoyar sara-yin šine-yin nigen

The day of ancestral rites to the sun rising sky is on the first day of February

Saran tngri takiqu edür nayiman sara-yin arban tabun bui

And the day of ancestral rites to the moon rising sky is on the 15th of August.

of the old era. Therefore, even though some scholars, monks, and intellects knew the alphabet, they could not reveal it. In 1949, when representative nationalist scholars of Mongolia including Perler, Rinchin, Natsagdorj, Sodnom, and others defended the tradition, they were criticized of violating people's benefit. That is why many writers, artists, and scholars had to criticize tradition and praise socialism.

When Mongol Bichig is written in calligraphy, mostly it is written in "letter and image" form to match the letter shape to its meaning. For example, when writing "person" or "horse," it is written artistically to resemble its image. Also, when making a seal or an artistic work, the straight line is bent for decoration or as a pattern.

Mongolian Alphabet in Modern Life

In 1946, when the Mongolian People's Republic adopted Russian Cyrillic alphabet, it was a result of friendly advice from the powerful Soviet Union at that time. Therefore, there were cases when the same Mongolian language was used in two or three types of writing, and some words were used in other various ways. Also, by using the same Cyrillic alphabet, the traditional

Mongolian language pronunciation became more similar to the Russian pronunciation.

After democratization in 1990, there was a debate regarding whether to completely stop using the Cyrillic alphabet in order to revive Mongol Bichig, but this eventually died down.

In particular, as computers and mobile phones were supplied, sending and receiving e-mails or text messages in the Cyrillic alphabet was very inconvenient. Even though the Cyrillic Mongol alphabet font was ready, two letters, Ө and Ү, couldn't be written easily. So most young people and students use the Latin alphabet to send and receive e-mails or text messages. Because of this, the reality is that the grammar or spelling of the Mongolian language is almost disregarded.

一起

World's Oldest Chinese Characters

— Ryu Dongchoon

The Prevalent Square-Shaped Characters of East Asia

Among the 6,000 different languages on Earth, Chinese is the most used language, followed by English and Spanish. A little over 20% of the total population in the world are native Chinese speakers and over 30 countries use Chinese. Chinese characters are the letters used to record this Chinese language. Many foreign countries use Chinese characters, but it plays a particularly important role in sharing ideas and maintaining China's unity as a nation, even though people speak different dialects. Among the writing systems, Chinese characters are the oldest of their origin that are still used today. It's because Mesopotamian cuneiform characters and the Egyptian hieroglyphic characters are not used anymore. Of course, Chinese characters we use today have changed in form since they were created, but the basic form remains the same, connected to the original characters. Thus, among various letter forms of Chinese characters, when we see the letter 象 (*xiang*, elephant), we cannot know why it shows the meaning "elephant," but when we trace the letter to its past forms, we can easily spot the appearance of an elephant in the letter and how the long nose is described characteristically into an image.

chronicle of Chinese character type of 象 (elephant)

Letters used today can be divided into Semitic alphabets and Chinese characters. Out of the two writing systems, the alphabet is used in overwhelming majority, but before the industrial revolution of the early 18th century, more than half of all books published were recorded in Chinese characters. In the past, Chinese characters were the most commonly written language in East Asia as a tool of communication between many countries who could not otherwise understand one another due to different languages. Also in Korea, Japan, Vietnam, and other countries, before their own letters were designed, Chinese characters were borrowed, modified, or applied to record and communicate their languages. In other words, a cultural area employing Chinese characters was formed. Each country now has its own method of writing, and Chinese characters are either no longer used or in limited use. However, it is still needed as part of the education system because the literatures of the traditional times were recorded in Chinese characters. In these areas, Chinese characters are a common denominator in connecting each other's thoughts.

What does a Chinese character look like? All Chinese characters have a basic square shape. Therefore, it is convenient to count the number of characters. But one thing lacking is that we cannot know the pronunciation just by looking at the characters. Those who have studied Chinese for a long time can connect the pronunciation to its character, but most people have to memorize the pronunciation for each word. This is because Chinese characters draw from images. Although this is a drawback in reading the language, there is still the ability to know the meaning of the word by looking at its form. Of course, if you study characters, this difficulty can be overcome easily.

Then, shall we find out more about the convenience of Chinese characters? The characters representing numerals are very easy. One is represented by one line 一, two is two lines 二, three is three lines 三. From four, the character forms are different, but after ten, like 十一 (eleven), 十二 (twelve), 十三 (thirteen), we can just add the numerals between one and ten next to the characters.

Other than the square form, because Chinese characters do not use spacing, we can easily calculate how many letters are used in one page and use less space compared to other foreign letters. For punctuation marks, it is similar to other letters, but a period is written in a small circle (。), and a mark showing parallel (、) is rather unique. Long ago, the characters were written from top to bottom. For those who read left to right, there would have been some discomfort. But now, just like many other systems, it is written from left to right.

From Picture to Letter

Every ethnic group in the world has a legend about its letters. In the West, it is normally said that God created letters. In China, it is widely thought that Cangjie, a historian working for the Yellow Emperor, their ancestor, created Chinese characters. It is said that Cangjie had four eyes, so he had excellent observation abilities. It is said that he was inspired by looking at the changes of the moon in the sky and the different footprints of wild animals and winged animals on earth to create the characters. When Cangjie created Chinese characters, it is said that the sky was deeply moved and provided many crops, and the ghosts were very surprised and cried out in the night. When we see the portrait of Cangjie in books, he is portrayed with four eyes. Of course, there is no such person, but people of the past drew him this way to show that Cangjie had excellent observation abilities. In actuality, writing systems such as Chinese, which have many letters altered from images, are unlikely to be created by one person. Also, when we see traces of primitive letters revealed by archaeologists' excavations, we can see that Chinese characters have been created throughout a long period in time, as people's ways of expression developed in many stages.

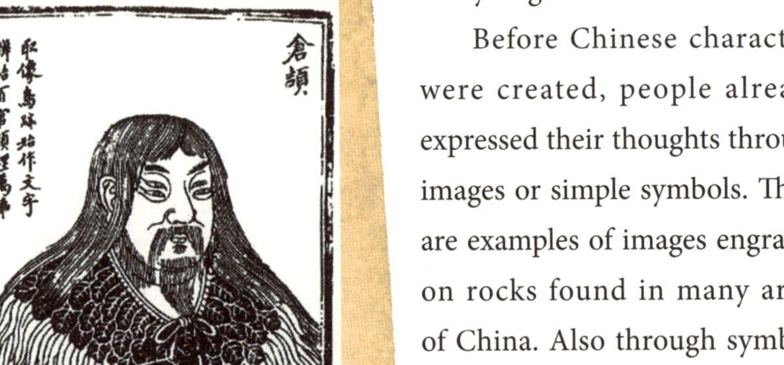

Portrait of Cangjie

Before Chinese characters were created, people already expressed their thoughts through images or simple symbols. There are examples of images engraved on rocks found in many areas of China. Also through symbols on the pottery of the New Stone Age and the tribal symbols in the

Bronze Age, we can see that the method of expressing meaning through visuals had developed. But as human society developed, social productivity and relationships between people changed, which the existing system could not express with limited images and simple symbolic forms. Therefore, people felt the necessity to record their words and communicate information through other means.

Letters are symbols that are recorded to read language, expressing sound through the eye. Therefore, it is difficult to distinguish from images, but the standard way to differentiate the two is by seeing whether it can be put into the same words or not. In other words, images are described differently in words depending on the person, but in the same group of speakers, letters are attributed to the same word. If we understand the difference between images and letters, the petroglyph of the image below showing a person hunting a tiger with a bow isn't

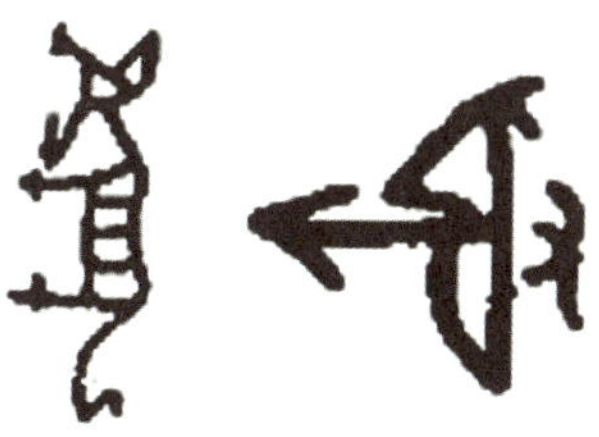

Petroglyph

oracle bone script 射虎 (She-hu)

much different from that in the oracle bone script 射虎 (*she-hu*, shooting the tiger), but we can easily understand that there is a characteristic difference between images and letters.

If so, what process did Chinese characters go through to change from image to a complete writing system? We divide Chinese characters according to the forms of ideogram (hieroglyphic, ideogram, and part abstract letters), symbolic character, rebus, and phono-semantic character. But these expression forms did not appear all at once. In the process of Chinese characters developing to become a complete writing system, they appeared in order of necessity. Among Chinese characters, letter images that have relation to the meanings but do not have relations to the pronunciation are called ideograms. Letters that have no relation between the image and meaning are called symbolic characters. These ideograms and symbolic characters first appeared not just in Chinese characters, but in all writing systems of the world. Among ideograms, each expression form did not appear at the same time. Like most ancient letters, initially, Chinese characters were also primarily hieroglyphics, so it is generally thought that the first letters created are hieroglyphics, but actually, it is not the case. As mentioned earlier, because the distinction between image and hieroglyphics is not clear, hieroglyphics were not deemed very necessary.

People felt the necessity to express numerals or objects with characteristics difficult to express with hieroglyphics. For example, by drawing figures and adding strokes in abstract expression method, numerals of 一 (one), 二 (two), 三 (three) were made. Using the symbolic expression method, the characteristics of an object were able to be articulated. For example, like an adult spreading two arms and standing still, there is a letter 大 (*da*) meaning "large." These letters still look like images, but there is a significant difference. When we express a big deer through an image, we can draw it big, but when we express it in letters, it's different. In other words, for a big deer, 大 (*da*) meaning "big," is connected to 鹿 (*lu*) meaning "deer," and is written 大鹿 (*da-lu*). On the two expression methods above, the symbol of the deer is similar in appearance, but essentially, one is an image and the others are characters. Thus, the concrete hieroglyphic mark of 鹿 (*lu*) became a true letter after the letter 大 (*da*), meaning "large," was used clearly distinguishable from its image.

As the world grew more complex, there was difficulty in recording all words with just ideograms and symbolic letters. With just ideograms, many languages cannot be expressed. Symbolic characters are only imbued with the meaning. Therefore, it is difficult to learn and remember. Thus, people came up with the phonetic representation method. This method borrows existing letters as pronunciation symbols to record the word. By this method, words that cannot be expressed with ideograms or symbolic letters could be recorded in letters. Letters recorded in this method are called "rebus." Greater use of this rebus method drastically strengthened the language writing function of Chinese characters and enabled all words to be written down. At last, the Chinese language was able to record the pronunciations of Chinese words.

As the usage of rebus increased, there were new problems. Because one character can represent several words, there were many cases in which we cannot know which word is written when we read. Therefore, to solve the problem of understanding the meaning, ideograms or symbols showing the meaning of the letter are added to the rebus to create new letters. Here is the example of the oracle bone script. The hieroglyphic of 翼 (*yi*, wing) is [oracle bone glyph], and in rebus, it also represents the word 翌 (*yi*, tomorrow). But when we see this word, there is confusion of whether it means "wing" or "tomorrow," so when we write "tomorrow," we add 日 (*ri*, day), to write [oracle bone glyph]. Also, in some cases, as the hieroglyphic [oracle bone glyph] drawn in the image of a phoenix 鳳 (*feng*) was written as 風 (*feng*), meaning "wind," the pronunciation part [oracle bone glyph] was added to create the new character form of [oracle bone glyph]. Phono-semantic characters are made by adding meaning or pronunciation indicators to the existing letter. After Phono-semantic characters were created, the number of Chinese characters increased by a lot, and the accuracy of expression also improved to become a comprehensive letter system recording the Chinese language.

When did Chinese characters become a complete letter system? Due to lack of data, it is difficult to reveal the exact period of creation for Chinese characters, but from data found in petroglyphs in many parts of China, pottery markings in the New Stone Age, tribal markings in the Bronze Age, and oracle bone scripts in Shang (商, or 殷 Yin) Dynasty period, we can estimate the approximate period. On the basis of these excavated data, scholars estimate that before 2800 BC and after agriculture developed in the New Stone Age, Chinese characters were first used in the plains of the Yellow River Valley. This presumption is right from the evidence in the oracle bone scripts of the latter Shang Dynasty; images are not shown true to their actual appearance, and instead, the directions of the characters are changed to write them more easily. For example, letters like (犬 *quan*, dog) and (豕 *shi*, pig) do not have legs facing down, but facing up. In the former petroglyph, animals living on land are described vividly, but in the oracle bone script, reality was abandoned to write with convenience. But on the other hand, we can still find trace of primitiveness of letters in the oracle bone script. Some ideograms change in shape depending on the situation. For example, 牢, meaning "cattle pen," was written based on the animal inside ∩ (宀) that changed from cow (牛), pig (豕), lamb (羊), to be written as ⿵宀牛, ⿵宀豕, ⿵宀羊, according to the type of animals specially raised as sacrifice in ancestral rites. In a perfect system, the character for the sacrificed animal would have been written as one character, but they are shown differently in images according to the animal. Because the oracle bone script has these conflicting characteristics, we can estimate that the oracle bone script was used not too long since the Chinese character formed its letter system.

Change of Handwriting

Chinese characters, forming their system during the latter period of Shang Dynasty, have changed their appearance as time passed. The appearance of Chinese characters in each period is called 字体 (*zi-ti*, character font). When we look at the change process of this character font, the ornamental seal type (隸書, *lishu*) created during the Han Dynasty especially brought innovative change to the structure of Chinese characters. Therefore, on the basis of the ornamental seal type, many handwritings are divided into old characters which are strong in pictures, such as the oracle bone script, bronze script, *dazhuan* (大篆), and *xiaozhuan* (小篆). Also, character fonts such as the ornamental seal type, printed style, cursive type, and semicursive style, which are prominent in signs, are classified as present letters. Now, we will see the characteristics of these representative character fonts.

Oracle bone script (甲骨文)

Oracle bone script is short for "tortoise shell letter and animal bone letter," which was used when people of the Shang Dynasty performed psychic and wrote its details on the shell of a turtle or on the bone of an animal. It was found at the end of Qing (清) Dynasty and about hundred thousand pieces have been found until now. Oracle bone script is known as letters related to the pyromantic divinations carved mostly on cow bones and turtle shells, but there were letters written in bones of other animals, and rarely, some were not engraved but written; also some were unrelated to pyromantic divination. Oracle bone scripts were mainly excavated in Yinxu (殷墟), the old capital of Shang Dynasty, but some were also found in outside of Yinxu, such as in Zhou (周) Dynasty.

Among the oracle bone scripts excavated, the most in

numbers and importance were from Yinxu, and these were used in some feudal dynasties of the latter Shang Dynasty, from about 3,100 to 3,500 years ago. The oracle bone scripts of Yinxu were perfect systems already using the method of six character classifications described in the scripts of the later generation's dictionary. On the right, you will see the examples of letters created according to the six classification methods seen in the oracle bone scripts.

Great Collection of Oracle Bone Script, No. 14294

Meanwhile, since the oracle bone script was an early Chinese character not fully standardized in its form structure, as seen in the image of the letter 鼎 (*ding*, caldron), there are still characteristics of an image, in which one letter uses several shapes or more than two letters are used in one character space.

- Pictograms

(象 *xiang*, elephant): elephant's characteristics of a long nose was expressed.

- Simple abstract ideograms

(上 *shang*, up): on the basis of the center line, a short stroke is inserted to mark the upper side.

- Compound ideograms

It is composed of (牧 *mu*, breed) and (牛 *niu*, cow), or (羊 *yang*, lamb) and (攴 *po*, hit). It means to grab a stick with a hand to beat a cow or a lamb.

- Phono-semantic compound characters

(星 *xing*, star): the shape and the pronunciation expressing the many stars in the sky is combined with (生, *sheng*, live).

- Derivative cognates

(老 *lao*, old) (考 *kao*, care): they are words for the elders, which can be used in exchange.

- Rebus (phonetic loan) characters

(其 *qi*, it): originally, it was drawn as a winnow basket which separates rock from the crop, but it is borrowed to the demonstration meaning "it."

various character fonts of 鼎 (*ding*, caldron) in the oracle bone script

There are examples of two letters used in one space: (十月, *shi-yue*), (祖丁, *zu-ding*), (十牢, *shi-lao*), (報丙, *bao-bing*), and using three letters in one space: (十三月, *shi-san-yue*), (七十人, *qi-shi-ren*), and (四祖丁, *si-zu-ding*).

Bronze script (金文)

Bronze scripts are inscriptions casted or engraved on bronze bowls. Initially, these letters were mainly shown on bells or cauldrons, therefore they were also called the bell-cauldron script (鍾鼎文). But because it was discovered in other bronze bowls, it came to be known as the bronze script. In the latter Shang Dynasty, which was the same period as the oracle bone script, there were some engraved with tribe marks or simple commemorative words on bronze bowls, but from the Zhou Dynasty, bronze scripts recording descriptions of achievements were found in large numbers.

bronze script
Dayuding (大盂鼎)

When we look at the letter form, the bronze script directly continued the oracle bone script through its resemblance, but

- Characteristics of bronze script

Because most bronze scripts were casted, the stroke is wider and thicker than the oracle bone script. The font is more fixed than the oracle bone script, and the direction of writing is also regular, from top to bottom, and from left to right. We can see that it has better form as a writing system.

Generally, the stroke structure of bronze script is more simplified than the oracle bone script. For example, the letter 囿 (*you*) meaning "hunting ground" is written [glyph] to directly draw the hunting land in oracle bone script, but in the bronze script, it is simply changed to phono-semantic compound character and combined 有 (*you*, exist) for pronunciation, and 囗 (*wei*, surrounding) meaning "ground," to be written as [glyph]. But not all fonts of the bronze script are more simplified than the oracle bone script. From the use of an object or from a characteristic of the writing material, there are some cases where the shape of bronze script shows earlier characteristic than the shape of an oracle bone script. The following is the comparison of the changing process in 天 (*tian*, sky). Bowel-carved bronze script and general bronze script, which are periodically later than the earlier and latter period's oracle bone script, show older letter-form characteristics.

types of the letter 天

Bowel-carved bronze script

Earlier oracle bone script

General bronze script

Latter period's oracle bone script

depending on the material and the periodic characteristic, it had other characteristics different from the oracle bone script.

Because collection and research of inscription from the Bronze Age started from the Song Dynasty, bronze script was the main subject of ancient letter research before oracle bone scripts were discovered.

Dazhuan (大篆)

Dazhuan is an ancient writing used between the bronze script and the *xiaozhuan* era. According to its geographical characteristic, it can be divided into the *zhouwen* of the Qin (秦) Dynasty in the west, and *guwen* of the six nations in the east.

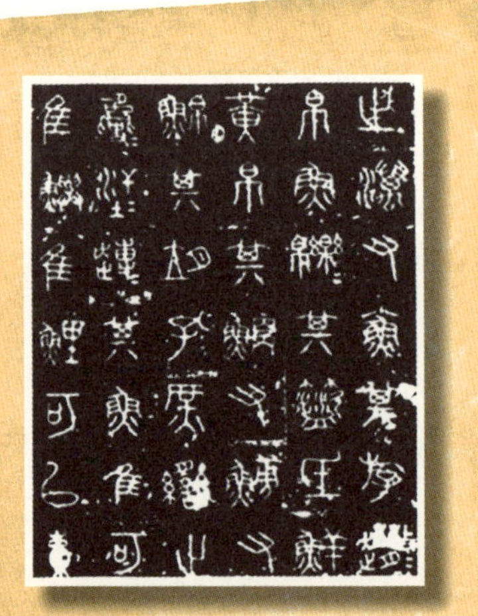

zhouwen
—Shiguwen

Zhouwen (籀文)

Zhouwen got its name of the letter scripts from the ancient dictionary, *Shizhoupian* (史籀篇). According to the statistics of Guowei Wang in Qing Dynasty, there are a total of 223 *zhouwens* in the *Shuowen Jiezi* (說文解字), which is important for studying *zhouwen* today. People of the Han Dynasty called scripts of

Shizhoupian, "*dazhuan*," and it is also called "*Qinxi dazhuan*" to distinguish itself from letters outside of Qin Dynasty. The representative letters of *dazhuan* which we can see today is the stone-drum inscription. These are the letters engraved into ten epitaphs found in earlier Tang Dynasty. On each epitaph, there were about 700 letters of four-character rhymed verses in the style of poetry. Because the epitaph looked like drums, it was called "*shigu*." When we see the stone-drum inscription itself, it looks like the letters of Qin Dynasty between the spring and autumn period and the Warring States period. Then we can say that the stone-drum inscription is a *dazhuan* letter of a relatively later period, inheriting *zhouwen* and influencing *xiaozhuan*.

Guwen of the six nations (六國古文)

In the period from Spring and Autumn to the Warring States period, productivity and economy developed to make academics flourish, and the class using letters expanded as well. To meet this demand, the form of the letters changed to a simplified form, and the material used to record letters

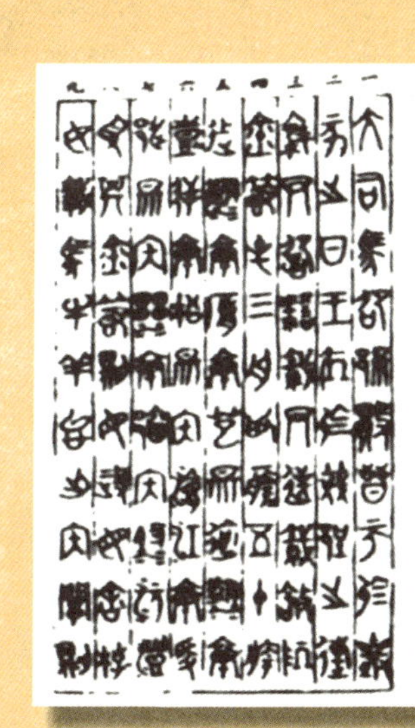

guwen
–Chu Ejungijie

were expanded to bamboo (bamboo pole) or silk. In the Warring States period, the power of the Zhou Dynasty weakened, and was divided into seven nations, which showed strong regional colors in areas such as politics, economics, and culture. Among these, Qin Dynasty-related letters inherited letters of *Shizhoupian* which were influenced by the bronze scripts of the West Zhou. Because Qin was in the same area, it naturally kept more letters of the Zhou Dynasty than the other six nations. As the other six nations were located in the east and the development speed of culture was faster than the Qin, the character font became more simplified than that of the Qin Dynasty. Of course, among the six nations, the form of the letters differed according to the degree of simplification, but we call them "ancient letters (*guwen*) of the six nations."

xiaozhuan – Qinliang

Xiaozhuan (小篆)

After Qinshihuangdi (秦始皇帝) united China, in order to arrange the confusing letter usages during the Warring States period, a letter reformation policy was strongly enforced. First of all, Qinshihuangdi ordered prime minister Li Si to fix and reduce the complicated character fonts to standardize the Qin Dynasty's letters and banned other writing systems of the six nations, which were different from Qin Dynasty's letters. Also, he published a letter dictionary imitating *Shizhoupian* to concentrate on

• Characteristics of *xiaozhuan*

Xiaozhuan set only one letter form as a standard for each letter; therefore, many letter forms of the ancient letters were arranged. For example, for the letter 逐 (*zhu,* chase), , , in the oracle bone script was fixed to , and for the letter 牝 (*pin,* female), , , in the oracle bone script was fixed to .

As *xiaozhuan* mostly exuviated from the appearance of an image to be symbolized, phono-semantic compound characters increased more compared to former letters. For example, the letter 聞 (*wen,* listen) looked like an image of a person and an ear in the oracle bone script, but in the *xiaozhuan*, it changed to a letter shape of , a combination of 門 (*men*) for pronunciation and 耳 (*er*) for the meaning.

In *xiaozhuan*, the stroke for writing the letter decreased greatly compared to former letters. The letter 中 (*zhong,* center) was written in oracle bone script, in bronze script, and in *zhouwen*, but in *xiaozhuan*, it was simplified to be written . The decrease in the number of strokes for writing a letter as time passes is a natural trend for the change of a letter. It is because people continuously search for convenience in writing.

propagating the new letter form. However, when we analyze the excavated data, it is seen that before Qinshihuangdi absorbed the six nations, there were already many *xiaozhuan* letter forms in the Qin Dynasty areas. Li Si and others only based on *zhuan* (篆) font used in Qin Dynasty's area and referred to *dazuan* in the *Shizhoupian* to arrange them. In any case, the standard letter form set by the nation at this time was *xiaozhuan*, and when we compare it with other earlier ancient letters, it has the following characteristics.

Lishu (隸書)

Lishu is a letter form modified from the public letter form (popular letter) of *xiaozhuan* which was widely used by people of the Qin Dynasty during the end of Warring States period. Because of its convenience, even the low level officials of the government used it frequently. In *Shouwen Jiezi*, it describes how Qinshihuangdi ordered Jeong-Mak to create *lishu*, but this whole writing system could not be undertaken by one person. Jeong-Mak was probably an officer in an important position to arrange the *lishu* formed in the public. Originally, the official letter form of Qin was *xiaozhuan*, but *lishu* was already widely used in normal life; in the Han Dynasty, it substituted *xiaozhuan* to become the main letter form. *Lishu* in the Qin Dynasty and the Former

Han Dynasty had much similarity to the *xiaozhuan*, and yet was different from the representative *lishu* seen in the tombstones of the Latter Han Dynasty. We call this the *lishu* of the beginning era, different from the Latter Han era's *lishu*, as *guli* (古隸) or *qinli* (秦隸).

On the Xiping 4th year of Emperor Ling of the Latter Han Dynasty, in order for the government to set a letter standard to record the *Six Scriptures*, a stone scripture in *lishu* was built in the highest educational institution of the nation, Taixue. *Lishu* in this stone scripture has a flat, square type letter form, and when finishing the inclined stroke or horizontal stroke, it is written in the upper direction to show that the end point is facing upward. Therefore, the entire form of the horizontal stroke pointed upward direction shows a wave form. This typical *lishu*

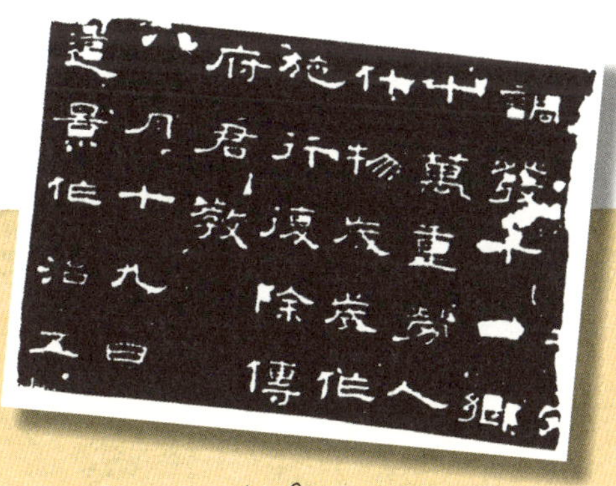

bafen
– Han zhang Jingbei

is distinguished from *guli* or *xinliti* (新隸體), popular from end of the Latter Han Dynasty to the Wei-Jin (魏晉) period, to be called *bafen* 八分 or *hanli* 漢隸.

Through *bafen*, the method of writing *lishu* was established. In other words, calligraphy had a clear standard. But people began to feel that even *bafen* was not convenient enough to be used in daily life. Hence, in the middle era of Latter Han Dynasty, a different popular letter shape appeared. Gentry of the Latter Han Dynasty still engraved stones with formal *bafen*, but *lishu* used by the general population already became the popular letter form. This popular letter form does not point the end in an upward direction like the typical *lishu* when finishing the stroke. It showed the trend of transitioning into a printed style of writing, affected by cursive characters. This letter form is *xinliti* (新隸體).

In the changing process of the Chinese character itself, the change from *xiaozhuan* to *lishu* was an epoch making incident. Former changes in letter forms decreased the number of strokes in writing, but the change to *lishu* was a structural change in form. Therefore, in graphonomy, this change is called *libian*. When we compare typical *lishu* with *xiaozhuan*, we can see the following changes.

In *lishu*, all letter forms are set by strokes. Later, Chinese character became a mark composed of strokes. In other words, the image type element remaining in *xiaozhuan* completely disappeared in *lishu*. The following is the comparison of *xiaozhuan* and *lishu* for 魚 (*yu*, fish), 燕 (*yan*, swallow), 馬 (*ma*, horse), 鳥 (*niao*, bird).

	魚	燕	馬	鳥
Xiaozhuan	魚	燕	馬	鳥
Lishu	魚	燕	馬	鳥

comparison of *xiaozhuan* and *lishu*

As 星 (*xing*, star) in *xiaozhuan* changed to 星 in *lishu*, Chinese character became more simplified in *lishu*.

The left or the right part of one character (radical) which was same in *xiaozhuan* divided into several forms in *lishu*, and originally different forms in *xiaozhuan* changed to the same form in *lishu*. This is conflicting direction of changes, but it coincides to the point that all original structural system of *xiaozhuan* was changed.

In *lishu*, to easily write the lines in *xiaozhuan*, it was changed to the strokes of dot, crossways, vertical, cut, and edge. Therefore, the round lines of *xiaozhuan* mostly changed to straight, short strokes. Accordingly, the appearance of Chinese characters changed from long square type to flat square type to form a unique style of *lishu*.

When changing the form of *xiaozhuan*, *lishu* only pursued convenience of writing, and the original purpose of Chinese character structure wasn't considered much. Therefore, in some process of changing to *lishu*, there were wrong changes in the character form. For example, the left part of *xiaozhuan* letter 折 (*zhe*, break) is a broken form of 木 (*mu*, tree), 折 but when changing to *lishu*, it changed to 扌 (手 *shou*, hand).

Regular script (楷書)

There is a dispute regarding the period of the development of regular script, or *kaishu*. But normally, it is seen based on *bafen* to be formed in the Former Han Dynasty and completed by the end of the Latter Han Dynasty. Regular script started to become popular from the Wei-Jin period and in the Tang Dynasty, when the most masters of regular script were generated. We can say that this period was the peak of regular script. From the Tang Dynasty, it secured its position as the standard letter form of Chinese characters. *Kai* in *kaishu* means rules and formalities. Therefore, *kaishu* means the letter form of examples or rules and formalities. When we compare it with *lishu*, its structure is basically the same with regular script. But the ends of regular script are not pointed upward when finishing the stroke, making it tidier and more convenient to use. Also, regular script is a square type form with only strokes, which is completely exuviated from the old image type of characters.

regular script
–Tang Yan Zengqing Shu

Cursive type

When *lishu* appeared, there were both block characters and popular characters. As the popular characters of *lishu* came into use, it became the cursive type in the Former Han era. This early cursive type was called *zhangcao* (章草), and it was popular among the lower levels of society, to be used mostly by minor officials when drafting an official document. For general documents, *lishu* was still used. But from the Han Dynasty, as there was mass copying of documents, the more convenient cursive type was developed. *Zhangcao* greatly modified the square type and structural system of Chinese characters by taking out one side (radical) or by leaving just the outline and changing dots and crossways to reduce the number of strokes from about ten to two or three. This enabled the structure of Chinese characters to be greatly simplified, making it faster and more efficient. But when we compare this to the cursive characters in the later period, *zhangcao* was not completely free from the effect of *lishu* of the Han Dynasty. The stroke did not connect in one stroke such as *jincao* (今草), and the strokes were completely independent, which did not maximize the efficiency of writing.

Jincao appeared in the Wei-Jin period, and *Qiuyuetie* (秋月帖) of Wang Xizhi (王羲之) was the representative work. The character

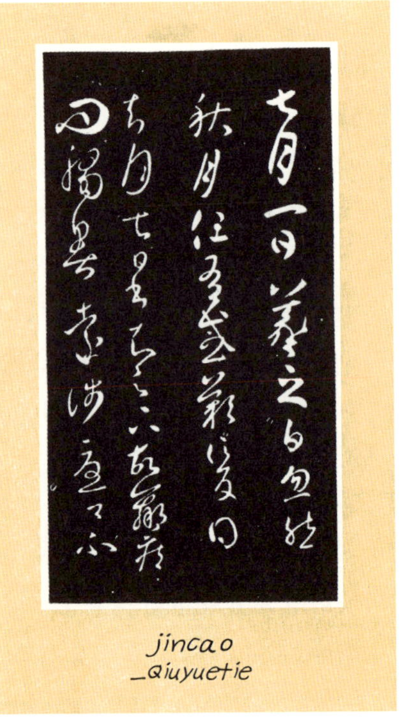
jincao _qiuyuetie

form of *jincao* mostly derived from *zhangcao*, but because the style of penmanship that was similar to *lishu*'s was modified, we can say that it is more affected by the printed style letter. *Jincao* greatly simplified the number of strokes, used several radicals for one part of a letter, and connected most letters to quicken the speed of writing. But because of this, decoding the words became more difficult, decreasing the practicality of the original letter and reducing the number of users.

In Tang Dynasty, with the base of this *jincao*, *kuangcao* (狂草) came into existence, letters became further simplified by being written in one stroke. *Jincao* was already difficult to decode, so *kuangcao* was even more difficult to recognize. It is thought that *jincao* and *kuangcao* no longer have practical value as a letter and have passed into the threshold of art, but we cannot neglect the effect of the simplification of Chinese characters.

Semicursive style letter (行書)

Semicursive style letters are an intermediate form of *jincao* and printed style letter, made in the Latter Han Dynasty. It was popular during the Jin (晉) Dynasty. The letter of Wang Xizhi and his son Wang Xianzhi is still the representative work of the semicursive style letter to this day. The characteristics of semicursive style letters can be summarized in two ways. First, it is somewhat similar to the printed style character, but is not straight, making it somewhat similar to *jincao*, but not free. Second, the strokes are connected, but the letters are separate to be easily distinguished, not difficult to recognize like *kuangcao*. Semicursive style letters are easy and quick to write, and decoding is also convenient, which exceeds printed style letter in practicality and usage in normal life.

Semicursive style
—Lantingxu

Simplified characters

Because Chinese characters are the letters of recording morphemes and words in the language, there has to be many letters. Also, each letter needs to be distinguished from others, which is complicated by the letter structure with many strokes. Some letters have over 60 strokes. Therefore, it is always said that there is an inconvenience due to difficulty in writing. Therefore, in the past, in regards to public and official government, there were continuous shortenings of characters when writing. This is because of the natural human nature of simplifying and minimizing the letter form through continuous usage of the letters. Due to these reasons, when the letter form was united with *xiaozhuan* in the Qin Dynasty through simplified *dazhuan* and among the ancient letters, simplified characters were selected to be arranged. Most simplified characters appeared from the public and had a strong presence; even the powers of the government couldn't suppress its use. In 1935, initiated by the Ministry of Education, the Ministry of State Affairs had several proclamations to announce the Total Table of Simplified Characters in 1946. This consisted of three tables; the first table had 352 simplified characters not used in sides (radicals), the second table had 132 simplified characters enabled to be used in sides and 14 simplified sides, and the third table had 1,754 simplified characters all inferenced from the simplified characters and simplified sides of the second table. The total table basically contained the range of *Xinhua Zidian* (新華字典) to list 2,238 simplified characters, which was actually 2,236 letters due to overlapping characters. By enforcing these simplified characters, China had the accomplishment of noticeably reducing illiteracy rate, but it is true there are also contrary effects in that the simplification discouraged the succession of traditional culture and idealized communication. Therefore, there are currently continuous debates regarding the use of traditional Chinese characters.

Story of the Sun and the Moon in Chinese Characters

The letter 日(*ri*, day) has an image of the sun in the sky. In the oracle bone script and in bronze script, the letter 日 is all marked as a round circle with a black dot inside. People say that this black dot symbolizes sunlight, or a sunspot inside the sun discovered by prehistoric people. At sunrise, the day becomes bright, and at sunset the day darkens, therefore aside from the meaning "bright," 日 is also used as a unit of time to express "day."

According to the Chinese legend, during the King Yao (堯) period, ten suns suddenly appeared in the sky. Originally, these ten suns were thought to be the sons of the God Di Jun and his wife Xi He, who lived in the ocean on the tree called Fusang (扶桑). Originally, each one per day comes up the Fusang to brighten the land, but on that day, the other nine also came up the Fusang. Therefore, the land boiled with heat and many living things died. So Di Jun sent down Houyi (后羿), who was skillful with a bow, to shoot down the nine suns, which left just the one sun we see today. This legend shows the fierce spirit of humans in the primitive age to overcome natural disasters. It shows that through our ancestor's efforts, we are continuing our lives today.

Now, let's go inside the letter 日 meaning the sun, to see some examples of the expression of time.

旦 (*dan,* morning) has the image of the sun rising. The line below the sun image is the shadow of the sun on the land or on the water. When we see the sunrise at early morning on the sea, we can easily understand the image of this letter.

The letter 暮 (*mu,* falling) meaning sunset was originally written as 莫. If we look at the ancient letter form, we can see the image of the sun falling between the woods in the evening. But as this letter was borrowed to represent the negative meaning "stop," the letter 日 related to time was added to create the letter 暮.

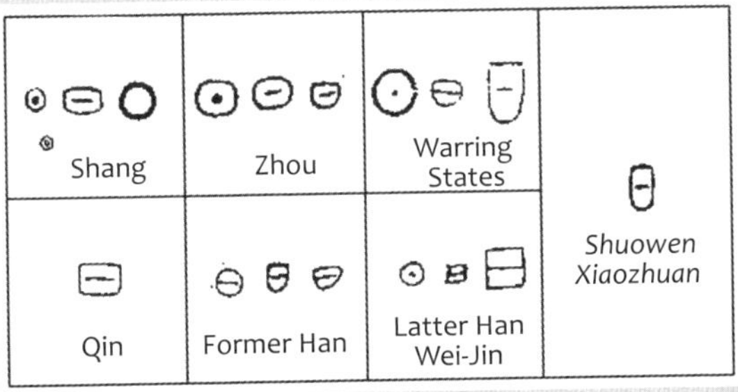

Shang	Zhou	Warring States	Shuowen Xiaozhuan
Qin	Former Han	Latter Han Wei-Jin	

日 (ri, day)

Shang	Zhou	Warring States	Shuowen Xiaozhuan
Qin	Former Han	Latter Han Wei-Jin	

旦 (dan, morning)

Shang	Zhou	Warring States	Shuowen Xiaozhuan
Qin	Former Han	Latter Han Wei-Jin	

暮 (mu, sunset)

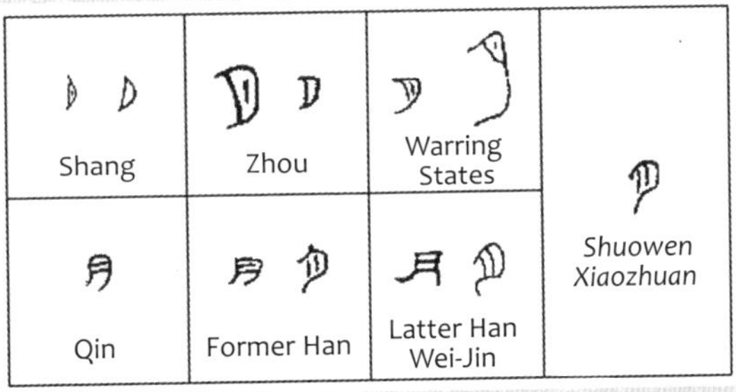

Shang	Zhou	Warring States	Shuowen Xiaozhuan
Qin	Former Han	Latter Han Wei-Jin	

月 (yue, moon)

The letter 月 (*yue*, moon) is a hieroglyphic in the image of the moon in the sky. The moon changes its shape periodically, but it is only round on the fifteenth day and the rest are all shown deformed. Therefore, it always seems empty or insufficient, as if lonesome. It is contrasted to the round image of the sun, representing that everything is satisfied.

月老 (Yue Lao) is short for 月下老人 (Yuexia Laoren, old man under the moon), who is a god of marriage in Chinese legend. In the books of Tang Dynasty, a person named Wigo was passing through Song Castle in the moonlit night to see an old man reading a book under the moonlight alone. Out of curiosity, Wigo went to the old man to ask what book he was reading, and the old man said, "This book is a record of relationships between men and women in the human world." So Wigo asked again, "What is the red string in your pocket?" the old man replied, "If this string is tied between a man and woman, even if they were once enemies, or no matter how far apart they are, they will become husband and wife." The Chinese call people who arrange marriages between men and women, Yue Lao.

If we look at the Chinese character now, the letter 明 (*ming*, bright) is a combination of 日 meaning the sun and 月 meaning the moon, but ancient oracle bone script shows a different form. Because the letter is not made by one person, some created 明

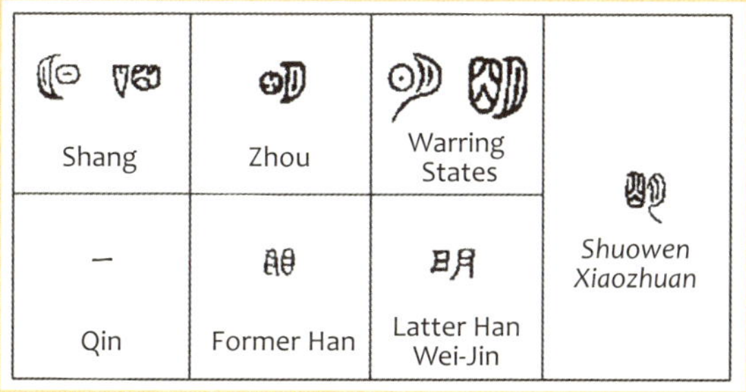

Shang	Zhou	Warring States	Shuowen Xiaozhuan
Qin	Former Han	Latter Han Wei-Jin	

明 (*ming*, bright)

by combining the brightest sun at noon and the brightest moon at night, but others express that it shows moonlight coming into the house in the dark night through a window. Afterwards, as it was united to become one letter form; only the character 明 exists today.

The letter 望 (*wang*, hope), meaning "look up to," shows the image of a person going up the heap of earth to look out into the distance. But afterwards, the subject "looking at" was added. The character 月, meaning the moon, was included. It is because the farthest thing that a person could see was probably the moon. This is the reason that the letter 望 means "to look far away" and also "to hope in abstract." Because the meaning could not be easily known from the image of the letter, this is an example showing later adjustments to the letter.

There is a letter that means early morning that uses the character 月. It is 夙 (*su*), meaning "early." When we see the oracle bone script and the bronze script of the 夙, it is an image of a person grabbing the moon. Of course, we can't really grab the moon, but what this letter shape shows is that, at dawn, when

<table>
<tr><td>Shang</td><td>Zhou</td><td>Warring States</td><td rowspan="2">Shuowen Xiaozhuan</td></tr>
<tr><td>–
Qin</td><td>Former Han</td><td>Latter Han Wei-Jin</td></tr>
</table>

望 (wang, desire)

<table>
<tr><td>Shang</td><td>Zhou</td><td>Warring States</td><td rowspan="2">Shuowen Xiaozhuan</td></tr>
<tr><td>Qin</td><td>Former Han</td><td>Latter Han Wei-Jin</td></tr>
</table>

夙 (su, early)

the moon from the night still shows, it could be low enough for a person to grab.

Reading About the Old Days of China Through Chinese Characters

The Chinese character is a combination of form, pronunciation, and meaning. This means that in the form of the letter, its unique pronunciation and the meaning are combined into one. Especially among the letters of Chinese characters, in ancient letters before *xiaozhuan*, they show the cultural information of that time through their form of images. It is like a living fossil showing the life style of the ancient people. The oldest oracle bone script reflects the lifestyle of ancient people 3,000 to 4,000 years ago. Through the old letters of Chinese characters, we can make assumptions about the lifestyles of the Chinese people in the old days.

There is a character that exemplifies the careful observation of the ancient Chinese. It is the oracle bone script of 臭 (*chou*), meaning

oracle bone script – 臭
(chou, smell / xiu, scent)

"smell." This letter emphasizes on the nose of a dog. It lacks reality, but the reason that the nose of a dog is drawn large with inappropriate body ratio was to emphasize the role of the nose in smelling. Through close observation of people during creation of Chinese characters, they discovered that the nose is responsible for olfactory function and also knew that dogs have a developed sense of smell compared to other animals, which is why they expressed "smell" as the nose of a dog. These characters of dogs are also shown in the letter 獸 (*shou*), which, as a hunting dog, became the right part of the character.

The image of the letter 得 (*de*) in bronze script shows the act of "picking up a clam from the road by hand." Clams were the currency at that time, and picking it up from the road means that there is no owner. It means to pick up money from the road. It's a windfall in some way. At the time, people expressed the abstract concept "obtain," by expressing a detailed incident in an image.

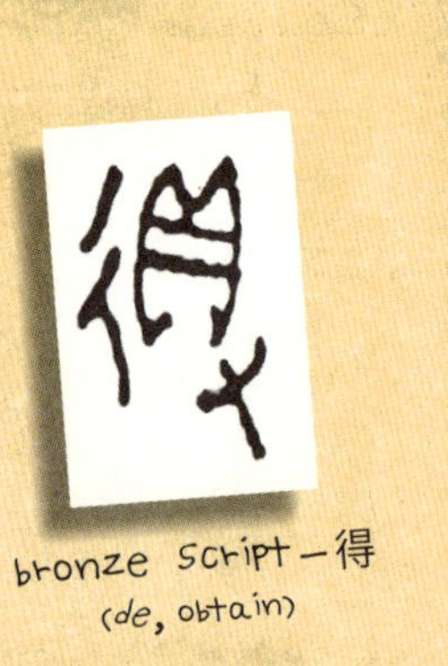

bronze script—得 (de, obtain)

We were able to obtain valuable information not only through analyzing each period of Chinese characters but also the changing process of Chinese character. The table on the right shows the letter 賓 (*bin*) meaning "guest," in the oracle bone script, bronze script, *xiaozhuan*, and ornamental seal type. The letter for the oracle bone script is composed of 口 (*kou,* mouth), meaning the entrance of a house and 止 (*zhi,* foot), meaning the "foot of the person visiting." In the bronze script and in *xiaozhuan*, along with 宀 meaning "house," 止 or 亻 meaning "guest," and 貝 meaning "money" was added. We can see through the change of this letter to understand that in the Zhou Dynasty, as the rules of decorum dictated, when a person visits another's house, a gift must be brought.

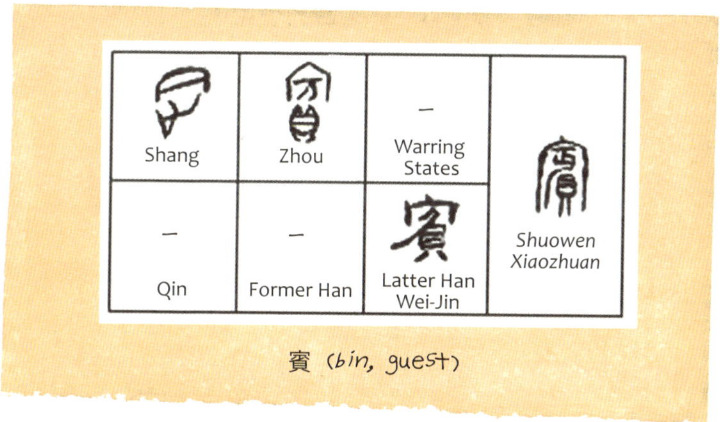

賓 (*bin,* guest)

Besides the letter form, we can also make assumptions about the aspects of the society of that time through the type of letters used in the ancient age. For example, in the literatures of Han Dynasty such as "Stonework" from *Erya* (爾雅), there are 51 proper nouns for "horse," 18 proper nouns for "cow," 13 proper nouns for "pig," 11 proper nouns for "lamb," ten proper nouns for "dog," and six proper nouns for "chicken." At that time, there are total 106 letters to express six main types of livestock. In the later period, these letters were eventually abandoned, not to be used, but the fact that there were various names of livestock reflects the stock farming society of that time. Also, characters expressing color in Chinese characters mostly have 糸 (*mi*, string) on one side. This enables us to assume that the original expression of colors came from the colors of silk. Actually, in the ancient letter dictionary *Shouwen Jiezi*, there are 24 letters expressing the color of silk. And among them, colors of 綠 (*lu*, blue), 紅 (*hong*, red), 紫 (*zi*, purple), 緋 (*fei*, silk) were often used as common nouns. From these letters, we can see the development of sericulture and dyeing in ancient China.

Chinese Characters in Modern Life

In the period of Chinese modernization, Chinese characters were identified by intellectuals as a main factor behind China's inferiority to Western powers. It was said that compared to the pinyin letters of the West, Chinese characters had too many in number, were difficult to learn, and lacked practicality. This was why one of the great scholars Lu Xun asserted, "If Chinese characters do not fail, China will fail." But now, by treasuring the characteristics of Chinese characters, it is actively applied in modern life. Shall we find out how it is being used?

Chinese character and image

Chinese characters, which originated from images, did not simply record language. In scripts such as cursive type in the latter period, the original practical function of the letter was set aside to be used for artistic enjoyment. The desire to beautifully decorate the letters already manifested in the period of the oracle bone script, but its genuine fanciness showed in *niaochongshu* (鳥蟲書), mostly seen on weapons of the Warring States period. Afterwards, the invention of the writing brush enabled the

niaochongshu

skillful expression of the stroke, allowing Chinese characters to pioneer the realm of calligraphy. Even today, the official script is the simplified Chinese character, but in calligraphy, the letters of the past are revived to show off the endless vitality.

On the other hand, different from the traditional calligraphy, practical application introducing the modern design method in Chinese characters was enacted. The design of the modern Chinese character called Art Letter, and corporate logos in the images of Chinese characters might be considered the new implementation of figure and ideograms of Chinese characters.

tribe mark of Bronze Age

logo of 2008 Beijing Olympics

bicycle brand logo

But actually, this technique is somewhat linked to the method used in tribal markings of the Bronze Age, traditional seal engravings, and in talismans. 2008 Beijing Olympic mark, which imaged the letter 京 (*jing*, capital) into a dynamic moving person, is a representative logo showing the figure of Chinese character. Also, the logo of a bicycle brand combining the two letters 永久 (*yougjin*, forever) is an example of applying the visibility of Chinese characters.

Chinese character and play

From long ago, there were plays using the ideogrammatic feature of Chinese characters. After the Zhou Dynasty when the usurpation of the throne became more politically significant, letters were used. In normal life, it was also used as a part of entertainment to fulfill the joy of writers. From what is told, when Qinshihuangdi unified China, the first name of the country was 琹 (*qin*, zither), but because the form of the letter had two kings (王) on one tree (木 symbolizes the chair that the King sits on), it was changed to the letter 秦 (at that time, the letter's pronunciation was same as 琹). It is said that this letter 秦 was also created by Qinshihuangdi in the history book of *Chunqiu* (春秋), taking half of each letter. Regardless of the truth, we can assume that at the time, many meanings were given to one Chinese character. A writer of great literature in Song Dynasty, Su Dongpo had a sister who was also very famous for her literature. There is a story of her competing with a close friend of her brother, Monk Foyin, who was a famous writer at that time. The phrase that the sister of Su Dongpo gave was "人曾是僧, 人弗能成佛 (*ren-ceng-shi-seng, ren-fu-neng-cheng-fo*: If a person was a monk before, this person cannot attain Buddhahood)." By separating parts (radicals) of the letter to get the meaning, in other words through a method of Chezi (坼字), she teased Monk Foyin. So he replied, "女卑爲婢, 女又可稱奴 (*nu-bei-wei-bi, nu-you-ke-cheng-nu*: If a woman is vulgar, she becomes a servant, and this woman is also called a slave)." Like this, these two people used the characteristics of Chinese characters to play with phrases that form antitheses. Today there is wordplay involving the arranging of letters using a poem form of four sentences in five letters each. For example, in the poem "前沒有后有, 左沒有右有, 家沒有國有, 弟沒有兄有 (*qian-mei-you-hou-you, zuo-mei-you-you-you, jia-mei-you-guo-you, di-mei-you-xiong-you*: Nothing in the front and something in the back, nothing on the left and something on the right, not in the house, but in the country, not within the younger brother, but within the older brother)." The Chinese character mentioned in the verse is 口 (*kou*, mouth), which is included in 后 (*hou*, back), 右 (*you*, right), 國 (*quo*, country), 兄 (*xiong*, brother). An example of a game arranging a Chinese character into four letters 旭 (*xu*, morning sun) (when it is written spread out, it is 九日 *jiuri*) expressing as 不足一旬 (*buzu yixun*: One day short of ten days). Also there is a game that uses the ambiguity of Chinese characters, such as 月 (*yue,* moon) interpreted as 朝前走 [*chao qian zou*: meaning 'marching forward' and also 'front part (前) of the letter 朝 (*qian,* morning) disappeared (走)']. Also, there is a game of adding strokes to the letter, such as creating another character by adding two strokes in the letter 口. There are letters such as 田 (*tian,* field), 古 (*gu,* past), 囚 (*qiu,* lock), 兄 (*xiong,* brother), 只 (*zi,* only), etc. The various games involving characters provided considerable help in learning difficult Chinese characters.

Chinese character and computer

In the age of computers, the method of input is one of the main concerns. There are two methods of inputting Chinese characters, one by using the keyboard, or by using something other than the keyboard. Generally, the keyboard method is mainly used. In the early period of computer use, in the 1980s, large keyboards were used. This large keyboard was similar to the blueprint keyboard in the printing house, with thousands of commonly used Chinese characters allocated on the keyboard. Afterwards, it was modified into a middle sized keyboard, but there was a problem of manufacturing this keyboard with many

Chinese characters, making it inconvenient to use as well.

Therefore, on the base of English keyboard commonly used worldwide, the way of inputting Chinese characters was invented. This input method uses the form and pronunciation of Chinese characters. That is to say, everything aside from the meaning when analyzing the three elements of Chinese characters. When using the form, just like how alphabets input the initial consonant, vowel, and final consonant, the parts of Chinese characters are inputted separately using *fujian* (radical). But because there are too many *fujian* in Chinese characters, they cannot all be shown on the keyboard. Normally, similar *fujian* use one key, and the computer has to choose *fujian* which can be combined. For example, 日, 曰, 口 are all allocated to one key. When using pronunciation, the alphabet is used to input Romanized Chinese characters. Among letters that are pronounced the same way, there is a method of selecting the relevant letter or inputting the first letter of the initial consonant and final sound (vowel and final consonant). Also, there are various input methods, such as applying both form and pronunciation, and inputting per word unit. However, because Chinese characters have many letters with the same pronunciation, there is the inconvenience of looking at the monitor to select one of many letters. Of course, it cannot be written as quickly as English.

To overcome this problem of speed, recently, methods not involving keyboards and instead, inputting by voice or through electronic pen, scanning and inputting the document are used. However, these methods have a long way to go to increase the rate of recognition. Along with the artistic application of Chinese character, the problem of Chinese characters harmonizing with the computer is an important task which will determine the status of Chinese characters in the future.

Japanese Letters: Representing Both Sound and Meaning

— Oh Miyoung

一緒に

Japanese Uses a Variety of Letters

Japan is an island nation made up of Hokkaido, Honshu, Shikoku, Kyushu, Okinawa, and other islands. It is the place where most speakers of Japanese live.

The population of the country is 120 million. Since there are a lot of people living in a large area, each region has its own dialect despite the fact that the country's political, cultural, and economic core, Tokyo, has the standard dialect. In particular, the Kansai region with Osaka as its center has a dialect that is widely known in Japan. People living in Japan's old capital of Kyoto take pride in their region's unique dialect even today.

Currently in Japan, Kanji (Chinese characters) and Kana are used to write the Japanese language. Kana has two syllabaries, Hiragana and Katakana. Looking at the signs in the first picture on the right, you would see a mix of Kanji, Hiragana, Katakana, and the Latin alphabet. In this way, Japan uses various letters in their language usage. The picture at the bottom is the table of contents from the book, *Children's Analects of Confucius*. Even though it is a children's book, we can see that it uses Kanji, Hiragana, and Katakana.

Japanese letter usage
as seen from the streets of Japan

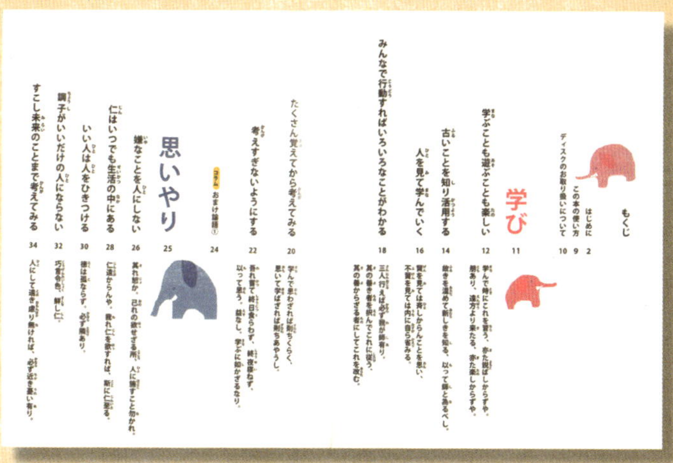

もくじ

はじめに	2	
この本の使い方	9	
ディスクのお取り扱いについて	10	
学び	11	
学ぶことも遊ぶことも楽しい	12	学んで時にこれを習う、亦た説ばしからずや。朋あり、遠方より来たる、亦た楽しからずや。
古いことを知り活用する	14	故きを温めて新しきを知る、以って師と為るべし。
人を見て学んでいく	16	賢を見ては斉しからんことを思い、不賢を見ては内に自ら省みる。
みんなで行動すればいろいろなことがわかる	18	三人行えば必ず我が師有り。其の善き者を択んでこれに従う、其の善からざる者にしてこれを改む。
たくさん覚えてから考えてみる	20	学んで思わざれば則ちくらく、思いて学ばざれば則ちあやうし。
考えすぎないようにする	22	吾れ嘗て終日食らわず、終夜寝ねず、以って思う。益なし、学ぶに如かざるなり。
コラム おまけ論語①	24	
思いやり	25	
嫌なことを人にしない	26	其れ恕か。己れの欲せざる所、人に施すこと勿かれ。
仁はいつでも生活の中にある	28	仁遠からんや。我れ仁を欲すれば、斯に仁至る。
いい人は人をひきつける	30	徳は孤ならず、必ず隣あり。
調子がいいだけの人にならない	32	巧言令色、鮮し仁。
すこし未来のことまで考えてみる	34	人にして遠き慮り無ければ、必ず近き憂い有り。

Japanese letter usage
as seen from a children's book

Kanji and Kokuji

Kanji are characters that were originally used in China, which passed through the Korean Peninsula to Japan around the late 3rd century and the 4th century. A record of Japan's history called the *Nihon Shoki* (translated as the *Chronicles of Japan*, finished in AD 720) reveals that two scholars from Baekje (an early Korean kingdom) named Wang-in and Ajikgi gave the *Analects of Confucius* and the *Thousand-Character Classic* to Japan. They also taught the contents of these books to the prince of Japan. Although there is no certain way to tell if this actually occurred, there is no question that "visitors" from the Korean Peninsula crossed over to Japan and influenced the writing system and culture.

There are more than 50,000 Chinese characters and various letter forms. Unsurprisingly it is impossible for all of the people to learn and use all of the many Chinese characters. Therefore, in modern Japan there is a list of Chinese Characters in Common Use that identifies the category of characters that are used in everyday life. In 2010, the list of commonly used Chinese characters contained 2,136 characters. The forms of Chinese characters (Kanji) used in Japan and the Chinese characters (Hanja) used in Korea are both different and similar to each other.

The method of writing Chinese characters in modern Japanese is called Shinjitai (a new type of calligraphic style), which has a more simple form than the Chinese characters used in Korea. Chinese characters were implemented in both Korea and Japan. The Jeongjache (traditional type of calligraphic style in Korea) was used until the middle of the 20th century in Japan. After using Jeongjache, which Koreans now use, Sinjache was adopted in Japan. In other words, the Japanese had used the same Chinese characters that were first introduced from China through Korea. In comparison to the Shinjitai, it is called Kyujitai.

Other than the Chinese characters taken from China, there were also characters originally made in Japan. Since Japan and China had different natural environments, different cultures, and methods of livelihood, there was a limit to what could be expressed with Chinese characters, so characters unique to

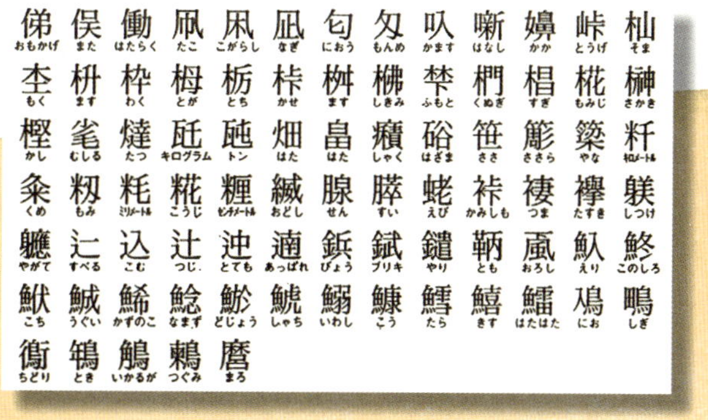

俤	俣	働	凧	凩	凪	匂	匁	叺	噺	嬶	峠	杣
おもかげ	また	はたらく	たこ	こがらし	なぎ	におう	もんめ	かます	はなし	かか	とうげ	そま
杢	枡	枠	栂	栃	桛	桝	柫	梺	椚	椙	椛	榊
もく	ます	わく	とが	とち	かせ	ます	しきみ	ふもと	くぬぎ	すぎ	もみじ	さかき
樫	毟	燵	瓩	瓲	畑	畠	癪	硲	笹	簓	簗	粁
かし	むしる	たつ	キログラム	トン	はた	はた	しゃく	はざま	ささ	ささら	やな	キロメートル
粂	籾	粍	糀	糎	縅	腺	膵	蛯	裃	褄	襷	躾
くめ	もみ	ミリメートル	こうじ	センチメートル	おどし	せん	すい	えび	かみしも	つま	たすき	しつけ
軈	辷	込	辻	迚	遖	鋲	錻	鑓	鞆	颪	魞	鮗
やがて	すべる	こむ	つじ	とても	あっぱれ	びょう	ブリキ	やり	とも	おろし	えり	このしろ
鯒	鯎	鯑	鯰	鯲	鯱	鰯	鱇	鱈	鱚	鱩	鳰	鴫
こち	うぐい	かずのこ	なまず	どじょう	しゃち	いわし	こう	たら	きす	はたはた	にお	しぎ
鵆	鴇	鵤	鶫	麿								
ちどり	とき	いかるが	つぐみ	まろ								

Kokuji: Chinese characters invented in Japan

Japan were made. These type of characters are called Kokuji (国字, national characters). Let's look at the representative characters of Kokuji.

Out of Kokuji, the character 魚 (meaning fish) was often used. Since Japan was an island nation surrounded by the ocean, fish was very common and was eaten often. It seems that in the original Chinese characters, there weren't enough individual characters to symbolize each type of fish. Also, we can say that due to differences in the region and climate, the fish living in China and the fish living in Japan were different. It is likely that Kokuji was made for these reasons.

After Chinese characters were first introduced to Japan, it is likely that the Chinese characters were considered to be foreign letters for a long time and were pronounced in Chinese. Eventually, the Chinese characters were used to write Japanese and the pronunciation of the Chinese Characters was also changed to a Japanese style as well. As these changes were established, it became Japan's Chinese character sounds.

Out of the Chinese character sounds, the one with the longest history is the Go-on (呉音, sound from the Wu region, China), which was passed over through the Korean Peninsula. Since it was introduced with Buddhism, today, there are many terms in Buddhism that are read in Go-on. Also, there are lots of Chinese character sounds to express words in one's daily life.

The situation of reading Chinese characters with Chinese character sounds is very similar to that of Korea. However, it is very different in that when one reads Japanese, one also reads the Chinese character's meaning. When Koreans study the Chinese character 學 they would read *bae-ul hak*. *Bae-ul* means learning in Korean, while *hak* is Chinese character sound. When a Korean sees this Chinese character, he or she may think of *hak* as meaning "learning," but would know not to read it that way. On the other hand, learning, which is まなぶ (pronounced *manabu*) in Japanese will also read the character as *manabu*. We call this *kundoku* (pronouncing Chinese character's meaning). Furthermore, the character is also read as the Chinese character sound of がく (pronounced *gaku*). This is called *ondoku* (reading Chinese characters by their traditional Chinese pronunciation).

In this way, Chinese characters were introduced to Japan and established as a writing method for the Japanese language, which is being used even today. This is quite different from the way Chinese characters were used in other surrounding countries. In the case of Vietnam, Chinese characters ceased to be used after colonization. In the case of Korea, although Chinese characters partly form the basis of the Korean language, all of the characters are now rendered in Korea's own alphabet Hangeul, and as a

Katakana was recognized as a character system and put into common use in society around the 10th century. Compared to Hiragana which was considered a writing system for women, Katakana was mostly used in scholarly works, official documents, and other such mediums. Like Hiragana, Katakana used several character forms which were arranged in 1900 and have been used since then.

Modern Japanese Katakana (clear voice) Table

	ア [a]	カ [ka]	サ [sa]	タ [ta]	ナ [na]	ハ [ha]	マ [ma]	ヤ [ya]	ラ [ra]	ワ [wa]	
ア [a]	ア	カ	サ	タ	ナ	ハ	マ	ヤ	ラ	ワ	ン
イ [i]	イ	キ	シ	チ	ニ	ヒ	ミ		リ		
ウ [u]	ウ	ク	ス	ツ	ヌ	フ	ム	ユ	ル		
エ [e]	エ	ケ	セ	テ	ネ	ヘ	メ		レ		
オ [o]	オ	コ	ソ	ト	ノ	ホ	モ	ヨ	ロ	ヲ	

Japanese Writing System

Mojie: Japanese letter turned into picture

Since the old days, letters were used like pictures or used as part of pictures in Japan. This is called *mojie* (文字絵, letter picture).

During Japan's modern Edo period (1603-1867), common peasants and children were educated at the *terakoya*, an educational institute. At this time *mojie* was also taught with a textbook. It is said that not just educational *mojie* were popularly used but also entertaining *mojie* were popular as well.

It can be said that the present day computer emoticons like [* ˆ ˆ *], which combines letter symbols, are related to *mojie*. Therefore, the *henohenomoheji* (へのへのもへじ) used today can also be considered a type of *mojie*. Also the other letter art such as *chirashigaki* (散らし書き) and *ashide* (葦手) also belong to *mojie*.

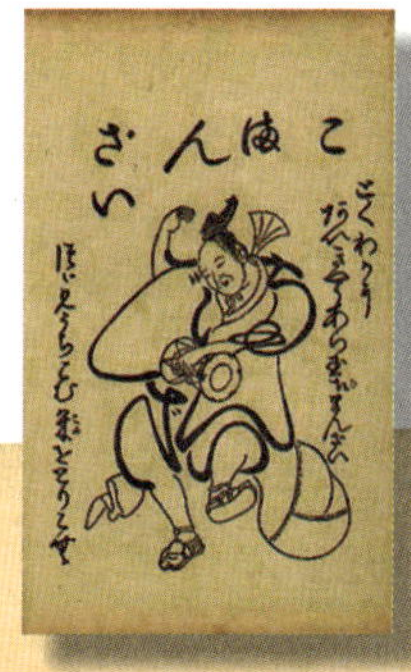

terakoya's mojie textbook

Henohenomoheji

Henohenomoheji is a *mojie* in which letters are used to draw pictures. The *mojie* is a combination of characters and sometimes also completed by drawing hands and feet.

The picture below is an example of *henohenomoheji*. It is a play on letters that only uses seven Hiragana characters to draw a face. Although we don't know for sure when it exactly began, it can be considered the original emoticon.

There are also other similar character combinations such as *henohenomoheno* (へのへのもへの), *hemehemeshikoji* (へめへめしこじ), and *heneheneshikoshi* (へねへねしこし). There is also something called the *tsuruniha-marumaru-mushi* (つるニハ○○ムし). The Hiragana character of つ [*tsu*] forms the bald head, the Hiragana る [*ru*] forms the ears, the Katakana ニ [*ni*] forms the wrinkles on the forehead, the Katakana ハ [*ha*] forms the two eyebrows, ○○ [*marumaru*], or two circles for the two eyes, the Katakana ム [*mu*] forms the nose, し [*shi*] forms the outline of the face, and combining all of these characters together creates an old man's face without a mouth.

henohenomoheji

Chirashigaki

Chirashigaki was used when writing letters or traditional poetry in Kana. It is a calligraphy style that only exists in Japan in which a character is expanded to the whole page. In the picture below, the background is written in *chirashigaki*.

Chirashigaki is written on a picture, and by becoming part of the picture, it is devised to make the picture artistically beautiful. It contains a person's artistic vision with various elements including the ink concentration and color, the thickness of the line, and whether the characters are written in a straight line with all elements beautifully combined. It is now considered very important in Kana calligraphy, being developed and reborn since it appeared in the middle of the 10th century.

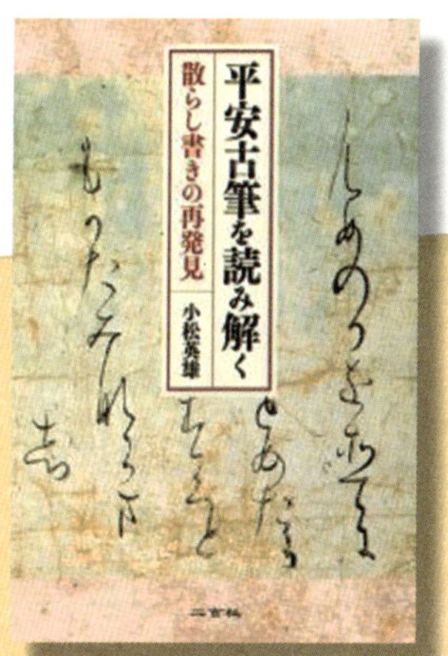

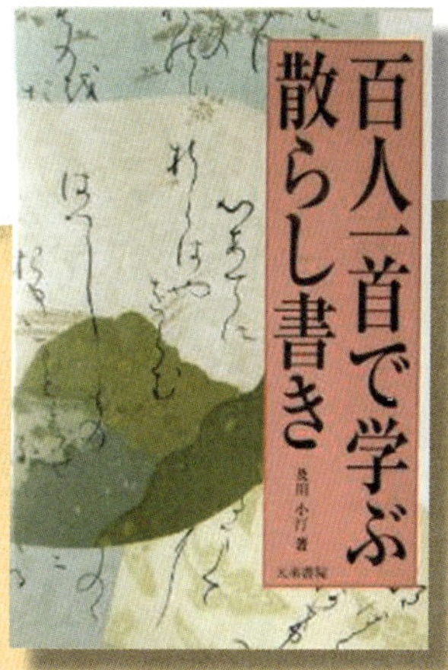

Chirashigaki

Ashide

Ashide is the transformation of a letter into an illustration by integrating a character to become part of a picture. The characters are written so that they are hidden in the streams, reed, sea birds, stones, or other objects in the picture. It is a calligraphy form that provides insight into the games the aristocracy played using letters and pictures during Japan's Heian period (9th-12th century). It is also called *ashide-e* or *ashidegaki*.

Although *ashide* was also used in ordinary pictures, they were usually used when the Buddhist scriptures were published. The pictures were added within the title page, and the picture below is an example of that. In the middle of the picture the Chinese characters 終 (end), 今 (now), 此 (this) can be seen while the Chinese characters 樂 (happy), 安 (comfortable) can be seen on the bottom right of Buddha.

ashide

Turning letters into art, *edomoji*

In Japan, the most representative means of turning letters into art is *edomoji* (江戸文字). It is the generic term for the ornamental characters that were popularly used during the Edo period. As seen in the picture below, each of the handwriting styles has its own name and usage.

The first handwriting style is *shibaimoji*. It is used when writing signs or programs for *kabuki*. The second style is *yosemoji*. It is used when writing signs for performance halls or programs, invitation letters and others for so-called *rakugo* story telling performances. The third style is *kagomoji*, the fourth is *higemoji*, and the fifth is *chochinmoji*. The sixth style, *sumomoji*, is used in *sumo* wrestling matches for writing the order or for advertising. The last style is called *kakuji*, which is used for one's legal seal.

Even now, *edomoji* is used for their original purposes at various places.

Witty Japanese letter games

Tawamuregaki

In the previous paragraphs, Manyogana, the source of Hiragana and Katakana, was explained. One of the uses for Manyogana was *tawamuregaki* (戯れ書き), which is an interesting example of letter management that reflects the Japanese people's playful side.

In Manyogana, one Chinese character represents one sound, but can also represent more than two sounds. Also, several Chinese characters can also represent one fixed sound. There is a book called *Manyosyu* (compiled in the 8th century) that was made up of songs written in Manyogana. This book shows innovative ideas by using numerals and animals for symbols. Let's look at the examples below.

First look at characters using numerals; some examples are 二二・重二・并二：し(*shi*, 4), 二五：とを(*to-o*, 10), 十六：しし(*shishi*, 4×4), 八十一：くく(*kuku*, 9×9). All of them use the principle of the multiplication table. In 二二・重二・并二 because there are two twos it becomes 2×2=4 and it is written as 二二・重二・并二 in Chinese characters while it is read as four し(*shi*) in Japanese. Since 二五 is 2×5 which equals 10, it is read in the old language of the pass centuries とを(とお in modern language, pronounced as *to-o*). 十六 (16) and 八十一 (81) is the opposite of that. In order to make 16, 4 must be multiplied with 4 and as a result it is read as しし (*shishi*). Also for the numeral 81, 9 must be multiplied with 9 and is read くく (*kuku*).

Examples of characters that use the sounds of animals are 牛鳴む and 蜂音ぶ. At the time, the sound of a cow was thought to be む (*mu*) and the sound of a bee was ぶ (*bu*). Therefore, 牛鳴 and 蜂音 is written while it is read as む (*mu*) and ぶ (*bu*).

Other characters related to animals are 追馬そ and 喚犬ま. It seems that the 追馬 was read as そ (*so*), which was the sound made from chasing horses. While 喚犬 was read as ま (*ma*), which is what dogs were called. So the characters 追馬 and 喚犬 were written and read as そ (*so*) and ま (*ma*).

There are many other characters that playfully mix characters with sounds. Through this type of writing system, it can be said that the Japanese people from the old days were witty and thoughtful.

Jinazo

There is something called *hanjimono* (判じ物). Much like today's quizzes, it hides meanings in pictures or characters and requires one to figure out the meaning. The type that is made from pictures is called *hanjie*, while the type made from characters is called *jinazo* (字謎). Therefore, you could say that it was a riddle concerning characters.

An example of a simple *jinazo* riddle is, "別れると一人、これはな~に? (*wakareruto hitori, korewa nani*: if you break, it will become one person (一人), what is it)." The answer is 大 (big). If you divide up the character 大 then you get the characters 一 (one) and 人 (person). Another riddle is "人のためと書いて偽りと読む。(*hitono tameto kaite itsuwarito yomu*: one writes saying that they are for a person but reads that it is a lie)." The character 爲 (=為) means "to do something" or means "for-" in Japanese and can also be read as ため (*tame*). However if you put together the character "person" with the character "for," it becomes "lie" or 僞 (=偽). This is how you understand this riddle.

Here are more riddles. Try solving it.

Examples of Jinajo

一つだと一本、(*hitotsudato ippon*: if it's one, it's one tree)

二つだとけっこう増えて、(*futatsudato gekkou fuete*: if it's two, it increases quite a bit)

三つだとたくさん。(*mittsudato takusan*: if it's three, it's a lot)

これはなに？ (*korewa nan*: what is it?)

Have you figured out the answer? That's right, it's "木 (tree), 林 (grove or group of trees), 森 (forest)." The Chinese character 木 tree is one, so it's one thing. If two 木 tree characters combine it becomes a grove 林. If it is made of three of the 木 tree characters, then it becomes a forest or 森. Simple isn't it?

Another *jinazo* that has become used in daily life is the word *beiju* (米寿). It means the age of 88. Why do they call the age of 88 *beiju*? The Chinese character 米 means rice, and if broken up the characters 八(8), 十(10), 八(8) can be seen. Therefore, the age of 88 is called *beiju*, and in that year a special birthday party is held to celebrate one's longevity.

It is said these kinds of *jinazo* also developed in China.

In Japan, *jinazo* started to become popular with comedy play writers during the Edo period. Even now, it is commonly used as humor in daily life.

Card games

One of the traditional games of Japan is the *hyakunin isshu* (百人一首). Since the old days, families or friends played and enjoyed this game when gathering during the New Year's holidays. Actually, the *hyakunin isshu* is compilation of poems written by 100 poets. In other words, it is a poetry book compiling traditional Japanese poems called Waka. This eventually developed into card games. In the card games, cards with poems written on them are spread out on the floor. One person would read a poem and the players would quickly find the card that contains the poem. Obviously, the player who collects the most cards wins the game. Players who remember the poem will be able to find the card even before the person finishes reading the poem. Also, like the picture on the left, each card has

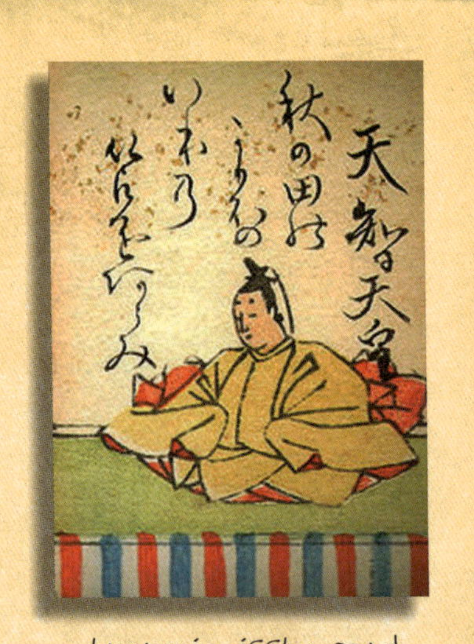

hyakunin isshu card

a picture and players who remember the picture can also quickly take the card as well.

Nowadays, the *hyakunin isshu* card game method is also being used to teach children Japanese characters. The picture below shows children's character study card. On one side are cards with sentences written in Japanese while on the other side are cards with pictures. The Hiragana character of へ (*he*) card starts with へびが (*hebiga*), and the content for that card is illustrated in another card. Of course, the character of へ (*he*) is written on both cards. The picture cards are spread out on a table or floor and the teacher or mother reads the card's sentence. The children then find the picture card with the content of the sentence. Through this process, children learn both Hiragana and Katakana. It can be said that this was devised so that children could have fun while learning characters by combining a traditional game with studying.

children's character study cards

Chinese character puzzle

In Japan, Chinese characters play an important part in writing Japanese. Although the letters are originally from China, historically, various considerations were added and revisions were made several times, and through that process, they became letters specifically for writing Japanese. The Japanese don't just use Chinese characters for writing but also use Chinese characters to make game, such as the *jinazo* mentioned earlier. Currently, Japanese people are enjoying Chinese character puzzles that try to develop the mind and combine fun using Chinese characters.

The picture on the left is the cover of a Chinese character

cover of
Kanji puzzle magazine

contents of
Kanji puzzle magazine

puzzle magazine. It looks very difficult. These sorts of magazines are released to the public in various types. The puzzle magazines were created so that the Chinese characters aren't only studied out of necessity, but can also be used to help one have fun and develop one's mind and one's intelligence. The puzzle magazines were created for adults in general rather than for students. The way that the Japanese create games using characters and transcendentalize and publish it into a magazine shows the way the Japanese are able to professionally develop a certain idea.

Japanese Letters in the Digital Era

Since the Japanese language uses Kanji (Chinese characters), Hiragana, and Katakana for writing, the system for typing letters on the computer can be very complicated. Not only does Japanese have a limited number of syllables, as a result have many homonyms in which the sounds are the same, but the meanings are also different. This is especially the case with words derived from Chinese characters. In that sense, it is very difficult to understand if it is only written in Kana. Also, because there are no spaces between words, where one pauses between characters changes the meaning of the text.

There are two ways to type Japanese on computers. One method is by typing it using the Roman alphabet. For example, if one types the Roman alphabet letters *s* and *a*, the character さ (*sa*) will be entered on the computer. Also typing *r* and *i* will cause the り (*ri*) to be entered into the computer. The second method is by typing Kana directly. When Kana is typed directly, characters are arranged on the keyboard. but there are only 33 keys for the almost 50 characters. In other words, there aren't enough keys for the characters, and thus, the characters are also arranged on number keys. After the characters are input this way and a word is finished, the space bar is pressed. When the space bar is pressed, Chinese characters will appear for the Kana typed in. If there are three Chinese character words, then three will appear, and if there are five Chinese characters, five will appear. The user then selects one of the words. When the user hits the enter key, the selected Chinese character is input into the computer. Compared to English, typing in Japanese requires much time and effort.

Typing Japanese on the computer is very inconvenient. However, this process takes even more time and effort on a mobile phone. Although, there is the way of typing using the Latin alphabet, the method of entering characters directly in Japanese requires that each of the buttons on a mobile phone contain all of the characters for each type of character, such as あ (*a*), か (*ga*), さ (*sa*), and others. So if one wanted to type a character that was at the end of the category, such as お (*o*) and そ (*so*), then they would have to press the same button five times. And if you enter a *dakuten* (Japanese voicing mark), you would have to press another button. After entering the Kana, the user would have to change the Kana into Chinese characters. It can be said that writing a mobile phone text message quickly is impossible.

During the beginning of the development of computers when the number of Chinese characters that could be entered was much fewer than that of today, there were scholars who were sure that Chinese characters would have no place to stand in the world of technology. However, as technology advanced the number of Chinese characters that computers could handle increased dramatically. Instead of being lost, in Japan, Chinese characters are being used more often compared to the days when Chinese characters were handwritten. This does not mean, however, that the Chinese character skills of Japanese users improved. It is because many are able to read Chinese characters, yet are unable to write them down. In this way, data processing technology has developed so that Chinese characters can be actively used without much change.

Korea's Creative and Scientific Alphabet, Hangeul

— Chung Byoung-Kyoo

함께

Letter Designed for Korean Speech

Letters are the visual record of a language. Although speech and writing may fundamentally be the same, they differ greatly in that speech disappears as soon as it leaves a person's lips, while most writings last for a long time as documents. Unlike writing, however, speaking is special in that a person's gestures, facial expression, intonation, speed, and gender will slightly change the meaning of what he or she is communicating. These aspects of language are innate to us. We cannot pick the language that we are born into. With the exception of special cases, people are born within their native language. However, not all of the world's languages have writing systems to document language. For Korea, there is a special script to record Korean language called Hangeul (Korean alphabet). Therefore, it can be said that Korean citizens are born in the world of writing known as Hangeul.

It wasn't until the reign of the Joseon Dynasty's (1392-1910) King Sejong the Great (who reigned from 1418 to 1450) that the Korean language acquired letters for writing with the invention of Hunmin Jeongeum (the original name of Hangeul). With the creation of Hunmin Jeongeum, now called Hangeul, King Sejong brought another aspect of culture into the lives of the Korean people. As a result, Koreans are born into the Korean language and Hangeul, learning and using both while living in the Hangeul culture. Aside from Koreans who live in other countries who may learn other languages as their mother tongue, most Koreans cannot live without the Korean language and Hangeul.

The Korean language existed before the creation of the Hunmin Jeongeum, but only in speech as there were no letters to write with. Even before Hunmin Jeongeum, there were many efforts made to create a (borrowed) character writing system like Hyangchal, Idu, and Gugyeol that borrowed the meaning and pronunciation of Chinese characters, called Hanja, to write Korean. But this writing system did not naturally suit the Korean language and, therefore, was quite limited. In the acknowledgement of the *Hunmin Jeongeum*, a Joseon Dynasty scholar named Jeong In-ji wrote about the trouble of using the borrowed writing system, stating that using Chinese characters for the Korean language was like "trying to fit an angular stick into a round hole."

However, the continuous attempts of the Korean ancestors to create a borrowed character writing system should be noted. This is because, at that time, the borrowed character writing system had a huge influence on the creation of Japan's Kana letters. More importantly, to write the Korean language, Korean ancestors made continual attempts to develop a writing system. These accumulated results greatly influenced King Sejong's creation of Hunmin Jeongeum. In this historical context, the creation of Hunmin Jeongeum in East Asia in the 15th century was praised as a miracle.

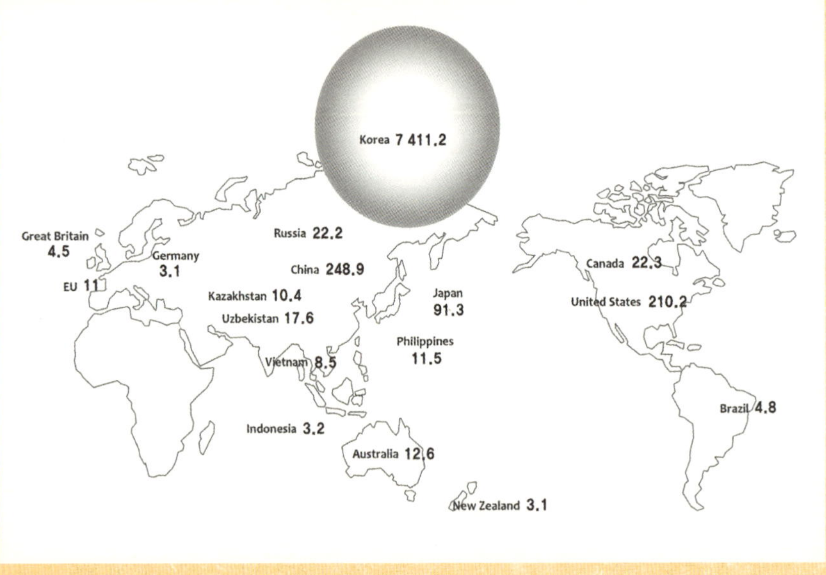

world usage of Hangeul distribution (unit: ten thousand)

UNESCO's Memory of the World Honors Hunmin Jeongeum

Although Hunmin Jeongeum was invented in the year 1443, it was revealed to the world through the book *Hunmin Jeongeum*, also translated as *The Proper Sounds for the Instruction of the People*. (There is a need to distinguish the difference between the name of the Korean alphabet, Hunmin Jeongeum, and the book *Hunmin Jeongeum*, which explains the creation methods of the Korean alphabet and how to use it.) Most letters have thousands of years of history, making it difficult to deduct the origin of the letters. In comparison, Hunmin Jeongeum is relatively young. Therefore, Hunmin Jeongeum has many features different from those of other letters.

Firstly, Hunmin Jeongeum was a completely new alphabet that had not existed before. In other words, it was original and creative. Thus, it has many different features that are thought to be novel and unique among all of the world's letters. In this perspective, it can be said that Hunmin Jeongeum rewrote the history of the world's writing systems. Also, it is possible to know who developed it and exactly when it was made. In the 25th year (1443) of the *Annals of King Sejong the Great*, it was written that, "this month, the King has personally made 28 letters of the alphabet." Moreover, the purposes for the letter's creation, the principles behind the system, and the method of operation have all been documented. This type of extensive documentation does not exist for any of the writing systems of the world, and has been passed down only for Hangeul. Through the recognition of the value of its documentation, Hunmin Jeongeum was honored as part of UNESCO's Memory of the World in 1997. In 1940, a copy of the *Hunmin Jeongeum* was miraculously discovered at Andong in Gyeongsangbuk-do province. It is now stored in the Kansong Art Museum in Seoul.

Before the discovery, there were many different opinions

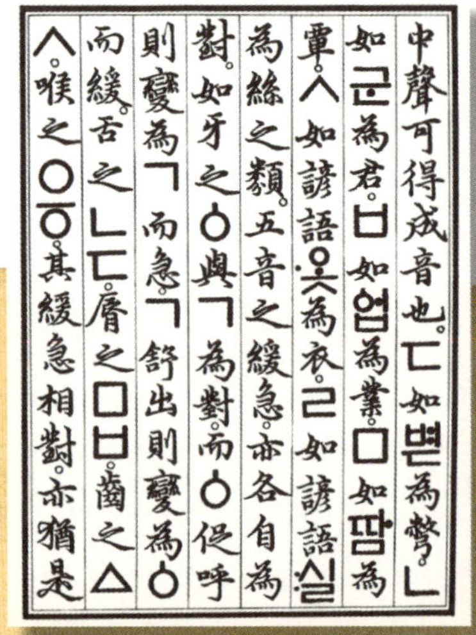
中聲可得成音也。ㄷ如볃爲彆。ㄴ
如군爲君。ㅂ如업爲業。ㅁ如땀爲
覃。ㅅ如諺語옷爲衣。ㄹ如諺語실
爲絲之類。五音之緩急亦各自爲
對。如牙之ㆁ與ㄱ爲對。而ㆁ促呼
則變爲ㄱ而急。ㄱ舒出則變爲ㆁ
而緩。舌之ㄴㄷ。脣之ㅁㅂ。齒之ㅿ
ㅅ。喉之ㅇㆆ。其緩急相對。亦猶是

Hunmin Jeongeum

concerning the origin of Hunmin Jeongeum. The reason for this was that most of the letters of the world were not originally made but instead were letters taken from other cultures and changed little by little to fit their languages. As a result, many academics also assumed that Hunmin Jeongeum would not be very different from other letters. Therefore, their prime concern was what letters Hunmin Jeongeum originated from. The claims called "Hunmin Jeongeum origin theory" were various, including theories that it was originally derived from India's letters Sanskrit, Tibet's letters, and Mongol's old letters Phags-pa. However, with the discovery of the *Hunmin Jeongeum*, all of the origin theories or imitation series were disproven. Through the information from the *Hunmin Jeongeum*, it was proven that none of the letters were taken from elsewhere and were completely original.

These facts provide for a unique position when researching Hunmin Jeongeum. Any disputes concerning the use of Hangeul or Hunmin Jeongeum, have to be based on the evidence in the book. This only applies to Hunmin Jeongeum and is impossible for other letters. This book, commonly called *Haeryebon* (*Explanation and Examples*), is a *Hunmin Jeongeum* document which details how the letters were originally and creatively made using scientific principles, along with the usage of the letters in the categories of Jejahae, Choseonghae, Jungseonghae, Habjahae, and Yongjarae. Also, the book starts with a preface written by King Sejong stating the reason and purpose for the creation of the letters, with examples of the letters in general usage frame. There is also Jeong In-ji's acknowledgement at the back, which summarizes the features of the alphabet.

King Sejong the Great, Creator of the New Letters

With King Sejong's creation of the Hunmin Jeongeum, the Korean people's longtime dream of a "complete Korean language letter" was at last fulfilled. However, there were two prominent theories as to the creator of Hunmin Jeongeum. One called the "royal creation theory," which claims that King Sejong personally created the letters by himself. The other theory called the "sponsorship theory," which claims that scholars of the Jiphyeonjeon (Hall of Worthies) created the letters with the cooperation of the king. However, there are no records in any of the documents related to Hunmin Jeongeum that suggests that King Sejong made the letters with the help of scholars. On the other hand, some believe that the process of creating something as complex as a letter system would be very difficult for any one person to do, and thus rebutted against the "royal creation theory." Particularly North Korea supports the claim that the letters were made with the help of scholars. However, recent support upholding King Sejong's personal creation of the letters has been gathering. Therefore, it wouldn't be strange to add the descriptor "great" to King Sejong's title.

One of the biggest features of King Sejong's Hunmin Jeongeum is that it extends from its originality to its scientific value. The fact that Hunmin Jeongeum is not based on any of the other letters of the world and is entirely original proves its creativity. It is the alphabet with a clear process of creation and letter-creating principle. It can be said that the letters are truly scientific in that the analysis of how Koreans made sounds was integrated into the way the letters were made. Academics around the world agree that this alphabet is scientific in that it clearly expressed the relation between letters and sounds to a degree that amazes linguists.

Hangeul, which was scientifically created with a sophisticated linguistic level, could be classified as a phonemic letters. It is different from Hanja, which is a system of ideograms. Hunmin Jeongeum, which was created in such a way that it could also be used to record foreign letters such as Hanja as well. Therefore, in order to record the sound of Hanja, characters that weren't necessary to the Korean language were also included.

Hangeul, Following the Rules and Steps

Hunmin Jeongeum, created by King Sejong, is made up of 28 letters consisting of 17 consonants and 11 vowels. The theoretical background of Hunmin Jeongeum's principle and method of creation is dividing each syllable in a word into three parts. In other words, it divides one syllable into an initial consonant, a medial (vowel), and a final consonant. This syllable trichotomy is the basis of Hunmin Jeongeum's creativity. At that time, the syllable division method in China was dichotomy (initial and final position of a syllable). For Korean, excluding the single consonant in the initial position of a syllable, whether it is a vowel or a vowel plus a consonant placed under a vowel, are added to be placed in the final position of a syllable. It is fitting to think that the syllable trichotomy is different from that of the Chinese division which divides the final position of a syllable again into a vowel and a final consonant placed under a vowel.

We can say that the planning of vowels is the most brilliant part of the Hunmin Jeongeum creation. Not only does it show it is of linguistically high caliber, created with the characteristics of Korean language syllables clearly in mind, but it also enabled the diving of the final consonant. The final consonant placed under a vowel takes a unique position in the Korean language. First, the shape of a final consonant is the same as the initial consonant. Looking at *Hunmin Jeongeum* Ye-eui part, there is a

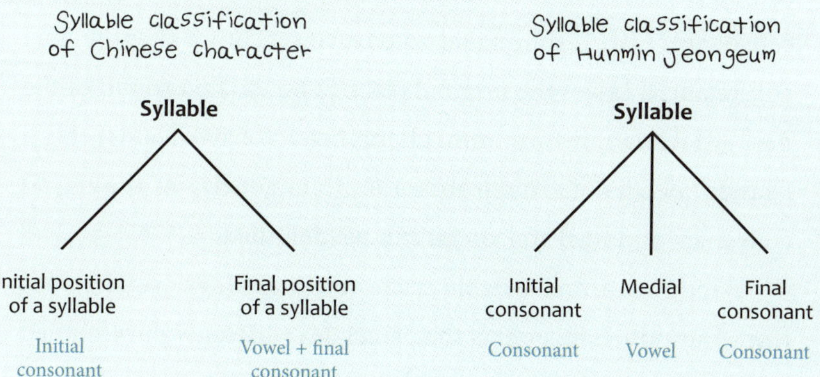

sentence, "종성부용초성 (終聲復用初聲: final consonant follows the initial consonant)." It says that the final consonant uses the initial consonant again, meaning that the shapes of the two are the same. Therefore, when the letters were made, the final consonant was not required to develop separately. Through this discovery, the number of letters required decreased greatly. In fact, only an initial consonant and vowels were required. An example showing this trait can be found in 밥을 먹다 (*bab-eul meok-da*). When we pronounce 밥을 (*bab-eul*), it is read 바블 (*babeul*), because the final consonant ㅂ[b] moves to next syllable's first consonant. The final consonant ㅂ[b] and ㅂ[b], the first consonant of 블 (beul) are the same.

This shows that the middle part and the final part of a syllable, which are difficult to divide in ordinary language, can be divided into an initial consonant, a vowel, and a final consonant. Also, it shows that when a vowel comes after the final consonant, it leaves the original place to be the first sound of the next syllable. In this way, the "phenomenon of syllable structural change" occurs. Through this, the homogeneity of the initial consonant and final consonant can be identified.

Along with this syllable trichotomy, another creative idea from Hunmin Jeongeum is the principle of hieroglyphics applied in letter creation. The definition of hieroglyphics is to "model

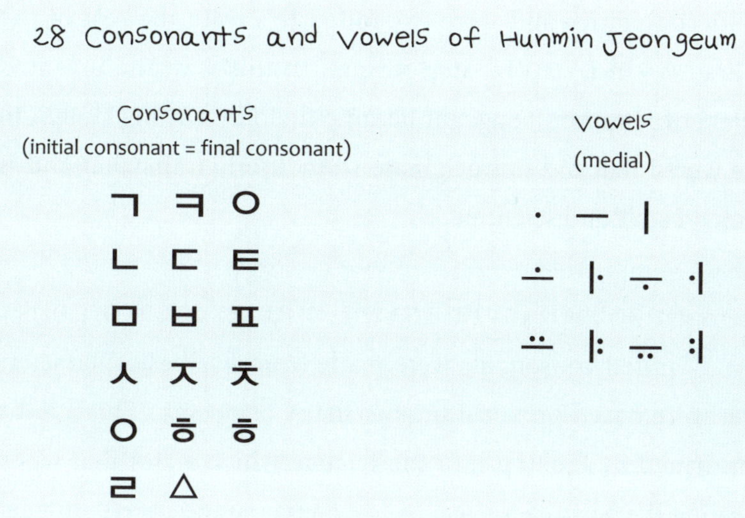

after something," which the 28 letters of the Hunmin Jeongeum exemplify by modeling after particular shapes. The subjects of the hieroglyphics differ for an initial consonant and a vowel. It is because the initial consonant (sound) is a consonant and the medial (sound) is a vowel, but both have subjects that they were modeled after for these sounds. This means that the symbols representing the sounds, or the letters, are not shaped arbitrarily.

Not all of the 28 characters of Hunmin Jeongeum were made from the principle of hieroglyphics. Some of the basic characters of the initial consonant and vowel were made from the principle of hieroglyphics and were expanded to create the rest of the characters in a step-by-step format. In this way, the invented letters of Hunmin Jeongeum became the only writing system in the world that did not originate from another alphabet and is both creative and scientific.

Consonants that imitate the human vocal organs

The 17 initial consonants were made from five basic characters that were based on vocal organ's shape of person. This can be confirmed by looking into the Jejahae which states that when creating the basic character ㄱ, "ㄱ, a velar sound (letter), imitates the way the root of the tongue closes the throat." It also mentions that the "ㄴ which is a tongue sound imitates the way the tongue touches the upper gums, the ㅁ which is a labial sound imitates

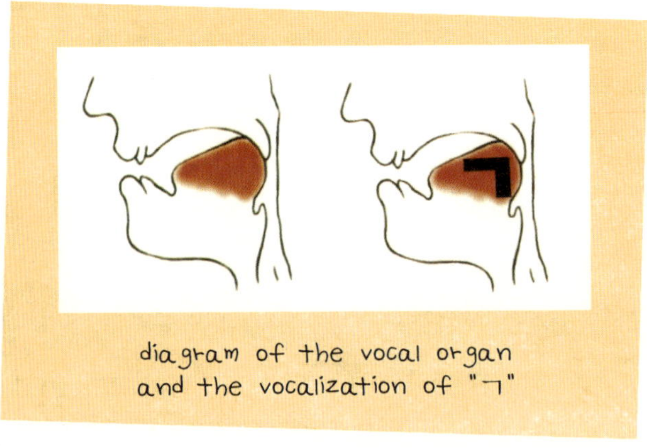

diagram of the vocal organ and the vocalization of "ㄱ"

Basic Characters and Combined Stroke Characters Consonants

Basic characters	Combined stroke characters
ㄱ	ㅋ
ㄴ	ㄷ ㅌ
ㅁ	ㅂ ㅍ
ㅅ	ㅈ ㅊ
ㅇ	ㆆ ㅎ

the shape of the lips, the ㅅ which is a dental sound imitates the shape of teeth, the ㅇ which is a throat sound imitates the shape of throat." This points out that the remaining basic characters of ㄴ, ㅁ, ㅅ, ㅇ were designed to imitate the way sound is made in the vocal organ.

With the basic five characters established, additional strokes were added respectively to create the remaining initial consonants.

Characters that were created by adding strokes to the basic

characters of ㄱ, ㄴ, ㅁ, ㅅ, ㅇ respectively are consonants of the same category. In this way, the characters which are of the same category of consonants have a stronger sound with each added stroke. The added strokes are displayed visually. Also there are three variant characters (ㆁ, ㄹ, ㅿ) that are completely separate and are not made from the hieroglyphic or the combined stroke principles. Although the basic shapes of the characters are derived from the basic characters, they are not the characters that have stronger sounds with additional strokes. Therefore, the five basic characters which imitate the vocal organs, the nine characters which have added strokes based on the basic

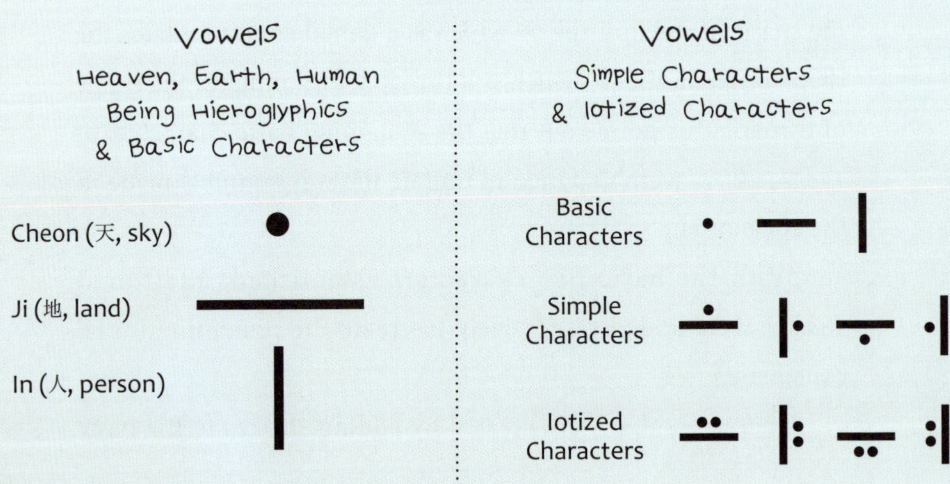

characters, and the three variant characters which have forms like combined strokes but do not have stronger sounds with additional strokes make up a total of 17 characters.

Vowels representing the shapes of the Heaven, the Earth, and the Human Being

There are three basic characters to the vowel. The vowel is different from the initial consonant and so the hieroglyphic origins are different as well. The vowels were created from each of the three elements consisting of Cheon (天, heaven), Ji (地, earth), In (人, human being) and are transformed into the Korean

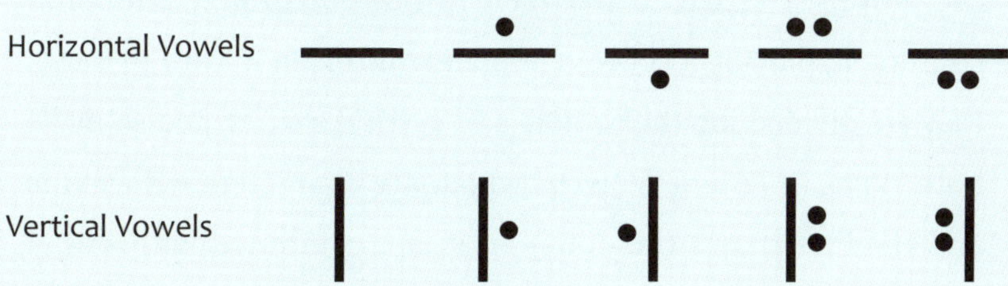

characters of sky (·), land (—), and person (|). These vowel characters contrast with the initial consonants which imitate the vocal organs. The eight other characters besides the three basic vowels are combined · with — and | . The upper half of the vowels combine with one · are called "simple characters." The lower half of the vowels combine with two · are called "iotized characters."

The invention of vowel characters applies the *yin* and *yang* concept of Neo-Confucianism, which was the prevalent philosophy at the time. This concept also has a deep relation to the Korean language's vowel harmony phenomenon. The · that is put on the right side of the | and on top of the — indicates *yang* vowels, and when it is put on the left side of the | and under the —, they are *yin* vowels. The form of the vowel includes the medial vocal features.

In the vowels, there are a total of 11 characters made up of three basic characters and eight iotized characters. In Hangeul, the vowels are placed between initial consonant and final consonant; playing a coordinate standard role in a word (syllable), they are divided into horizontal and vertical shapes, and so make both types of letters. Vowels, which are characters with a line and the line(s) and the dot(s) on it, are combined with initial and final consonants to create a syllable character. When this happens, there is an effect in which the characters can be easily distinguished from one another. In this way, it can be assumed that the vowels were made before the initial consonants.

Moreover, in the creation of Hunmin Jeongeum, the vowel was recognized for its originality. Through the uniformity of the medial's form and features, the medial, or vowel, can be easily identified. The fact that vowels can be easily read cannot be overemphasized. We can see this just by comparing it with Latin alphabet. The vowels in Latin alphabet include *a, e, i, o, u*. There is no relation in the forms of the vowel letters. Also there is little to distinguish the vowels from the consonants. In Korean, the consonants (initial, final) and vowel (medial) can be identified at a glance by their shape. Also, only in Hangeul does each character clearly show phonetic features.

Yeonseo and *Byeongseo*, Basic Characters Combined

Besides the 17 initial consonants and the 11 vowels, *Hunmin Jeongeum* contains another type of characters. They are the *yeonseo* and *byeongseo*. When two characters that are *sun-gyeong-eum* (light sounds that pass through the lips) ㅸ are combined

Types of *Yeonseo* and *Byeongseo*

Yeonseo	ㅸ	ㆄ	ㅹ	ㅱ		
Byeongseo	ㄲ	ㄸ	ㅃ	ㅉ	ㅆ	ㆅ
	ㅳ	ㅄ	ㅶ	ㅺ	ㅼ	ㅾ
	ㅽ	ㅴ	ㅵ			

from top to bottom, it is called *yeonseo*. When characters like the ㄲ have two characters consecutively written together, it is called *byeongseo*. When a *byeongseo* is made with the same characters such ㄲ, ㄸ, it is called *gakja byeongseo*. Also when it is made with different characters such as ㅺ, ㅳ, it is called *habyong byeongseo*.

The *byeongseo* and *yeonseo* are not new characters. They are simply combinations of existing characters. Characters that are made with suffix *seo* (書), meaning letter, in Hunmin Jeongeum are not new characters according to the terms of letter creation. Therefore, these characters are not included in the 28 characters of the alphabet. We can also confirm this fact by taking a look at *Hunmin Jeongeum*'s main text, which mentions that when an initial consonant and a vowel are combined and written together, it is called *buseo* (附書), meaning "letters written together." Horizontal vowels are placed under the initial consonant, while vertical vowels are placed on the right of the initial consonant.

The World's Only Constructed Letters, Hangeul's *Hapja*

In *Hunmin Jeongeum*, *hapja* (combined letters) is mentioned several times. It explains that in order for a word to depict a sound, the initial consonant, vowel, and final consonant must be combined. This is because the initial consonants and vowels are just phonemic scripts and thus cannot function alone. Therefore, with the vowel at the center, the initial consonant, vowel, and final consonant are combined, or just the initial consonant and vowel are combined. They then form letters into a syllable that represents a sound. As the alphabet was created as a phonemic script, it is used by combining letters

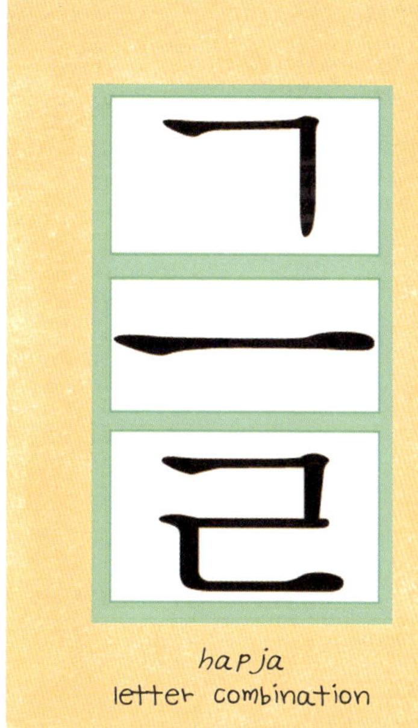

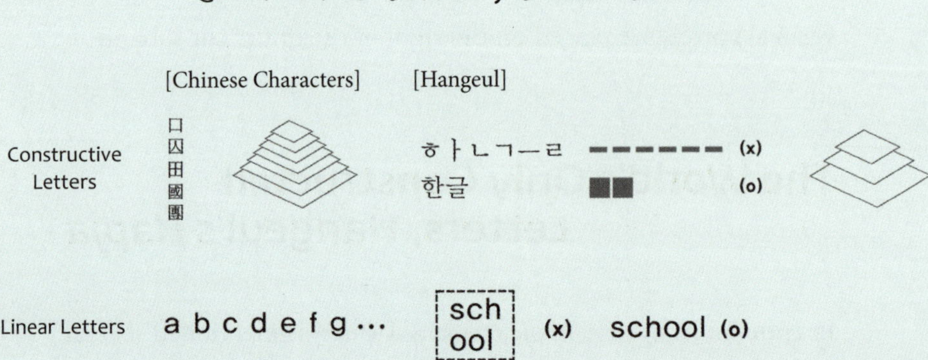

into syllables. Thus, Hunmin Jeongeum is a "phonemic and syllabic letter" that combines the features of phonemic script and syllabic script.

This was an unprecedented and groundbreaking method to manage and write letters. By the way, we generally call phonemic scripts "alphabets" or "letters," and syllabic scripts "alphabets" or "letters" as well. Until now, there weren't any terms to sufficiently describe the difference. Although Hunmin Jeongeum scholars were fully aware of this fact, they did not create any terms for this, which is quite strange. (As we have to note the difference between the scripts based on phoneme and scripts based on syllables; scripts based on phonemes are called letters, and scripts based on syllables are called syllabic blocks.) Through this we can see that Hangeul's letter combination is unique and this is one of Hangeul's most remarkable features.

Since syllabic blocks (*hapja*) are made through the combination of letters, many variations of the syllabic block can be made. Hunmin Jeongeum's initial consonant and vowel letters have their own vocal features respectively. The vocal features of the letters are easily viewed in the combined syllabic blocks. In the syllabic block 강 [*gang*] we can easily see the sounds for each letters ㄱ, ㅏ, and ㅇ. When the syllable 강 is spoken, phonemic order for the syllable is also easily seen. The only writing system in the world with these features is Hangeul. We have to once again acknowledge that this writing system is not based on any other and is innovative with its letter combination method.

Hunmin Jeongeum's letter combination was made so that Hanja (Chinese character) could be used in conjunction. This can be easily confirmed by looking through a printed copy of the *Hunmin Jeongeum*. The syllabic blocks are written in the same size as Hanja on square blocks. The reason that Hunmin Jeongeum was made was so that it could be easily used with

Hanja. The Latin alphabet is written on one line and is called "linear." However Eastern letters are written on square blocks with strokes added, so we can say that the main characteristic of Eastern letters is that it is like constructing a building. The Chinese character 鬱 meaning "depressed" is composed of 29 strokes. In terms of construction, you could say that it had 29 floors. In comparison, with Hangeul, you would have three or two floors. This is because Hangeul is a phonogram that can be

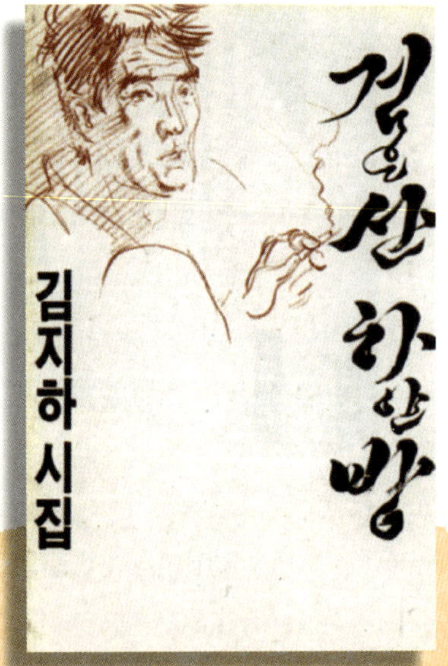

The Black Mountain, The White Room
renowned poet Kim Ji-ha's Hangeul calligraphy

made up of either a combination of initial consonant, vowel, and final consonant, or a combination of initial consonant and vowel. Meanwhile, Hanja is basically made up of ideograms in which one character represents one idea or concept. Still, both scripts can be written in the same square block. Also, they are both alike in that strokes are added the same way that floors are added to a building. This feature of Eastern letters is what makes calligraphy possible. The fact that calligraphy is possible for Hangeul, a phonemic letter, is because of the visual and formative characteristics of the Eastern letters.

World's Cultual Areas and Languages

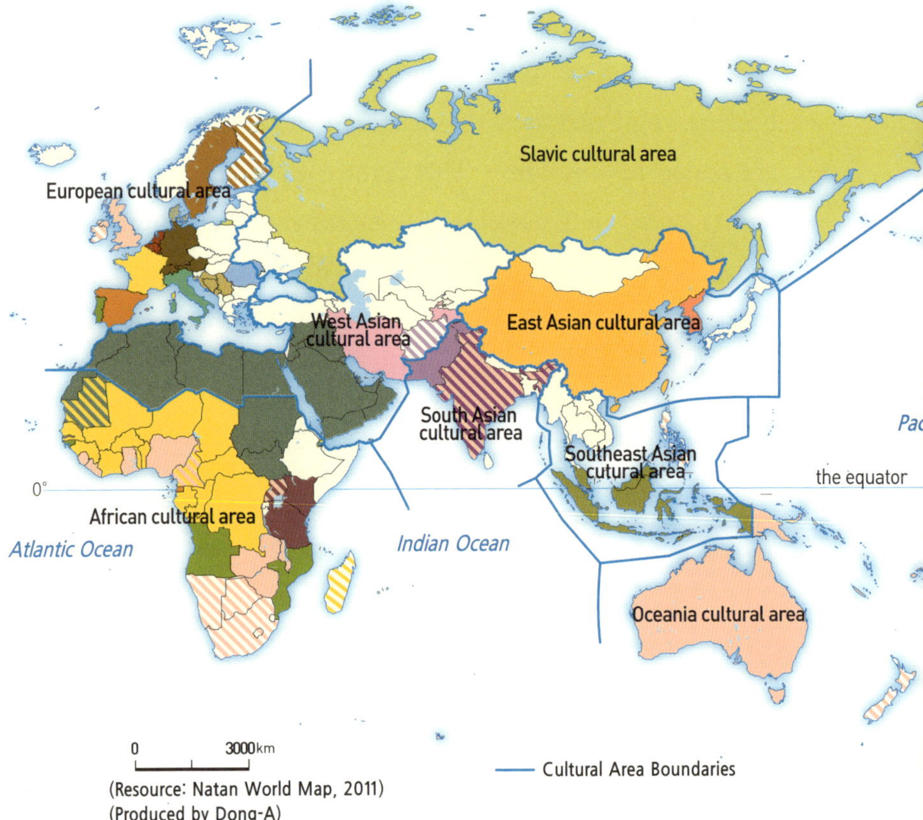

(Resource: Natan World Map, 2011)
(Produced by Dong-A)

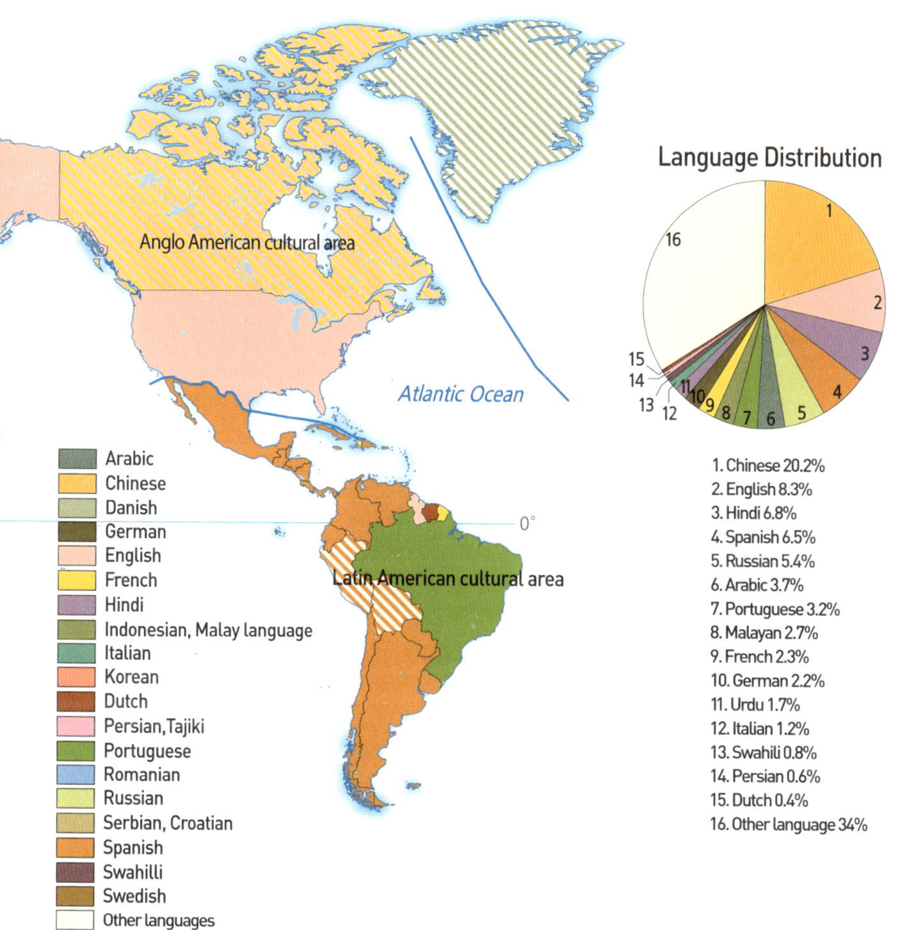
Anglo American cultural area
Atlantic Ocean
Latin American cultural area
0°
Arabic
Chinese
Danish
German
English
French
Hindi
Indonesian, Malay language
Italian
Korean
Dutch
Persian,Tajiki
Portuguese
Romanian
Russian
Serbian, Croatian
Spanish
Swahilli
Swedish
Other languages
Language Distribution
1
2
3
4
5
6
7
8
9
10
11
12
13
14
15
16
1. Chinese 20.2%
2. English 8.3%
3. Hindi 6.8%
4. Spanish 6.5%
5. Russian 5.4%
6. Arabic 3.7%
7. Portuguese 3.2%
8. Malayan 2.7%
9. French 2.3%
10. German 2.2%
11. Urdu 1.7%
12. Italian 1.2%
13. Swahili 0.8%
14. Persian 0.6%
15. Dutch 0.4%
16. Other language 34%

References

Hindi Alphabet of India, Where Gods Live

Kim, Yeong-gyu et al. *History of Hindi Language Development.* Seoul: Hankuk University of Foreign Studies Press, 2004.

Lee, Jae Sook. *Two-faced Ashoka.* Paju: Woongjinthinkbig, 2010.

____________. *1,000 Faces' Nations, Story of India.* Seoul: Mirae N, 2010.

The Mysterious and Beautiful Alphabet of Arabic

Sa, Hui-man. *Language and Literature of Arab.* Gwangju: Chosun University Press, 2000.

Song, Jeongseok. *World's Language Exploration.* Seoul: Jungin, 2008.

Yoon, Yongsu. *What Kinds of Language Is Arabic?: Sociolinguistical Focusing.* Seoul: Oedaemunhwasa, 2005.

____________. "Development Process of Arabic Letter and Type: With the Quran's Manuscript," *Mediterranean Review.* Pusan University of Foreign Studies, 11(3), pp. 31-51, 2009.

Fischer, Steven Roger. *A History of Writing.* Trans. Park, Sucheol. Paju: Book 21, 2010. Also available as an e-book.

Chejne, Anwar G. *The Arabic Languages: Its Role in History.* Minneapolis: University of Minneapolis Press, 1969.

Easy When You Know It, Thai Letters

Kim, Hongkoo et al. *Thai for Beginners.* Busan: Pusan University of Foreign Studies Press, 2001.

Kim, Hongkoo. *Understanding Thailand with a Snap.* Busan: Pusan University of Foreign Studies Press, 2006.

Chamberlain, James R, ed. *The Ram Khamhaeng Controversy.* Bangkok: The Siam Society under Royal Patronage, 1991.

松下正弘 編.『タイ文化ハンドブック』東京: 勁草書房, 1995.

Vietnamese Letters: Uncovering the Mystery Through Understanding Its History

Yu, Inseon. *New Version of Vietnamese History.* Seoul: Yeesan Publishing Co., 2002.

____________. *Vietnam and Her Neighbor China: Past and Present of the Two Countries.*

Paju: Changbi Publishers, Inc., 2012.

Choi, Byeong-uk. *Modern and Contemporary History of Vietnam*. Paju: Changbi Publishers, Inc, 2008.

Nguyễn Khuê. 『Những vấn đề cơ bản của Chữ Nôm』 Việt Nam: TĐH Tổng Hợp Tp. HCM, 1988.

Nguyễn Kim Thản, Nguyễn Trọng Báu, Nguyễn Văn Tu. 『Tiếng Việt trên đường pháttriển』 Việt Nam: Nxb. KHXH, 1982.

Nguyễn Thiện Giáp (chủ biên). 『Lược sử Việt Ngữ Học, Tập1』 Việt Nam: Nxb. Giáo dục, 2006.

Phụng Nghi. 『100 năm phát triển của tiếng Việt』 Việt Nam: Nxb. Tp. HCM, 1993.

Trần Trọng Kim. 『Việt Nam Sử Lược』 Việt Nam: Nxb. Văn hóa thông tin, 2002.

The Easiest to Learn: Indonesia's Language and Letters

Reid, Anthony. *Southeast Asia in the Age of Commerce, 1450-1650: The Lands below the Winds*. New Haven and London: Yale University Press, 1990.

Shin, Yoon Hwan. *Excursions to Southeast Asian Culture*. Paju: Changbi Publishers, 2008.

Sneddon, James. *The Indonesian Language: Its History and Role in Modern Society*. Sydney: University of New South Wales Press, 2003.

Mongolian Language and Alphabet: The United Nomads of Mongolia

Gantulga et al. *Mongolian History*. Trans. Kim, Janggoo et al. Seoul: Northeast Asian History Foundation, 2009.

Poppe, Nicholas. *Written Mongolian Grammar*. Trans. Yu Wonsu. Seoul: Minumsa, 1992.

Yu, Wonsu. *Mongolian for Beginners*. Seoul: Samjisa, 2006.

____________. *Language and Culture of Mongolia*. Seoul: Sonamoo, 2009.

Tumurtogoo, D. and Cecegdari, G, eds. *Mogolian Monuments in Uighur-Mongolian Script (XIII-XIV Centuries)*. Taipei: Institute of Linguistics, Academia Sinica, 2006.

____________. *Mogolian Monuments in Phags-pa Script*. Taipei: Institute of Linguistics, Academia Sinica, 2010.

Ц. Шагдарсүрэн (Ts. Shagdarsüren[g]). 『Монголчуудын үсэг бичигий н товчоон (Mongolchuudyn üseg bichigiin tobchoon)』 Улаанбаатар (Ulaanbaatar), 2001.

World's Oldest Chinese Characters

Ryu, Dongchoon et al. *An Introduction to Chinese Language Studies*. Seoul: Korea National

Open University Press, 2008.
Lee, Gyu-gap. *Teaching Method of Chinese Character Studies*. Seoul: Chinahouse Publishing Co., 2009.
龍宇純.『中國文字學』中國: 學生書局, 1982.
裘錫圭.『文字學概要』中國: 商務印書館, 1988.
許進雄.『中國古代社會』中國: 臺灣商務印書館, 1988.
劉志成.『文化文字學』中國: 巴蜀書社, 2003.
韓鑒堂.『漢字文化圖說』中國: 北京語言大學出版社, 2005.
殷寄明外.『現代漢語文字學』中國: 復旦大學出版社, 2007.
徐中舒主編.『漢語古文字字形表』中國: 四川人民出版社, 1980.
徐中舒主編.『秦漢魏晉篆隸字形表』中國: 上海辭書出版社, 1985.

Japanese Letters: Representing Both Sound and Meaning

Oh, Miyoung et al. *History of Japanese Language*. Seoul: J&C, 2006.
____________. *Introduction to Japanese*. Seoul: J&C, 2012.
沖森卓也編.『日本語史』日本: おうふう, 1989.
松村明編.『大辞林』日本: 三省堂, 2006.
朝日新聞出版.『週刊朝日百科書跡1 経典国宝の美』日本: 33, 朝日新聞出版, 2010. 4.
亀井孝外編.『言語学大辞典世界言語編2』日本: 三省堂, 1989.
第6回本の万華鏡 へのへのもじえ一文字で絵を描く. リサーチ·ナビ (Research·Navi).

Korea's Creative and Scientific Alphabet, Hangeul

Gang, Shinhang. *Reasearch on Hunmin Jeongeum*. Seoul: Sungkyunkwan University Press, 2003.
Gwon, Jaeseon. *Research on Analysis of Hunmin Jeongeum*. Daegu: Ugoltap, 1995.
Korean Studies Group, Graduate School of Seoul National University. *How Further Came Korean Studies?* Seoul: Dong-A Publishing, 1990.
An, Byeonghui. *Reasearch on Hunmin Jeongeum*. Seoul: Seoul National University Press, 2007.
Yu, Changgyun. *Hunmin Jeongeum*. Seoul: Hyungeseul Publishing Co., 1982.
____________. *History of Korean Linguistics*. Seoul: Hyungeseul Publishing Co., 1988.
Lee, Sangbaek. *Origin of Hangeul*. Seoul: Tongmungwan, 1957.
Lee, Ikseop. *Study on Korean Writing System*. Seoul: Seoul National University Press, 1997.
Hong, Gi-mun. *History of Development of Jeongeum, Proper Sounds*. Seoul: Seoul Newspaper Press, 1947.

Photo Credits

Hindi Alphabet of India, Where Gods Live

Indian buffalo; Taj Mahal in India; Feast of the Sacrifice, Eid al-Adha (p.24); Indian musician with a cobra (p.25) © Yonhap News

Curry and roti, Indian cuisine (p.24) © Kim Jihui

Traffic signs written in Hindi and English (p.27) © Charu Kapoor

Indian spices and herbs (p.24); Children in a Sari, Indian traditional cloth (p.25); Signpost of historic site written in Oriya, Hindi, and English (p.59); Rural bus in India (p.63); Poster advertising to eat milk and egg (p.63) © Park Jong-woo, APCEIU

Devanagari keypads (p.65) © Lee Jae Sook

The Mysterious and Beautiful Alphabet of Arabic

Petra in Jordan; Al Khazneh temples in Petra; Yemenite children; Islam Mosque (p.66); Haji in Saudi Arabia; The central religious text of Islam, Quran (p.67); Ancient remains of Petra (p.71) © Yonhap News

Figures made of Arabic alphabet (p.88) © Embassy of the Republic of Korea to United Arab Emirates

Easy When You Know It, Thai Letters

Wat Jong Kham, Buddhist temple in Thailand; Wat Phra Kaew, Buddhist temple in Thailand; Thai traditional dance (p.90) © Yonhap News

Tom Yum Kung 1, Thai cuisine (p.90) © Kim Injeong

Songkran festival in Thailand; Tom Yum Kung 2, Thai cuisine (p.90) © Tourism Authority of Thailand

Statue of King Ramkhamhaeng the Great (p.97); Epitaph of King Ramkhamhaeng the Great; Contents on epitaph of King Ramkhamhaeng the Great (p.98); Method of writing Thai consonants (p.102); Method of writing Thai vowels (p.105); Religious mendicancy (p.111) © Kim Hongkoo

Vietnamese Letters: Uncovering the Mystery Through Understanding Its History

Vietnamese water puppetry (p.116) © Kim Jong Uk

Vietnamese rice noodles, Pho (p.116) © Ha Jaehong

Woman in Ao dai, Vietnamese national costume; Boat vendor of Ha Long Bay in Vietnam; Ngoc Son Temple in Hanoi, Vietnam (p.116) © Yonhap News
Children of a minority ethnic group (p.122) © Nuguyen Bach Duong, APCEIU
Cover from the booklet introducing the Trường Sa Archipelagoes; Trường Sa Archipelagoes introduction program (p.123); Cover of Vietnam's greatest literature masterpiece *Truyenkieu* (p.124); Hanoi's 1000 Year Anniversary Memorial (p.127); Vietnamese which uses Latin alphabet (p.132); Vietnamese with its intonations; Hanoi TV's "The Regained Smile" special performance (p.134); E-mail written in Vietnamese letters (p.135) © Ahn Kyong Hwan

The Easiest to Learn: Indonesia's Language and Letters

Lion dance, New Year celebrations in Indonesia; Traditional Indonesian dance (p.136); Traditional fabric of Indonesia, Batik; Indonesian shadow puppet performance (p.137) © Yonhap News
Immigration at an Indonesian airport (p.138); Sign "Prioritize Malay Language" written both in the Jawi script and the Latin alphabet (p.145) © Min Seonhui
"Mental health" says an Indonesian sign written in the Latin alphabet (p.146); Students in Indonesia (p.149); A sign says "Hygiene is the key to health, diligence to fortune, faith to happiness" (p.153) © Nico R. Haryono, APCEIU
Epitaph in Jawi script (p.156) © APCEIU

Mongolian Language and Alphabet: The United Nomads of Mongolia

Traditional Mongolian instrument, Morin khuur performance (p.166); A statue of Genghis Khan (p.167) © Yonhap News
Mongolian traditional house, Ger; Mongolian camel; Mongolian Ger and cattle (p.166); A man in Deel, Mongolian traditional clothing (p.167) © Lee Inseong
"Mongol (Mongγol)" written in Mongol Bichig (p.175) © Jo Seong-geum
First chapter of *Secret History of Mongolia*; Mongol Bichig scripture; Mongol Bichig book cover published in Inner Mongolia (p.173); Cover of Mongol Bichig book *Mongolian Alphabet Classification Dictionary*; Contents of *Mongolian Alphabet Classification Dictionary*; Mongol Bichig in Mongol Ulaanbaatar Genghis Khan International Airport (p.174); Karakorum museum; Mongolian alphabet engraved in bronze kettle; The first newspaper in Mongol; Book cover in Mongol Bichig; Modern Mongol book cover (p.175); Part of a scripture written in Tod alphabet (p.178); Vagindra alphabet scripture published in 1907; Book cover in Mongol Latin alphabet (p.179); Russian Cyrillic Mongol alphabet (p.180); Manchurian

alphabet; Newspaper published in Mongol Bichig after adopting Cyrillic alphabet (p.181); *Kümün*, meaning person written in Mongol Bichig; *Mori*, meaning horse as decorative letter written artistically in Mongol Bichig (p.182); Handwriting written in Mongol Bichig; Mongol Bichig written with a typewriter (p.183) © Kim Janggoo

World's Oldest Chinese Characters

Shaolin Kung Fu; Chinese cuisine, Tangculiji; Chinese panda (p.186); Traditional Chinese Beijing Opera; Tiananmen (p.187) © Yonhap News

Chinese cuisine, Mapo doufu (p.187) © Choi Geumdan

Japanese Letters: Representing Both Sound and Meaning

Japanese food, Sushi; Japanese cherry blossoms; Ketataisya shrine in Japan; Japanese hot springs, Onsen (p.234) © Yonhap News

Japanese traditional dance; Women in Kimono, a Japanese traditional garment; Japanese dish, Ramen (p.234) © Japanese National Tourism Organization

Japanese letter usage as seen from the streets of Japan (p.237) © Kim Dayeong

Japanese letter usage as seen from a children's book (p.237); From Manyogana to Hiragana (p.243); From Manyogana to Katakana (p.245); *Terakoya*'s *mojie* textbook (p.247); *Chirashigaki* (p.249); *Hyakunin isshu* card (p.256); Children's character study cards (p.257); Cover and Contents of Kanji puzzle magazine (p.258) © Oh Miyoung

Korea's Creative and Scientific Alphabet, Hangeul

Hunmin Jeongeum and *The Story of Hong Gil-dong*; Goryeo celadon; Changdeokgung; Seokguram (p.262) © Seo, Jaesik

Hanok (p.262) © Lim, Seokjae

Bibimbap (p.262) © Korea Tourism Organization

Hanbok (p.262) © Shinsungjoodan

Map

Spread of Asian letters (p.15)

Noma Hideki. *The Birth of Hanguel*. Dolbegae, 2001, p. 126 which was revised and quoted from the picture by Gamei Dakasi, Oto Dokihiko, and Yamada Dosio (2007a: 117)

World's Cultural areas and Languages (pp. 288-289)

Produced by Dong-A refferring to the Natan World Map, 2011

About Education for International Understanding

Education for International Understanding (EIU) is UNESCO's important enterprise for dealing with various problems that the international society is facing. EIU which aims to build a Culture of Peace generically conducts education for multicultural understanding, peace education, human rights education, sustainable development education, globalization education and others to create a peaceful and inclusive world for sustainable development.

* The pictures in this book were made possible by the help of various organizations and individuals. We would like to thank all who provided pictures.